CW00820961

What

didn't

quite

Chris Ifso

www.nearlyology.net

Cover design by Bill Mayblin

ISBN: 978-1-9995990-1-0
The Nearly Project
127 Rathcoole Gardens
London N8 9PH
www.nearlyology.net

a project of if:book uk
exploring digital possibilities for literature
www.ifbook.co.uk

For Atlas, Vidar & Yuli

READER REVIEWS OF *WHAT DIDN'T QUITE*

"I really had fun reading about these quirky characters and their nearly experiences. The author knows his milieu very well - stressed middle-aged Londoners trying to be relentlessly innovative and entrepreneurial at a time when grants are hard to get and investment means playing a game they don't really understand. Couple that with mid-life crisis and a sprinkling of shamanism and the result is a funny and fast-moving story that you can't put down. And the bonus takeaway is that it really got me thinking about the 'nearly' moments in my own life. Food for thought indeed!

– Prof. Sue Thomas, author of *Technobiophilia*

"Funny, touching and clever, inhabited with recognisable characters reaching back and stumbling forwards in their lives, flopping towards some sort of redemption that just might come from the mysterious Carraday. So: mystery, wistfulness and topicality. Worked for me – no nearly about it."

– Joanna Klaces

"Characters who I cared about; a plot with strong momentum... a fascinating exploration of what nearly happens to us. Funny... a powerful rendition of its characters' (and our) lives and times... has the makings of a word-of-mouth hit (and/or a cult novel)."

– John Skelton

"Chris Ifso is an artistic explorer. It's great to see his work come to such vivid life. The Nearly Project is fascinating, playful, serious, wide-ranging, truly thought provoking. *What Didn't Quite* is beautifully written."

– David Almond, author of *Skellig, My Name is Mina*

"Bizarre outsider artist Carraday gathers Nearly Stories in the local library and lives with his aged mum in an imaginary aboriginal Nearlyverse somewhere in post-Crash, pre-referendum England. Freya and Jamie find him and their lives explode. This compelling and darkly funny novel involves secrets, strange desires and alternative selves. There are dodgy deals and nearlysex, puppetry and passing times, songs, psychedelics and a campervan."

– R. Emington

By the same author:

IN SEARCH OF LOST TIM

"The story of a blogger who is contacted by a boy who claims he lives in the 1960s and is communicating via his 'Futuriser'. It's a jeu d'esprit and, just possibly, the future of fiction."

– Suzy Feay, Independent on Sunday

"I love Lost Tim... the story is masterful."

– William Shaw, author of *The Birdwatcher*

ACKNOWLEDGMENTS

Many thanks to Hattie Coppard, Bill Mayblin, to Dora Meade for advice and liking the trippy bit, Dan Visel for beta app version, Jia-Yu Corti for the Nearly Dance, Joe Coppard for advice on transmedia, Carol Laidler for alldaybreakfasting, Lily McLeish for Nearly Acting workshop, Bee Peak for puppets, Kayt Lackie for song & fellow studently support, Abbie Coppard for song and proofing, Peter Forbes, Alistair McEachern, Iain Stewart, the Ifso Band, all those who participated in Nearly Workshops and Events at Bath Literary Festival, Rich Mix Festival, Royal Society of Arts, Poetry Café, Ruby Rose Café and contributed Nearlies, some of which feature in the book, all those involved in the Creative Writing PhD at Bath Spa University including supervisors Philip Hensher and Donna Hancox and above all Kate Pullinger, supportive supervisor supreme. Useful sources of information and ideas have included the Campaign Against Living Miserably (CALM), and peyroniessociety.info, providing invaluable support to those with a condition somewhat like the fictitious Hinchcliffe's, The Little Angel and City Lit for training in puppetry, dance and animation, Academy Inegales for the Nearly Music, Tino Sehgal's These Associations and the amazing Associates it assembled, James Paul, Alex Zika, the Schmiedes of Hallein, Luke Roberts, Kirsten Irving and The Ifso Writers, Justine and Caroline of Byte The Book, Bob Stein and all my if:book collaborators exploring the future of the book - and many more.

This is a book. The Nearly Project is a transmedia project. To find out more, hear nearly songs and soundscapes, read and contribute your own accounts of what didn't quite – or hasn't yet – please go to www.nearlyology.net

WHAT DIDN'T QUITE

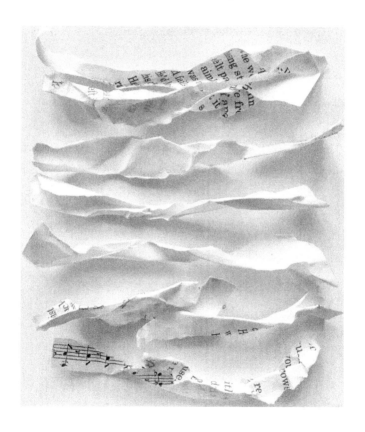

THE NEARLY NOVEL

THE NEARLY MANIFESTO

*Nearlyologists call on all people to share freely and openly
one with another who they really and nearly are.*

*In the analogue age we led linear lives with beginnings,
middles and ends.
In digital times we can be nearly many
in various virtual spaces.*

*In the age of austerity there's much we may want
but not actually get; these un-actable desires deserve
to be acknowledged as part of our being.*

We are what we eat – and what we've nearly eaten.

*Once others decided who were real writers
deserving reproduction. Today we are Nearlywriters,
able to amplify and illuminate words and pictures
but responsible for deciding when our work
is cooked enough to show and to whom to show it.*

*We learn constantly, approximately,
way outside the confines of formal institutions.
We are students of the Nearlyversity.
Only through conversation with others can we decide
which nearlies we might still want to realise.*

*In the middle of the journey of life
the line between what we've done and nearly done
begins to blur.*

*Far more things nearly happen than happen.
The universe is held together by the dust of
humankind's Nearlyincidence.
Embrace your Nearlies. Be Nearlyer.*

FINGERS NUDGING

Freya Seward sat at the kitchen table, fingers nudging the screen of her mobile, texting her friend Yasmine to say she "nearly died" this morning when she opened the BBC News app and saw the story about the baggage handlers' strike and all flights to Marseilles being cancelled. She didn't mention the letter from the bank that now lay spread-eagled on the pine table alongside her coffee cup, cereal bowl and laptop. The computer screen displayed a steady pulse of travel news, Twitter stream, Facebook updates with click bait links to fattest celebrities and secrets of star infidelities. Freya stared out of the window. The radiant morning shone brilliant blue, the garden golden with strewn leaves from last night's storm, but all she saw was red.

From the hall came the sound of a key in the lock. "Hello?" Nothing. "Who's there?" No sound except the thud of her heartbeat and the ping of a notification. The handle of the kitchen door twitched, began to turn, creaked slowly open. "Hello?" Silence. Through that crack her every terror prepared to pour.

"Who's there?"

A small felt woman in superhero garb poked her head round the door, mouth opening and closing as a voice called out: "It's... Wonderdaughter!"

Freya stifled a gasp as Pippa, tall and skinny in blue jeans and black leather jacket, walked in, and bowed theatrically, pulling the glove puppet carefully off her arm. Freya slammed both hands down to cover the letter.

"Pip! Bloody hell!"

OUT INTO THE WIND

Carraday knackered from wayfaring,
frantic with worrying, round round the town centre,
come back back to the homestead.
The Mumma she sleep in her chair, daytimetelly babbling
as ever, but he feeling her fading, skin dry as bark, slack
jaw, breath rasping. He push gently cushion more under her
head, gatherup mugs and detritus. In the kitchen he
washup, open the cupboard, lifting down and unscrewing
the Nearly Jar.
Time to open wide the window, whisper
getbetterwellpleaseplease
and sprinkling the grindings out out into the wind
which blow em up over the top of the
Spar Mini Store opposite
and away.

GAGGING

"…and…with…more…train…"
Jamie tried not to gasp for breath as they clambered up to
the top of the ridge and stopped to look down on the huge
beautiful gloom of grey sky, gritstone and dark evergreen
forestry. A group of white-haired women clattered past,
fully kitted out in North Face branded fleeces, Ordinance
Survey maps in plastic holders round their necks, chatting
and clutching those ski pole things walkers used now,
zipped into their waterproofs of khaki and mauve. And
whereas Martin had stout walking boots and a large
backpack, Jamie wore ordinary shoes and a raincoat, a
stuffed and stained Playfest International tote bag over his
shoulder, like he'd that minute strolled out of a city-centre
office for his lunch hour and found himself transported here
by magic. This pleasant walk in the countryside was feeling
like a very earnest undertaking, good for the health but a

bit bloody joyless, chillier now the sun had gone in. Martin was ahead, Jamie talking to his shoulders about the central themes of the play strategy and plans for rationalising the workforce while remaining true to the Department's core values.

"…ing…the…team…could…be…more…"

Martin stopped, wiped his brow.

"I'm gagging for a pint."

"Efficient. I think I'm getting a blister."

"And a big bowl of chips."

"Should've put talc in my socks." Leaning against the moss-covered remains of an old dry-stone wall, Jamie felt the film of hot sweat between his tee-shirt and his body begin to cool. He peered over the edge at a huge expanse of landscape; birch trees, fields, rolling hills and valleys fading into the drizzle. Good to get away and look down from a height on things, to gain some perspective.

"But Jamie mate, don't you think: what's the sodding point?"

"Stops friction apparently."

"Of helping the bosses make cuts."

"It's not simply about cuts."

"Yeah, right. Dismantling local services, that's what it's about."

Jamie opened his mouth, then closed it again. He considered himself to be fundamentally still just as much of a lefty as Martin, but felt oh so fed up with this constant negativity about how everything actually *was* in the messy, compromised world we all actually had to live and work and make decisions in.

"Come on, Comrade. The bitter beckons." Martin's mobile rang. He strode off, murmuring endearments to his lovely wife Connie, babbling at Stan, their cute little son. Martin walked with that bouncy strut of his which always made Jamie want to kick him hard up the arse. It took Jamie a moment longer to set off again. Puffed out and damp with sweat, trying to catch his breath, he stood as if surveying the dazzling sweep of nature's grandeur.

"Definitely – a blister."

SOBBING FRENCH EMOTICONS

"Didn't mean to scare you, Mum."

"Jesus, Pip!"

"Sorry."

"Bloody hell. Give me a hug." Freya reached out her arms and Pip leant down to be embraced. "That's better. Can you stay for a coffee?"

"Not now, I'm afraid. Need to get my alter ego to rehearsals. Mind if I leave the van outside?"

"Superpower: free parking. That's OK. But leave the keys. Your Dad's away." She proffered her cheek, which Pippa kissed lightly. "Off walking with Martin."

"Walking? You're joking me." Pippa carefully folded the Superwoman puppet, star of her company's next production, stuffed it into her backpack, zipped it up, hoiked it onto her shoulder, dropped the car keys on the table and headed for the front door.

"See you later, honey."

"I may have to pick up the car and just go to be honest. Sophe's invited the writer round tonight. See you, Mum."

A few seconds later and the door slammed. Freya sighed, looked back at her phone, heart still thudding. She could do with a superhero right now to save her from ruin, but Pip might not be the best person to confide in about that.

Yasmine, on the other hand: she'd been a confidante ever since the days of The Rainbow Garden. They'd stayed in touch through the decades, after Freya and Jamie bought the place and it reverted to being plain 10

Rayner Gdns. Then Yas moved back to France to find work. Freya missed her like mad, needed so badly to share her woes with someone she trusted. A few weeks ago she'd fixed a weekend to visit Marseille, booked a plane ticket and a cheap hotel near Yasmine's tiny bedsit, downloaded a Lonely Planet Guide – and now this bloody strike, which of course she supported but wasn't half a drag, and this letter from the bank too, and everything was screwed. OK, she was skint, her business teetering closer to the brink than she'd told Jamie yet – or realised herself really, until this letter and its fierce red demands – but dammit, she wasn't going to let the bastard bankers rob her of all life's pleasures. And anyway, the new website was finally ready, almost. Zane still hadn't got back to her re. the launch day, nor acknowledged final payment. Freya prodded the screen to put in a password and log onto her account online. Yes, she was still just as broke.

With bag packed and husband already bundled off for his walking weekend, she'd seize the time. While Yas was texting back a row of sobbing French emoticons, Freya was emailing the organisers of that conference on *Futurising Social Media* which Zane had recommended so highly during their last coaching session at Webberations. A few seconds later the phone pinged with a reply to say, what a coincidence, they'd had a cancellation from a French academic, so Freya could pay a reduced fee and go in her place, back into what was her comfort zone these days: digital seminars and workshops and edgy conversations with competitive collaborators over warm white wine and crudités with hummus and yoghurt dips. Even the discounted conference fees were still expensive, but hey, this one was bound to generate business. It bloody well had to. And she'd catch up with Zane.

What a shame, though. She'd been poring over the guidebook and had such a clear image of strolling through the charming Vieux-Port, the main harbour and marina of the city guarded by two imposing forts (Fort St Nicolas and

Fort Saint Jean), stopping for lunch where dozens of stylish cafés line the quayside area, much of which was rebuilt by the architect Fernand Pouillon after its destruction by the Nazis in 1943, then ambling pleasantly to the magnificent new Museum of the Mediterranean, opened as flagship of the city's year as cultural capital, and visiting the Radiant City, Le Corbusier's stunning modernist experiment in communal living recently damaged by fire, with its newly restored spacious corridors, rooftop playground and views over the turquoise sea.

The ping of another notification brought her back to the room and the screen and the To Do List of her woes. No more avoiding. Some days the bear can eat you. Today she bloody well had to start eating the bear.

**

"I nearly... learnt to tapdance but my grandfather died."
"I was on my way to be interviewed for the job of my dreams – then my wife's waters broke."
"I nearly... filmed Roger Bannister run the four-minute mile, but my friend and I bumped into some girls who asked us to tea so we went with them instead."

**

NESTLINGS

Secretly Jamie relished the exercise of rethinking the Recreation Department for changing times. An opportunity to rejig roles, shift people about, weed out dead wood and help others play to their strengths. It wasn't such a different process from expanding the team actually, and more interesting than simply running things day to day. Martin was always so negative. Then again Jamie rather enjoyed Martin's breezy, over the shoulder diatribe against Neo-Liberalism, Climate Change, The Parlous State of

Contemporary Pop Music, Tory Education Cuts, The Twat Who Was Head of The School where Martin Worked Teaching A Level Art & Design.

After a gruelling descent through drizzling rain, they checked in at The Nestlings B&B, a whitewashed cottage smelling of bleach and synthetic roses, took scalding power showers and creaked over to the pub across the road for a dinner of pie and peas and a pint or two.

"No wonder the kids are so bloody ignorant, bombarded with shit pop, online porn and cyber bullying. It's enough to fuse anyone's brain cells."

"Is there nothing you can do to make an actual difference, Mart. Instead of ranting?"

"I'm not ranting, I'm opining, critiquing."

"OK. Anyway."

"Really I'm not."

"You used to want to change the world, not just moan about it."

"Yeah yeah, OK. How's the family?"

"Freya's OK. We don't see much of Pip but she seems very happy with Sophie and all."

"I know I'm supposed to be responsible for her moral development, but whenever we meet, Pippa always ends up advising me. Great lass." Martin was Pip's unofficial, atheist godfather. "Stan's fantastic, and Connie's girls are a bit less angry with me now. Her ex is calming down too. Connie's mum's been staying – she's almost civil these days."

"O, lucky man."

"Connie is the most amazing, beautiful woman I've ever known and I can't believe she married me."

"I agree, she's lovely and neither can I." Jamie took a final mouthful of locally sourced beef pie, pushed his knife and fork together and smiled up at his reassuringly annoying best friend. To Jamie's surprise Martin looked genuinely miserable.

"But it's mangled us, mate: her splitting up with the twins' dad, the horrible divorce, then us having Stanley. We don't have time or patience for each other any more."

"Really?"

"I can't remember when we last had sex. Well – actually I can, vividly. But that was months ago. And like now, when Connie's mother's staying and gagging to do babysitting, she wants to get away from me."

"Enjoyed your pies, gents? Care to look at the desserts menu?" The publican loomed wheezingly over them, waiting to clear their plates. One eye on the TV over the bar, he ran through his patter. "Go on – I'm sure you can handle a brownie and ice cream, two strapping young chaps like yourselves." They were full already, but the challenge was irresistible. They ordered one portion with two spoons.

"So where is Connie then?"

"On a hen weekend. Not the wild sort. These days brides go for detox and saunas."

"Well that sounds reviving, like this is for you I hope. Maybe when you get home..."

"Maybe." Martin scruddled his hand through his hair and sighed. "Except she looks at me and sees the man who screwed up her dull but cosy marriage. I look at her and see a gorgeous romance that's – turned to stone."

Martin clammed up, muttered apologies for "going on" about his problems. They were both too exhausted to talk much more and ate their shared brownie then finished off their pints in silent rumination, trying not to overhear the publican and two locals griping about a Polish family recently arrived in the village. Uttering deep and involuntary groans, the two men raised themselves up out of their chairs, plonked empties on the bar and went to bed.

Back in his tiny floral wallpapered, fake oak-beamed guest room, Jamie couldn't sleep. He switched on the lamp, sat up in the voluminous bed swallowing back the metallic taste of reflux and began drawing alternative staff structures in his Moleskine notebook, seeking SMART ways to deliver better for less. For over a decade Jamie had been the Council's Co-ordinator of Play in the Recreation Services Department, with a team of five, a budget of, well, several thousands, a reassuringly quite senior position in a field which sounded like it was all about fun. "What a wonderful job that must be!" friends and relations enthused, picturing him running joyfully around playgrounds for a living, instead of writing funding bids at a cramped desk in the back of the Council House. When was the last time he'd come back from work babbling about some hilarious and touching comment a kid had made about their tree house? He still took pride in the mission of *providing creative and fulfilling leisure possibilities to the citizens of tomorrow*. But Martin wouldn't be the only one howling once the cuts were announced. Jamie yawned, dropped his book and pen onto the floor, switched off the light and rolled over.

from THE LITTLE BOOK OF NEARLY

Close your eyes
Run on the spot as fast as possible for 20 seconds
Freeze
Run on the spot as fast as possible for 20 seconds
Freeze
Run on the spot as fast as possible for 20 seconds
Freeze.
In your mind carry on running.
Thus you may enter the Nearlyverse.

ACCORDING TO STICKERS

"That's me." In the foyer of the Hotel on Brighton Grand Parade, Freya leant over the table to pick up her badge and welcome pack while the young intern faffed through a list of names. She stuck the rectangular name badge onto her jacket, noticed that Zane's hadn't been picked up, snatched a Danish from the white table-clothed counter, managed to pump a black coffee out of the thermos jug, then headed through to the conference hall, stopping to add a stack of her smart little business cards to a table laden with leaflets and flyers. During the morning's presentations she tapped and clicked on the laptop, its heat radiating into her knees till she felt it would melt itself through her dark suit skirt to her flesh, then weld with her bones. Once logged onto the wi-fi and her Twitter account, Freya sent out copious notes and comments about the speakers she was half listening to, added a hashtag to attract fellow #fsm delegates, then waited like a fisherwoman for new contacts to nibble on her pithy asides. Every re-tweeter or new follower she hooked was promptly emailed a PDF copy of her brochure, with a friendly, self-deprecating note attached. Freya looked up from the screen, ran her fingers carefully through her recently tinted hair, marvelled again at how conversant she'd become with the habits and acronyms of digital times, then dived back into her Macbook for more key tapping and hash tagging. This room was a pond of new contacts and today she'd be reeling in plenty of juicy new clients for sure.

Conference sessions took place in different zones, highlighted with big cardboard signs: "Argue", "Energise", "Empathise", "Futurise", "Toilets". In the Argue Zone the facilitator threw a red foam football at any members of the audience who dared raise their hands to speak. Inside the ball was a microphone to record the questions for the podcast. But the presenter's aim was poor and the ball kept bouncing off the heads of those it was aimed at. Between the zones you could queue up to sit in a chair and be stroked by prosthetic robot arms, taste chocolates manufactured by a 3D printer, watch demos of new digital tools for political engagement in the dawning clickocracy, refill with coffee and increasingly stale Danish pastries. At the evening Tweet Up, a perfectly normal reception except all wore stickers with their Twitter names felt-tipped on, after wandering lonely round the edges of the room, Freya popped into the Toilet Zone to re-apply lipstick, then re-entered to approach an interesting trio of chatters called @digisamp, @wibbliblob and @astrobanana. She stood next to them smiling knowingly, trying to exude the sense that she was someone they should know, interjecting odd murmurs of assent, a witty aside, then plunging in with a full-length comment. Her fellow networkers shifted to make room for her and conversation rumbled on.

"There's a lot happening in that space right now," said Astrobanana to nods of agreement, gazing into the middle distance.

Freya turned to see what he was looking at. It wasn't a space, but the backside of a waitress. "Sorry. Which space?"

"The whole VR thing meets the retail experience?"

"OK. Yes. That space. Very exciting. My company's primed to move into it. We're working with the people at Webberation. You know Zane?"

@astrobanana eyed her coldly through trendy red spectacles.

The young man next to her smiled down. "Sorry – I don't think we've been introduced. I'm Dan Sampson."

"Freya. Seward Associates." Out with the business cards and the spiel about how her company was currently actively seeking additional clients to add to their varied portfolio, partnering with Webberations on a total reboot package including a dynamic new site about to go live. It soon became apparent that @astrobanana's circle were fishing for clients too, not holders of budgets themselves.

Dan was tall, stubbly, gorgeous, with gelled, wild hair and probably twenty years younger than Freya. What was weird about him: as they chatted he seemed to be enjoying her company. He scratched his designer hair and fidgeted in his designer tight-legged, baggy-crotched jeans, looked Freya straight in the eye and laughed warmly at her jokes. He asked her name and then used it frequently. And,

Freya thought to herself, he has brown eyes to die for. O, but she didn't think things like *brown eyes to die for,* didn't use the word 'gorgeous' about men of any age, or didn't any more, if she ever had, her being middle aged and pretty much happily married of course and a professional and – well, not someone who thought like that. Then again, by rights she should've been in France on this beautiful if chilly weekend, so didn't she bloody well deserve a bit of flirtation?

@digisamp butted in."Dan, how up are you on Oculus Rift?"

Freya stepped back, walked again around the room, half smile in place, but found no sign of Zane or any Webberation stand, and no other huddles she could edge her way into. She was about to make her excuses when something nudged her in the ribs. She turned to find Dan, a glass of wine in each hand, using his elbow to catch her attention.

"Want one of these? I see you've run dry."

She placed her empty glass on a passing waiter's tray and took the new one he proffered.

"God, some tweeters are twats," said Dan and smiled that smile. They talked, Freya's eyes glistening with the urgency of her need to generate income, staring into his, leaning in close to be heard over the hubble [hubbub?] of the room, pulling nicely conspiratorial faces about colleagues around them. The conversation almost died when they moved onto the dearth of investors in start-ups these days, livened up nicely over the pros and cons of the new iPhone and what signing online petitions actually achieved, even more so as they discussed some of the fruitier uses of VR they'd seen clips about on YouTube and laughed as Freya envisaged the commercial potential for more women-centred apps.

Then Dan said, "I do like you."

Was that what he said? The acoustics in the room weren't good, but that's what she thought he said. It was how he said it that mattered.

And she actually replied, "Hey – I'm old enough to be your mother."

And he said, or had he? Had he? Maybe she'd misheard. "I don't care." And there was a moment – or perhaps not – when, if the room hadn't been filled with yattering digi-people, he might have leant down and kissed her, she was – almost – sure of it. But the room was full and he didn't, and the conversation moved onto issues surrounding the policing of the dark web, and then @astrobanana reappeared with @donatojojo and @ifbook, talking about people she didn't know and acronyms that meant nothing to her, and she excused herself, slipped out to the loo feeling old and dull and out of touch and afterwards found herself taking the lift up to her cramped, viewless hotel room.

She locked the door, breathless and intoxicated, took a shower, heart hammering, dried her hair with a device which made her feel like she was being breathed on by a sweaty stranger. Next Freya texted a picture of the seafront and a message to Pippa about the lovely view and boring conference, hoped the rehearsals went well. She plugged in her laptop and phone to recharge, hammered out another angry email to zane@webberation.net. Next she prepared for bed, switched on the tiny TV which loomed over her on its rickety shelf and, thinking she'd be awake all night, drifted off to fitful sleep with the shopping channel burbling about exercise machines, woke up unrested for another tepid shower and down to a dining room smelling of bleach. Here conferees sipped horrible coffee, flicked through the delegate pack or huddled panicky over iPads doing final honings of their Powerpoint presentations.

INTO TO THE NEARLYWHEN

All fizzing as ever, Mumma sicker and sicker,
due to the buzz getting louder and louder. He trying to fill in
the space between,
but not stopping that crackling of the cosmic almost,
head close to explode with the pressure of it now,
the whole wide Nearlyverse pressing down
on this eggshell skull.
He think going strollabout and telling might help.
The big reveal.
But the space leaky these days and oozing, power draining
like hot piss into cold earth. In his locked room he paint
himself good, spots and swirls of inked possibles.
Takes blinking ages.
In the next room the Mumma's dry coughing.
In the glass see the inner jive, the Nearly to really
as dancing to walking,
the writing with his body in the air help help and go to
flashbackbackback
over the days, undulating a way through into to to the
Nearlywhen.

COOL TOOL & EYEBEAMS

And here was Freya at breakfast discussing the potential
for start-ups in the mindfulness app space with this young
man Dan again. His smile was as dazzling as a burst of
winter sun. Her morning grumpiness evaporated, hope
rekindled.

   "Where did you get to last night? Did you find your
website designer guy? I was thinking – you know you were
saying about designing a tool to help people concentrate? Do
you ever use Self Control? It's an app, downloadable free,
lets you block access to distracting websites for up to one
day, so you can get on with the task in hand. Maybe you

could make something like that – with a guided meditation and diet tips too?" said Dan. He smiled broadly, without irony, then took another hearty mouthful of muesli. Freya watched his warm, moist lips as they worked on the cereal and felt herself melting inside like a character from a novel she wouldn't dream of reading. She was on the verge of swooning. No, really – actually close to fainting suddenly, the smell of bleach in the dining room overwhelming, catching in her throat, making her gag. She forced herself to turn and wrench open a window onto a bleak service area of humming generators. Dan looked on concerned as she sat back and gulped in air, a hot flush sweeping through her body.

Like Google Earth when you click on a place and go zooming out and up, into the dark stratosphere then down again, zoning in on the turning globe, on one continent, one country, one town, one street, one moment, she was thrown back to another time more than two decades ago when she'd clutched at her throat and felt herself on the edge of passing out. On her way to a band practice, carrying an electric guitar under one arm, wearing, she remembered, bright pink tights, leopard skin shorts, Doc Martins sprayed green and a red leather jacket studded with women's symbols and anarchist badges, hair electric blue, pondering how she felt about this Jamie guy, with his big, bear-like body and curly blonde locks, who she'd spent the night with, even though The Longstockings were riven with arguments about sexual politics and musical directions, struggling to hurry while rolling up a cigarette with a wad of tobacco she had filched from his heavy greatcoat as she left his place on another bright winter's day. She put the roll-up between her lips and lit it, coughed, coughed again, stopped off at the corner shop for a breakfast apple and KitKat which she slipped into her jacket pocket, and rushed on towards The Premises where they'd hired a practice room for the day. What caused the reaction they'd never discover; afterwards she underwent tests for allergies to all sorts of foods and fibres, but it was never pinned down. In the street she bent down, clutching her throat, disbelieving the strength of what was wracking her body, terrified but also assuming it would pass at any moment. Shoppers passed her by assuming drugs were involved. Then a face loomed over: Chunk Webster, the band's drummer, bending down, eyes wide.

"You OK, Freya, pet?"

And Freya found herself replying, "Yeah, no worries, I'll be fine." But realised she was fainting, op art patterns of light superimposing themselves across her view of the street. Suffocating. Freya tried to scream but the sound was muffled in her ballooning throat. Going going. Game Over. And yes, out of this fear something else emerged: that overwhelming sense of peace which so many experiencers of near death talk about. She was letting go, setting sail, flying beyond. Still hearing the murmur of voices, street commotion, and a deep voice full of concern. "Are you sure you're OK, Frey?" It was Martin the bass player speaking now. The psychedelic swirls faded and she pretty much was.

And dropping down into this century and the restaurant of this soulless Brighton Hotel, all that energy having rushed back into Freya's brain, filling her with a storm of memories and emotions, her eyes settled again on young @DigiDan sitting across the table, scratching his chin with his iPhone, within reach of her arms yet many virtual miles away. He whose sparkly smile and firm shoulders she'd been so pleasantly aware of since setting eyes on him at the previous night's opening reception and whose workshop on the Twittersphere had been so particularly uplifting, his lilting voice making turgid facts about analytics and bounce rates sound almost poetic, everything he said so new and ringing and green and wise in a young kind of way – and so full of income generation potential.

She glanced at Dan and in that moment, like a line from a metaphysical sonnet or the script from the adventures of a shapeshifting TV time-traveller, their eyebeams met and something happened between them, or at least so it seemed to Freya. And she dropped the spoon into her bowl of sugar-free Alpen and walked out with Dan to start *Day Two: Beyond The Network.*

They went together into the packed conference hall where she managed to bag a seat next to him and buzzed at his proximity. It was a talk on *Futureproofing your Social Enterprise.* Freya could feel him breathing and fidgeting beside her, felt her skin tingle dangerously when he glanced at her and smiled.

From THE LITTLE BOOK OF NEARLY

Stand still, legs apart, slightly bent.
Put your hands up high
then push them down slowly
as if pressing the coffee grounds in a cafetière,
in this way straining yourself
for remnants of regrets
traces of desire.

GET YOU OUT OF MY HEAD

When driving long distances alone, it was Freya's practice to make optimum use of the time by holding a meeting with herself. Often she wrote an agenda before setting off, presented a Director's Report and then discussed key issues, sometimes out loud. Plenary over and conference closed, she drove back from Brighton intent on netting new custom, brainstorming new products and services she could develop with Zane, or that Dan guy, to save her ailing company. Panic began to overtake her; she blocked it by imagining the affair she might have with young Dan.

Was she completely blind with infatuation, or had he been coming onto her? No – he can't have been; she must have misheard. It must have been him responding to her weird looks and – oh God, how embarrassing – Freya beaming back at him like a mad lady. But last night it felt so possible. On that dark car journey home Freya turned up the radio and imagined the young man sat beside her in the dark, his hands resting on her thigh as she changed gears, his voice thick with longing, them discussing breathlessly how she had to leave her old life behind to love again, how that shocking news would spread.

"I can't bear this, Dan – I need to be with you."

"You bring me alive, Freya. We've got a future together."

"Don't leave me!"

"But I love this guy."

"How could you do this, after all we've been through?"

"What about me? Imagine how your daughter feels."

"And me, your so-called best friend! I'm shocked, Frey. Then again, he is hot."

"Your own mother forced to watch you destroy the family for the sake of some mad, selfish midlife crisis!"

"Mum, I just can't get him out of my head."

"At her age: mum in some pop song romance with a toyboy…"

"Stupid woman!"

"Lucky cow!"

By the time Freya turned off the slip road onto the M25 the dark car was packed with ghosts of family and friends and acquaintances gabbling horrified, eyes wide and chins wagging.

She parked the car in the drive, locked the demons inside to argue amongst themselves, unlocked the front door, dumped her bags in the hall and tiptoed up to wash, brush her teeth in the painted round mirror with seagull atop which they'd bought one wet weekend in Scarborough, change into her nightie in the dark of the bedroom without waking Jamie. She slipped beneath the duvet, curled around the warm bulk of her slumbering husband briefly, then rolled over.

"You all right Frey?" Jamie mumured.

"Wha..?"

"You keep sighing."

"I'm fine, fine... shouldn't have bought a coffee when I stopped for petrol."

"Mmm. How was the conference?"

"Oh, you know. How was your weekend with Mart?"

"Good. I'm one big ache though."

The familiar clicks and rumbles of the family house. Jamie's wheezy breathing, a short fart as he stirred. Occasional shadows and lights on the ceiling from passing cars. The same orange street-light as back when consciousness-raising groups and rehearsals for the Benefit Band took place weekly, and house meetings were held to debate what to order from the veg collective and who was responsible for the stains in the bath and the smell of bacon last Sunday morning. Things had changed so much since then: the commune dispersed. Jamie and Freya stayed on and made an offer to buy the place from their elderly landlord. Negotiations were engaged in, aided by Jamie's half-brother Tyler who, when asked for advice, came eagerly round to their scruffy home in his smart city suit to blind them with figures, make dubious remarks about the number of immigrants in the area, give Freya more supportive hugs and touches than was necessary and thrash out what, looking back now, had been a bloody good deal. It seemed a terrifying price at the time, mind you, their collectively shared monthly rent replaced by a hefty mortgage for two.

Rooms were painted white, then magnolia, then grey, then sunshine yellow then brilliant white again. Walls were knocked through and extensions built, parties held for children's birthdays and their own decades passing. Still there were improvements they'd not yet got around to. Next she was planning to tackle the front yard. But now Freya remembered The Rainbow Garden, the name a sort of ironic but respectful dig at old hippiedom. It was such a special place then, where a group of close friends lived sort of communally and held meetings where they sat in circles on the lumpy sofa and cushions on the floor debating issues like whether to protest against nuclear disarmament by refusing to pay the gas bill, and how the copy of Mayfair found under the bed of a departing house member perpetuated the patriarchy and violence against women. They went out dancing together, not to night clubs but Women's Aid Discos and fundraisers for 'Rise!', the ever-endangered Community Arts Centre. Here lentil lasagne was cooked and served under a bare light bulb. In the kitchen a Bertolt Brecht poster poem silkscreened in dark green ink told them, *"You'll go down if you don't stand up for yourself / Surely you see that'.*

Remembering how the house smelt, how it hummed with the thrill of all kinds of revolutions preparing to happen, she pictured not the young Jamie but instead her new friend Dan. He fitted in very well, except she envisaged him fiddling anachronistically with his iPhone, absent-mindedly reaching his arm out and around her waist to pull her towards him, his hands slipping under that thin cotton blouse to the warmth of her soft young skin beneath. Dan's dream phone rang. He answered it, frowned. "The bank. For you, Freya." And she jolted awake.

MOJO THESE DAYS

In the light of cutbacks blah blah blah, priorities shifting blah blah blah, redundancies needed to be made.

"But I gave you my plan for scaling back the team."

"Which was useful, Jamie. However, the Councillors argued cutting one senior post lets us keep more frontline staff."

"What about freelance projects for the department, Graham? I mean, with all my experience here, I could work on training, strategy implementation?"

Graham Stone, Head of L/CE, folded his arms, leant right back in his black leather chair, widened his eyes in panic for an instant as he thought he was tipping over, managed to rectify himself, looked Jamie in the eye and sighed deeply. "To be honest? No. I'm sorry. For the foreseeable it seems to me that nobody up there is in a position to give a toss about what this team does. Across Leisure slash Comm Ed. I used to have all sorts of targets, now the aim is to 'implement' as little as possible, spend as little as possible, create as little impression as possible, achieve..."

"Yes. OK, Graham, I get your drift. We're a waste of space."

"Exactly, Jamie."

"I was kind of joking."

"Ah."

Unlike his wife, Jamie was no entrepreneur. But reckoned he'd done OK at his management role. Fundamentally it was about sitting in the midst of whatever debacles occurred around him and doing nothing much except taking responsibility. There were days when all kinds of crap happened: a flash flood hit the storage area; Rita the grumpy receptionist threw a hissy fit; a favourite team member knocked on the door of his office and entered sheepish but glowing with excitement to announce she was pregnant or leaving to travel or marry; the team failed to win a major grant they'd been relying on. In these circumstances it was Jamie's job to say, "OK well, phone a plumber / start formal proceedings / advertise for a replacement / start redrafting and research other charitable trusts". He took the flak, stated the obvious and moved things on. The good news was he could delegate any task to others, the bad was that The Head of Leisure / Community Education was on his back constantly, while only Jamie lay awake at night worrying about the fate of his beloved Local Play Strategy, fear gnawing at his bones. Well, now it need gnaw no more.

Graham Stone smiled benignly at him across the desk. Time passed. Someone opened the door behind Jamie's back. A woman's voice muttered, "Sorry," and began to close it again.

"That's OK, Aditi, we're about done here."

"I'd better go," said Jamie, smiling at the young office assistant as if nothing out of the ordinary had occurred. He squeezed past her, walked out of the office and straight out of the building, stepped into the street and began on autopilot to walk home. The conversation with his boss replayed over and over, Jamie brimming with winning arguments he'd failed to make. Tomorrow he'd go back to Graham and plead, shout his case. He wasn't going to take this lying down.

As he crossed at the lights on the corner of West Street, his eyes fell on the Oxfam shop window and in it, *Freewheelin' Bob Dylan*, secondhand 12-inch vinyl, with that cover photo of Dylan and his radical girlfriend called Suze Rotolo laughing in loving conspiracy as they ambled, eyes on the sidewalk, down Bleecker Street in the Manhattan snow. The album came out when Jamie was a small boy. But his best mate's elder brother had a copy. Jamie was fascinated by that picture, a window onto a life he might somehow have led, a street he could have travelled down, guitar on his back, if a few things had gone differently. Well, OK, quite a few.

Spotting the record seemed like a sign. He turned to walk into the shop.

From THE LITTLE BOOK OF NEARLY

Close your eyes.
Relax.

Clear your mind.
Concentrate on your breathing.

O well then don't bother.

WHACKED

And found himself lying in the street clutching at his groin
from where a searing pain emanated. And couldn't fathom
what had hit him. Then he saw twisted round his leg a
metal A-frame chalkboard, the words "Vinyl Sale Inside"
written on it, now blurry, smudged by his trousers.

"All right, sunbeam?" enquired an old bloke
walking past with his boxer dog which strained on its leash
wanting to investigate, and possibly piss on, the fallen man.

"Fine. Sorry. Stupid of me," Jamie gasped, pulled
himself up as quickly as his bulk allowed, brushed chalk
dust off his legs and walked on as if nothing had happened,
but round the corner stopped, leant against the wall and put
his hands on his knees, pulsating with adrenaline and
shock. Whacked in the balls by a chalkboard. Like when
he'd been hit by a wave that time in Cornwall, caught by a
breaker, a massive wall of water which drew him inexorably
under, gripped and scraped him hard along the shingle bed.
He'd hauled himself out of the magnetism of the surf and
rushed back to find Pippa paddling safely in the shallows.
Then realised his trunks had been sucked from his body by
the backwash. He was in pain and stark bollock naked.

Freya was clipping the hedge when Jamie limped
home. She wore an old white tee-shirt bearing the faded
remains of the logo of the local Women's Festival which had
folded years ago. His wife was a great acquirer of items
bearing slogans and emblems, using her body as an
advertising hoarding for her beliefs. Their wardrobe was
filled with mostly lost causes. Now she wiped a soil-stained

31

arm across her brow, sighed and smiled at her husband, then noticed his distress. "Hi love. You OK?"

Jamie had an urge to laugh. Having this big news to impart gave him an almost comical power to change the mood. Any second Freya will look shocked, will ply him with outraged questions, urge him to sue, to protest, to fight back.

"I've been made redundant." He waited for her to erupt.

"Oh." She stood frozen, gripping her shears. "Oh."

"Bit of a shock," he said, needlessly.

"Oh," she said again, turned on her heels and walked back into the house. Not the reaction he'd expected. But that evening she was more herself. Showered and changed, she poured two glasses of wine, handed one to Jamie, asked for all the details of what that bastard boss of his had said and done, and then about notice leave, redundancy packages etc.

"We can fight it. Get the union..."

"No chance. It's over." Thank heavens we've got some savings – and your income of course, my darling." Freya smiled wanly, knocked back her Merlot. They went to bed, Jamie undressed and Freya gasped consolingly at the bruise forming on his leg. He explained what had happened with the chalkboard, tried to laugh off how he'd knackered himself on the sign, how much it still hurt but should be OK in the morning.

But it wasn't OK. How to describe it? Something felt different. Next morning he sat on the toilet feeling jarred and aged from his tumble. He read over and over the back of a shampoo bottle which promised *healthy-looking shiny hair from the very first wash*. As he tensed his pelvic floor to pee, he felt aware of some subtle connection severed between brain and groin, a blunting of nerve endings. When husband and wife snuggled up together that night, Jamie pecked Freya on the cheek and turned away.

WAVE

"Blue, Mum?"

"Well I like it, Pippa."

"It's great, it's just..."

"Blue."

"Yes, very."

"Electric it's called. I used to have it like this."

"Yeah, when you were young and in a punk band."

"New wave."

"And it was in fashion. But no, I think it looks rather cool actually. I wouldn't call it electric, though. More blue-black, like Superman's hair in the comics. A bit kind of cosplay."

"Whatever that is. Well I like it and I needed a pick-me-up."

"OK."

"And a USP. Anything to make Seward Associates stick out from the crowd. You don't know how hard it is to get work at my age, Pip."

"Come off it, Mum, you always attract attention. But blue hair – a selling point? Really?"

"My new business card's the same colour. My website too, when I get round to it."

"Uhuh."

"Well I like it. Futuristic. Anyway, not so way out that your Dad's even noticed."

"You look great, Mum. So is that OK if I park in the drive again?"

"What do you mean 'attract attention'?"

AND

The next night and the night after that, and the night after that one. Sometimes in the early morning Jamie awoke with some kind of erection, but, to his increasing horror, his cock was becoming bent now and shrinking, gradually twisting

33

up in a curl like a question mark pointing at his chest. And it didn't half hurt.

From THE LITTLE BOOK OF NEARLY

Now
find a space.
Write the first word that come to mind
to describe who you nearly are.
Write it in the air
with any part of your body.
Write the word
as big as you can.

STAPLER PROBABLY

Jamie cleared his desk, removed his blu-tacked assemblage of photos, inspiring quotes, postcards from exhibitions of art that seemed relevant to the work. He'd imagined the whole department collapsing utterly after he left, but now the redundancies had been agreed, those remaining looked rather perky. He said farewell to his colleagues, including Rachel who'd started the same day as him all those years ago, sad mousy Rachel who'd sat quietly beside him all that time, gradually greying.

"Well, all the best Rache."

"I'm looking forward to getting out of this shit hole soon myself frankly, Jamie. My husband's got a new job in Paris and he's offered to help me realise my dream of setting up a Dance Company working in schools and prisons."

"I never knew you were..."

"Married?"

"Interested in dance."

Office assistant Aditi had the wholesome attractiveness of a Blue Peter presenter, and Jamie struggled to stop himself staring as she bent to collect the post from the out-tray each afternoon.

"I've never felt in a position to say it before, being your line manager and all, but now I'm off, let me say it's been really wonderful working with you, Aditi, and I do wish you the very best in your career."

He opened his arms and stepped forward for a hug, his body making brief contact with hers. But instead of embracing, Aditi mirrored his movement and they stood opposite each other, arms flapping like distressed penguins, uttering squawks of mock sorrow. She said crisply, "Well, good luck with retirement or whatever," and popped back into the office, to claim his stapler probably, move her desk so she had a better view of the street, and prepare to be restructured into a slightly less badly paid role with far more responsibilities.

SPOOKY DARLING

"I was thinking, Mum, I could make you a puppet.

"That's very sweet of you darling... Why?"

"Yeah, like an avatar, a logo. A mysterious character you could put on your website and use for promotions."

"OK. Well I don't think a blue-haired glove puppet's going to help my image much."

"I was trying to be helpful. You sounded so down."

"Sorry. I love your puppets, Pip, really I do, but some people do find them a bit – spooky, darling."

"That's because puppets are so powerful, they seize attention. Nobody notices the puppeteer running around moving their parts. Nobody notices the strings or the mouth that doesn't open. People find them riveting."

"I'm sure they do, love."

"You see we're being encouraged by the Arts Council to look at income generation."

"It'll take more than a bloody puppet."

"Mum!"

"Sorry love, sorry. Thanks but..."

"No thanks. Yeah. OK."

INSUFFERABLE

"Don't worry – I'll have a filter coffee if that's easier. Or maybe an orange juice."

"Cappuccino. No problem, sir. Thank you very much." In the mirror behind the counter of the Café Del Mondo, Jamie caught sight of his reflection: a fat, bald man, getting on a bit, one hand making vague keyboard chord shapes on the counter top, waving a five-pound note in the other while the stressed Italian waitress struggled with a Gaggia machine, under the steely gaze of her boss, a middle-aged blonde woman standing underneath a canvas-printed photo of herself when younger and less nasty.

"Sorry."

"Not your fault. They should give you proper training." He dropped a pound coin in the tips jar and felt his spirits lifted by the manager's scowl and the waitress's smile.

"Thankyouverymuch."

He took his cup of coffee from the flushed and flustered barista with the kind eyes. Shouldering open the glass door he found a seat outside the café overlooking the hospital and prepared to die.

Since redundancy he'd been insufferable, Jamie knew it, holed up in his den watching the Council website, stomping about muttering imaginary speeches to his ex-bosses about the appalling small mindedness of local government, the transformative power of play for community cohesion, education and economic development, the blatant ageism of their employment practices. Jamie had become a kind of Shadow Minister of Play, tracking the decisions of the remaining team and drafting his radical alternative strategy for the sector he'd been so rudely ejected from. He used the web to stay up to date with Council doings and emailed Graham to gripe and moan about what he found there. He knew his old boss wouldn't give a damn, but he couldn't stop himself. Taking a slurp of coffee, he used his mobile to log on yet again to the Council website now, muttered, "Bastards!" pressed in a number and put the phone to his ear.

"They're recruiting for a Senior Policy Officer with responsibility for Play. That's tantamount to illegal!"

"Hi Jamie. Absolutely typical of this local authority. But, mate, you've got to kick the Social Notworking. Where are you?" Martin's voice was tinny amidst the din of playing children.

"In the Del Mondo."

"The bad news is you're out of work; the good news is you can hang out in cafés and forget about all the wage slavery some of us are still in the thick of." Jamie hadn't told his friend or his wife about this twisty genital issue. If only they knew. Instead he poured out bile about his redundancy, watched Freya losing patience with him, watched himself failing to apologise, watched himself not reaching out, but curling up instead tighter and tighter around his secret pain.

"Out on my ear," muttered Jamie to Martin. "I should never have turned down that job in New York."

"You've been offered a job? When did that happen?"

"Chunk Webster sent me details, it was at the New York Public Library, Head of... Community Engagement or something or rather. He said I'd have walked it."

"You didn't get offered it? Look I must go soon. The bell's going."

"I didn't actually apply in the end. This job here came up, but..."

"Hang on – this was all...bloody decades ago?"

"Freya kept on at me to go for it. We'd be living in Brooklyn, earning a fortune."

"Oh come off it."

"It's all my fault, I didn't have the guts for all that upheaval."

"Jesus, Jamie. Listen to yourself." Down the phone the roar of charging schoolchildren. "Look, sorry, got to go."

The café door swung open as another customer barged out, a fraught young man holding paper cup and cinnamon swirl. A burst of babble from a local DJ spilt from the radio playing inside, and that catchy, synthy opening riff of The Eurythmics' *Sweet Dreams Are Made of This,* Annie Lennox wailing high as the door clicked shut again. Without the routine of paid employment, he had no anchor to tie him to the present; lately old songs like this sent him flying back in time.

Here with pregnant Freya discussing nuclear Armageddon and the pros and cons of towelling versus paper nappies. The café was called The Silver Spoon back then and served Nescaff in glass cups alongside plates of baked beans on toasted Wonderloaf. Here with baby Pippa in her buggy when he would cajole a rubber teat between her budding lips and watch while she gulped on the bottle and he tried with his other hand to guide the coffee cup safely to his own mouth. Years of family snack breaks, laden down with bags of shopping, hard-earned salary being spent on trainers and lampshades and gadgets from portable music centres to Walkmen to iPods, and God knows how many tons of groceries, the same items bought and consumed over and over.

Pippa turned from squirming toddler clutching Blabamus the stuffed bunny, to lithe child with her family of dolls and cuddly toys each with their own voice and characteristics, to grumpy teenager, lonely but ever online, chatting into the ether. Freya plumped and wrinkled up a bit, but still looked pretty fanciable, while Jamie evolved

38

from a longhaired hunk – that's what Freya used to call him, said he was her Norse God, her Thor – to big, balding Dad and manager tipped to go so far. Now he'd turned to this obese, featureless blob of a bloke who hadn't gone anywhere much after all. And his mojo wasn't working. But then neither Freya nor anyone else seemed interested in his mojo these days.

The door swung open again. Today the music was Beyoncé singing about putting a ring on it. The waitress smiled, pushed a strand of hair behind her ear, began wiping the tables and collecting up cups.

"Enjoying the sunshine, sir?"

"Yes. Bit chilly though." Wow. Killer chat-up line. Such sparkling wit and repartee. Jamie shivered, looked at his watch. Appointment in 30 mins. An old man sat hunched opposite, cigarette between his lips, perusing red top headlines about Jihadi Brides and the sins of old Deejays. Everyone else he could see was plugged into a mobile, gawping into their personalised screens. "Actually, I lost my job," said Jamie.

"Tell me about it," said the waitress. Of course she meant, don't. She knew about shit wages and long hours and racist asides and instant dismissals. Passers-by passed by with eyes downcast, squeezed and stretched and pummeled by this age of austerity. Now a woman with sunshades and earbuds, cigarette and painted nails, stopped still to chat into the air. In Greece, thinks Jamie, they've been throwing bricks, in Syria facing bullets, in the Café Del Mondo across from the Hospital drinking grey coffee and staring into their phones. Life on the streets in the 21st century at five to eleven. Jamie's smartphone had been a leaving present from the Council, given at a brief event featuring a lemon drizzle cake and card signed by lots of people he hardly knew. "All best from I.T. Support :) xxx." Up pinged new emails: all spam.

OK so he'd lost his job – but like Martin said, perhaps he could think of it as having been freed up to retire early. They could cut back and get by. And now he could find the time to do all those things he'd always wanted to, had been meaning to get round to since before family life happened. He just couldn't remember quite what those were.

Please let him not be dying, though. Twisted willy cancer – was that, as they say, a Thing? Today he promised himself to chart a new course to see him through economic downturn and physical dysfunction, the thickening of his arteries and swelling of the stomach region and all the tedious rest of it. Today he will decide how to proceed. He will consider his options. He will write lists. Please let him not be dying. Let him please please be well be well and all manner of things be well.

From *THE LITTLE BOOK OF NEARLY*

Now
run through the letters of the alphabet quickly
saying an adjective that starts with each letter.
'I am Angry / Beautiful / Confused / Desperate / Energetic...'

How nearly are you which of these today?

SHADOW MINISTER

"We're going to insert a camera into your penis sir," said the Doctor cheerfully, rubbing his hands together to warm them. While the gadgetry was assembled, the team chatted about CCTV and social media and today's surveillance culture. Jamie was asked to strip bare except for shoes and socks, to put on surgical gown, lie on a paper-covered day bed, have willy washed, prodded and discussed by Doctor Gunawardena and his trainees, like restaurant hygiene inspectors around a dead rat.

"We could live stream these images on your Facebook page," said a spotty young male trainee, then, hurriedly, "Joke." But the Doctor frowned.

"I'm afraid this will sting rather but it won't take long. Then we will inform you of the results in a week or so. But please – you mustn't worry."

"You don't think it's serious?"

"I mean whatever it is, worrying won't help."

TRACKING GAME

Spotted her first in the outback, walking in drizzle.
He loiter there plenty him, sweet with the mulch of autumn,
and a whiff of dogshit. Budding trees flowering blue plastic
bags, lager cans caught in their branches.
Down by the barbed wire fence where dead fridges
and DVD players lie, innards spilled.
Rare birds and crapping doggies walking their owners,
the brisk-before-work ones, the leisurely-time-to-kill types,
the strange ones and saddoes.
This his haunt and see her there sighing, putting wires in
her ears, pulling phone from her pocket. A glint as
something metal drop as she doing
the handsfreephonething,the big arguing.
Then she head back across the grass to the road.
He walk to the point where that something fell.
In the mud right there
a bunch of keys on a chain with a stone attached.
Feel like he's dreaming it, that she's his Nearlyincident all
set to really happen. Knowing it with a certainty.
So he go find and do his following game:
walking behind copying the way she walk. That telling you
a lot, how people carry themselves.
Catch site of the special one again at the lights by the
Kebab shop. Bright stripy scarf, slim, almost skinny,
neatly bobbed black hair

And o the most startling eyes,
looking up at crossing's red man/green man,
then standing rooted, staring.
Eventually she walk over the road, bit stiff,
showing stirrings of mid-life creakiness,
all the way up the road through to the high street, and then
well well
round the corner into the library.
And he follow.

DEBTS AND DESIRES

"As I told you, Madam, this is Axis Business Hub, we have a wide range of companies registered here."

"But this is the number I've always used. They can't just've vanished."

"As I say, we're a virtual hub. As in we don't actually occupy the same physical space?" There was a delay on this woman's voice with its annoying rising inflection. The line had a pingy acoustic, like she was speaking from a toilet.

"Well can you please tell me what physical space they do bloody occupy? Emails bounce back, their number has a pre-recorded message, their website's down. I urgently need to talk to them and at least you're a real person – I hope. The company's called Webberations. Please can you…"

"I'm afraid once a company is deregistered with the Axis Hub, terms and conditions stipulate we are not at liberty to disclose details madam, thank you have a good day." The number went dead. When Freya called back she was being held in a queue, told to press hash for further options, thanked for her patience, then cut off.

She'd been too absorbed in her furious phone call to notice where she was walking. Now she looked around her, it seemed right that she'd ended up here: outside the library. As a kid Freya would bunk off school and hang out in her local one, where the lovely librarian didn't shop her but instead pointed out books that shaped her imagination ever after. The plaque on the wall said this Central Library had opened in the Sixties as a focal point for the community of the future. It was a spacious and bold building, a red brick exterior dominated by a green bronze statue of Progress flying, clench-fist forward like a bare-breasted Supergirl sculpted by someone not as good as Henry Moore. Through the glass window, directly in her line of vision stood a display board on which was written:

BUSINESS HUB
The resources you need to:
Write a business plan
Raise finance
Build your brand
FREE TO USE

She stepped closer to read the small print and the glass doors slid welcomingly open before her. Inside the building, the walls were papered in flyers for Council recycling initiatives and freelance colour therapists, its spaces sparse and shabby. Directly ahead stood a new pine and steel display stand of brand-new paperbacks with titles like '5 Minute Marketing' and 'Making It Big with Little'. As she headed towards it a tall man in a dark suit materialised in front of her. He put down the leather suitcase he was carrying, took something out of his pocket.

"Excuse me, miss, believe you dropping these."

"Excuse me?"

"Your keys. Outside." He held them in his cupped hands. She recognised the pebble with a hole through it which she'd found on a Cornish beach once and attached to the bunch. Freya was aghast.

"Oh, good heavens. Wow. How very kind." Freya cupped her hands too and reached out to him, like Oliver Twist asking for more. He dropped them into her open palms. And then rubbed his fingers together over them briefly, as if he was sprinkling something.

Perplexed but overwhelmed with gratitude, marvelling at all the trouble saved, the locks not needing changing, the keys not needing to be cut, the burglars unable to gain entry to her home, the money, valuables and cherished ornaments neither stolen nor broken, Freya stowed the keyring in her handbag, grabbed the man's hand and shook it hard, beaming at him.

"Thank you so much."

"Pleasure, lady," the man said, his voice gravelly, with an unusual lilt in his accent, a tinge of Welsh perhaps, or was it South African? Maybe Eastern European. He was probably in his mid-sixties, wore a slightly crumpled black suit and tie, white shirt, grey hair cropped neatly, deep-set eyes green with a disconcerting fleck of amber. The man smelt of soap, twisted his stubbly neck nervously as if it might be itchy under his collar, seemed highly embarrassed. His eyes fixed on hers, then widened, sparkled, eyebrows lifted, wrinkles rippling like the stirred surface of a deep, clear pond. His features opened themselves to her, lips forming into a beatific, spirit-lifting gift of a smile. A moment later he reverted to the shy frown. "Must get on. Excuse me."

Debts and desire, fear and frustration. Breathless, tense, with shoulders like iron, Freya stared straight at and through this chap as he walked away, panic engulfing her again. She sat herself down at a desk, pulled a notebook and pencil from her handbag and tried to write an analysis of her Strengths, Weaknesses, Opportunities, Threats, but could only think of one big threat: how Jamie would discover that all their joint savings, which he basically relied on his businesslike wife to look after, had been eaten up her own business over these recession-hit years. The bank was demanding repayment on the loan she'd taken out to repay the family nest egg. And now the company she'd spent the last of the money on had vanished into thin bloody air.

44

Webberations had sounded so convincing about how their package of shiny new site design, ongoing analytics support and business coaching was precisely what was needed to thrive in the age of austerity. Oh god and now – she knew it was some kind of displacement activity but that didn't stop the intensity of the passion – now she was besotted with this guy Dan from the conference. Their brief flirtation had drained all the colour from her life and shrouded it with a multi-coloured, utterly imaginary existence in which everything was easier and sexier and fully funded. Freya's SWOT Analysis became a doodled letter T exuding drops of sweat. She scribbled over the drawing, closed the notebook, stood up to leave, then noticed what that gentleman was doing.

He had taken his suitcase over to one of the white formica-topped library tables. Opening it with a loud click, he carefully removed felt tip pens, paper, a large reference book, and a pack of white file cards. He spread some out on the table, wrote neatly in felt tip on one clean card and propped this up against the book. It read: WHAT HAS *NEARLY* HAPPENED TO YOU? THANK YOU IN ANTICIPATION. – G. Carraday. Reaching back into the case he hauled out a heavy, black laptop and prised it open, placed it in front of him, sat, upright and focused, glaring hard at the screen.

**

"I nearly... grew up in another country – the country I was born in but moved away from at a young age. This other me, however, still lives there. I am quite sure of it."
"I nearly... never won a race. I started before the whistle."
"I nearly... had a career in biscuit marketing (I was headhunted by McVities and very nearly took the job)."
"I nearly... became a badass gang leader (at primary school) who was afraid of nuthin'."

45

"I nearly… didn't burn the wedding photos."

**

From THE LITTLE BOOK OF NEARLY

Walking together in a line
everyone mimics the walk of one person,
then another
feeling how it is to inhabit them,
Nearly being them,
Nearly feeling what they feel.

PINNINGDOWNING

"Do you mind if I have a look…?" She pointed at the outspread cards.

"No, no… Yes. No. Do." The man looked down at his screen leaving Freya to read. The cards were written in a variety of hands, some scribbled in biro, some carefully lettered, some of what was written amused her, some was affecting. Then, "I'm nearly broke," she thought and gazed at the wall, frozen in thought until she noticed the man was watching her strangely. She shook her head, put down the card in her hand, said,

"So, do explain: you're a researcher?"

"Umm."

"A psychologist?"

"Gathering nearly stories, madam. I believe this is necessary."

"Really?"

"Nearly."

"I'm sure it's very therapeutic."

The library security man ambled over to look at the cards also. He turned to the man and said,

"Still doing your thing, eh, Professor? Had any contributions?"

"Not today, Mister Carl."

"Hope the Professor isn't bothering you, Madam."

"Far from it."

"That's good. Well, as long as you've made it clear you're not staff, Professor. Of course, it's library policy to promote local businesses and – creatives, like the Prof." The security man sauntered away again.

"I'm Freya Seward, Professor. So pleased to meet you."

"Carraday."

"And these are fun. I mean, touching rather," she said, pointing to the cards. "Or maybe you find them funny."

"No, no, no."

"Sorry, I didn't mean..."

"Nearlies need to be attended to. To cleanse the air. And so I gathering them."

"Clearing the air. Yes I can see that. A 'Nearlyologist'! Is that what you are?" She laughed at her own idea and he did too, seeming pleased with that title. Nearlyologist. Oh yes, exactly. She rummaged in her bag. "And my knight in shining armour, Professor, for finding my keys." He was beaming now. "Well, please allow me to contribute. I've got a pen... Yes." She clicked it and scribbled on the back of the envelope from the bank. Carraday handed her a card. He sat still until she finished writing. He took the card from her and put it into his suitcase.

"Are you going to read it?"

"Yes. If you wanting that." And he opened the case, but Freya chose that moment to turn and go, slipping away so that when he looked up again, shocked by what he'd read, she had disappeared.

EX EX EX

"He does what?"

"Collects Nearly stories."

"And why does he do whatever that is?"

"He's a Professor. From overseas. Doing a kind of research residency at the library." Whether this was true or not, she wasn't really in a position to say, but neither was she going to let Jamie make fun of the kind gentleman who had returned her keys and intrigued her with his file cards in the midst of her worries. "Or something." She peered at the recipe book and sprinkled garam masala onto a teaspoon then stirred it into the onions while Jamie sliced green pepper. Freya was smaller than her husband, a few years younger and, she reminded herself, a good deal slimmer, slipping around the bulk of him to reach for more olive oil. Radio 4 News was on and they laughed and sighed and howled with outrage in unnoticed harmony at items about an embarrassing scandal for the Conservatives, a lethal bomb in Baghdad, a protest against cuts to benefits. Freya squeezed past Jamie to adjust the gas. She wrapped his [her?] arms around him and kissed his neck lightly. He smiled but squirmed out of reach.

"This Professor's cheered you up. I was going to phone Pip today to see how her rehearsal went. But I didn't want to look like a pestering parent."

"I texted her at lunchtime and she seems fine." Freya pulled her mobile out of her jeans pocket and clicked it on to check the message. "All good, pee ex ex ex" it says."

"She really paints a word picture of the experience there doesn't she."

They cooked on in silence, concentrating on news and ingredients. What Freya had written on a white file card in the library had left her elated with relief. Even if it might not be really true at all.

"I nearly... had an affair."

Unburdened of guilt about her feelings for Dan, distracted temporarily from her money worries, she was hungry for intimacy, wanted to cuddle up with Jamie and get down to it right now like they used to. She squeezed his lardy arse as he bent down to put the Le Creuset in the oven, but he only let out a yelp and stood up again.

"So he sits in the library and people tell him about things they didn't actually do?"

"Kind of." The perfect place to gather Nearlies is the library, the residence of so many who are in a state of imminence: students nearly qualified, outcasts on the borders of homelessness, Nearlywriters forever about to start work on their opuses, a woman realizing she's almost bankrupt.

From THE LITTLE BOOK OF NEARLY

Close your eyes.
Remember a dream you had recently.
Make something from it happen
today or whenever.

BURST

"Are there things we nearly did in our lives which we need to acknowledge – as important to us as what actually happened? I mean, come on love, tell me: what are your Nearlies?" Freya asked her husband.

Jamie saw himself, guitar in hand, under the spotlights, and knew this was another thing he couldn't talk to his wife about. Like the letter from the hospital which he'd pocketed that morning when it landed on the mat and hadn't dared to open yet. Now he asked if she'd seen the backdoor key, then hauled the bin liner out to put in the recycling. In his mind he heard the bass line throb, gripped tight the neck of his guitar, looked out across a sea of upturned faces, a broiling sea of swayers and dancers churning in the hazy dark, and when the drums rolled and cymbal crashed, stepped up to the microphone, into the spotlight, and burst into song.

**

"I nearly... flew to Sri Lanka on the morning of the tsunami."
"I nearly... told my parents that I'm not a virgin."
"I nearly... moved away. Nearly packed it all in, gave up, let the tides and trials wash me away. I didn't though, I didn't let it beat me. Now I never settle I always strive for hope."
"I nearly... stayed in my perfect life with my wrong husband."

**

LIKE TELLING

It was nicotine that did it. Freya's concentration was shot, fantasies of passion with Dan mixed with nightmares involving bank managers waving summonses. And she knew she ought to be more sympathetic to Jamie, but really, he was driving her crazy. Meanwhile the library provided a bolt-hole
when she became too fidgety to sit alone in the tiny office which she rented on the run-down section of the High Street now designated the Enterprise Quarter. At the Business Hub she researched funding possibilities from on-line and printed funding directories. Also in the library she found Professor Carraday in place with his suitcase and laptop open. That security man, Carl, asked her each time, 'Come to see the Professor again, Madam?"

"No no, I'm consulting the resources." The big man grinned. Amidst the silent library users, the Nearlyologist gave a shy glance from across the room and turned back to the screen of his laptop. Freya surveyed the shelves, not sure now quite what to look for now she'd consumed most of the books of top tips for budding entrepreneurs. She'd been telling herself she really ought to start reading proper novels again but began to flick through racks of DVD movies and box sets instead. And keeping an eye on Carraday who she noticed had taken out of his pocket a plastic lighter and a shiny silver cigarette case. She hadn't seen one of those for years.

A few minutes later he clicked the lid of the case, which sprang open. Another five minutes passed before he pulled out one cigarette and placed it on the desk next to his computer. Freya didn't smoke, not really, not any more, but in her life had been round and round the cycle of giving up and caving in, the horrible buzz of withdrawal and the miserably delicious succumbing again. She was pretty sure Carraday was engaged in some private ritual to limit his own intake of nicotine. But this little bit of theatre reminded her of so much from her past that was illicit and pleasurable: being one of the huddle of dissidents who bonded on the steps puffing outside meetings; the roll-ups and spliffs to concentrate the mind whilst writing songs with The Longstockings; post-coital ciggies in bed; the days of playing gigs then dancing, trying to steer clear of the groping blokes, but copping off with someone maybe, or taking speed and staying up all night talking; the days of not giving a damn.

At last Carraday stood up, walked to the exit, muttered as he passed her. Outside the glass door he put the cigarette in his mouth and lit up. Freya slipped out to join him.

"Professor? I wonder if I could possibly cadge a...?" She pressed two fingers to her lips, mimed inhalation. "I left

51

mine at home." He flipped open the battered case and held it out to her, smiled his smile, so welcoming and warm.

"Come for a walkingabout, Mrs Seward?" And she followed him like a lamb.

Who else did she know who smoked any more? Pip apparently, but not much and never in front of her mum. Rosalind said she'd really given up this time, thanks to vaping. Both of them would be horrified to discover Freya was sneaking crafty cigs again. One, though – what was the harm in that? Carraday took tiny, delicate puffs as they walked around the little municipal park behind the library, its hedges dripping from an earlier downpour. Head spinning from the first toke, she found herself telling this stranger about the Dan incident and her irritation with Jamie. The Professor of Nearlyology was tactful, non-judgemental – didn't say much at all actually, but looked at her with his big green, mesmerising eyes. As if he was her therapist or something, she voiced whatever thoughts bubbled up.

"I suppose you could say I *nearly* had a second child. But I needed to get back to some kind of work after Pippa was born. I do sometimes imagine that other one and wonder if I should've. And I work in Nearlies myself in a way. I'm a communications coach – a digital consultant. Which means I work with clients who tell me who they'd like to be. I help them use the Internet to pretend that's who they really are!"

"Oh?" He looked rather troubled by this.

"No. Well. Sort of." Freya was dressed in her professional get-up, crisp and clean in jeans and blouse and light make-up, a thin, brightly coloured Indian cotton scarf around her to cover any sags or bulges, though she hoped there weren't too many of those she hadn't managed to exercise away. Mister Carraday was stiff in his dark suit and walked fast. She followed, jabbering away to fill up his silences.

"It feels that way sometimes. Do you live around here, Professor?"

He stopped in his tracks to listen to her, then strode on without answering. When she assumed he hadn't heard, Carraday stopped again, said, "Living with my mumma. She not well."

"You're her carer?"

"Yes. Is why I gathering the Nearlies. Fending off the baddest of the possibles."

"Professor Carraday, may I ask where you're from?"

"What you meaning, Mrs Seward?"

"Your – way of speaking." He looked surprise. "You lived abroad, perhaps?"

"Never," said Carraday, frowning.

"Neither of your parents are – were – from overseas or anything?"

"No. But my father gone faraway." He looked as if he'd been accused of something.

"I didn't mean to pry." She crushed her cigarette end against the bark of a tree, laughed. "I wonder if I could rebrand myself a Nearlyologist."

OVER THRASHING GUITAR

Jamie was hunting for something but had no idea what – like trying to reconstruct the remnants of a dream. All morning he'd been rummaging frantically through lever arch files and IKEA storage boxes up in the spare room. Now he pulled out from under the bed an old Crawford's Rover Biscuit tin, bright red with a faded picture of pink wafers and custard creams printed on, and prised off the lid. There! He unfolded and held aloft a wrinkled, silkscreen-printed poster for a gig by The Longstockings, featuring punky young Freya, in cut-off jeans and fishnets, ripped tee-shirt and mouth open in angry song, a dark inky blur in the background which might have been him posing with his

Fender Telecaster. And here was a smaller flyer, glossy this time, with The Longstocks' logo, a photo with singers Helen and Spacey, sullen in matching baggy suits, a blank space underneath for adding the venue and date of the gig.

The Longstockings used to rehearse in the cellar at The Rainbow Garden. Formed by Jamie – then known as Jimmy – and fronted by the purple-haired Freya who had responded to his postcard in the music shop and agreed to join if they changed their name from The Upshuts to something more feministy. The renamed band knocked out three-minute rants against sexism, war and unfairness in general, howled by Freya over his thrashing rhythm guitar, Martin thumbing away on bass, Chunk flailing about in a Keith Moon-like frenzy on drums, Freya playing slow, twangling atonal lead guitar solos. Then two mates of Chunk's muscled their way in, brought in their synths and backing singer girlfriends, sneaked songs onto the repertoire which made no mention of reclaiming the night or bringing down Thatcher. Annoyingly these had catchy tunes and infectious beats, got the dancers going at benefits for the miners' wives against violence against women. Musical differences occurred. Backing singer split with synth player and copped off with bassist. A shouting match between Freya and Chunk on the steps of The Premises led to letters in the local Free Press and Women's Newsletter. Somewhere in the midst of this furore, Jimmy/Jamie turned up at Freya's place, a shared house in the student district near the cemetery, with a bottle of wine, an ounce of Old Holborn, a bag of grass, and stayed the night.

They lolled on the floor around her gas fire for hours, talking, rolling joints, playing records and cassettes on her music centre. The Au Pairs, The Slits, Joan Armatrading, Rip Rig & Panic, Comsat Angels played, an eclectic mix tape of hard and soft, old and new. Hours passed by and their bodies inched closer, Freya's scent and heat mingled with the cannabis, the chill of the night air through wonky window frames drawing them closer. Then

Freya scrunched her face up, said, "Ooh, I'm numb. Think my brain's got pins and needles." And they burst out laughing.

He offered to rub some warmth back into her shoulders and she pulled off her jumper, bent her neck forward for the massage. They sat still for a while longer, his arm around her, till finally she curled in and raised her face to be kissed. And then there was the deliciousness of necking and exploring, hands reaching where they'd been yearning to reach, conversation replaced by sighs and murmurs. Eventually they went to bed, drawing the curtains on a new day beginning to dawn. They stripped off quickly, slipped between ice cold sheets and, between giggles and gasps, he felt the blissful naked length of her, reached above, behind, below and dot dot bloody lovely dot.

In the morning over breakfast of porridge and instant coffee, ethical and tasteless, Freya loudly denounced rock music and men, announced her decision to give both up in favour of pursuing her art and political aims. Present company didn't seem to be excepted. On the way home Jimmy – that's what he called himself then – stopped off in his favourite greasy spoon café on Market Road for a bacon sandwich, dejected though still buzzing, glowing and sticky. He smelt her on his fingers, hummed Joni Mitchell's *Coyote* to himself and tried to put the night down to sexy experience, though he knew already he was lost in love.

Jamie/Jimmy was astounded when Freya appeared at his place three nights later. The bell rang and he found her on the dark front step, bronzed under the street lights, wrapped up against the cold in a thick tweed coat with fake fur collar, an old lady's garment from the local Oxfam shop, decorated with badges and brooches, a woollen hat covering her spikey, now grass-green dyed hair.

She glowered at him, said, "Well, can I come in then?" and pushed past into the hall. He made a pot of tea which they carried up to his room. Clearing a space amidst the debris of books, clothes, albums, magazines and cassettes, he sat on the bed and asked how she was. Freya ignored him, stared out of the window sullenly, shrugged off the big coat, stubbed out her roll-up, then snogged him. They carried on where they'd left off, and did so on an irregular basis after that. No commitment, no arranging of next times.

This Longstockings flyer was a rarity. That line-up didn't last long. Soon after their next gig, Freya stormed out of the band telling Chunk to go shove his sodding drumsticks up his pop-picking, patriarchal middle-class arse. The band had been renamed Longstock, which didn't mean anything but they thought sounded quite cool. Martin had also denounced Chunk as a sexist but not made any signs of leaving, and miraculously Jimmy managed to remain Freya's lover and a band member by adopting a non-committal smile when being harangued by one side about the other.

One day Freya announced to him that she was pregnant. He was thrilled, delighted, overjoyed – amazed to realise how he felt, stunned also that Frey, ten years younger, so smart and talented and full of potential, was delighted too. She seemed nervous as hell when she told him, but as time passed and what was going to be Pippa grew in her womb, Freya assured her boyfriend that she knew with burning certainty this child was to be kept and treasured, short-term artistic plans worth shelving for the sake of this new life growing.

"I'm a shit singer anyway. Gawd knows what I'm doing trying to play guitar. I'm going to channel my energy into radical fucking mothering instead." All would be well. Jimmy was impressed and relieved by her certainty.

Nineteen Eighty Something, The Premises, *(We Don't Need This) Fascist Groove Thang* by Heaven 17 pounded out into the cavernous bar where a row of student bar staff struggled to pour pints for a swarm of radical music lovers, tee-shirted in slogans and band names. Jimmy had been waggling his tenner ineffectively for ages when Chunk the drummer appeared at his side, immediately caught a barman's eye and mimed his order.

"FOUR PINTS. OF BEST."

"HI CHUNK."

"FUCKING AMAZING!?"

"WHA??"

"THE NEWS!!" This exchange over the racket of talk and music.

"WHAT. NEWS??" Chunk took his clutch of drinks back to the table, sticky with lager spills, handed them out to the rest of the band and waited while Jimmy waved his tenner to attract attention, and eventually managed to be served, then sat down opposite.

"That management guy. He's only offered us a deal. A tour and a single."

The bassist, Martin, was not so impressed. He unwrapped himself from the embrace of backing singer Helen and said, "We got to watch these capitalist arseholes. They'll rip us off."

"Yeah but at least it's a deal,' said Spacey and stubbed out her cigarette on the table top. The boys stared at her, taken aback by this intervention. "Well it is." She scratched her cropped pink hair and scowled.

"Better be ripped off and famous than never be famous at all," said Chunk with gravity.

And at that moment in The Premises when the passageway to fame opened before him, Jamie slammed the door on the possibility without giving it conscious thought. "Well good luck you guys, but sorry, I'm leaving. I'm going to be a Dad." And so he'd quit the band. It felt like he hadn't found the time to reflect on that decision since. Until now as he stood in the spare room and a wave of long suppressed regret engulfed him. Jamie folded up the poster and flyer, dropped the papers back into the box which he raised high above his head and tipped up, pouring a shower of their old letters, postcards, magazines and god knows what else onto the floor. Then he flung the empty tin at the wall.

JUNK OF THE PLANNING

Freya was preparing for her meeting with the bank and wanted to re-read a chapter she'd found in the library on business plans. As she walked in, Professor Carraday leapt to his feet and hurried over, looking determined, whispering loudly.

"MrsSeward. I would like to be telling you."

"Excuse me? Sorry, Prof, I'm a bit pressured this morning."

"Cigarette? Walk around about maybe?"

"Not really time, I'm afraid."

"OK."

"Is everything all right, Professor?"

"Madam, I am not a Professor."

"Oh, but I thought."

"Mister Carl calling me that."

"OK. Look I am running a bit late."

"I wanting to explain." None of his gravitas – today he was like a schoolboy, bursting to tell. Despite her lack of time, she was intrigued.

"Sorry?"

"I nearly move to Australia – to the city of Brisbane – some years back. But then my Mumma getting crook. She frail, housebound. I know I cannot be leaving her. Brenda, my... fiancé then, would not wait. She go on her own."

"And your mother – is she? – how is she..."

"Mumma still ill. Worse. Mind wandering bad. Surrounded by Nearlies needing dispelling. I need to clear more faster. Cannot move so I nearly did. In my... mind." He stared at the floor long enough for Freya to wonder if he was going to speak again. She scanned the shelves as she spoke.

"My husband and I talked about moving to New York at one time. Never got round to it either," she sighed. "I still have an image of me with a coffee in one of those New York paper cups walking out of the subway on the corner of Broadway and 12th or whatever on my way to work. Feeling so cool. It never happened but I can picture it vividly. Did you keep in touch with your fiancé? Never any chance of joining up again later?"

Carraday scowled.

"She meet a man from Tasmania on the plane over. Still living there I believe. Leaving I with the mess of the plans we been making together."

Freya headed for the Business Hub and Mister Carraday followed, walking sideways like a crab alongside her, in staccato sentences explaining how he'd been left with guidebooks to Brisbane and all the information on which areas were affordable. They'd spotted a district Brenda thought sounded lively; it was called the West End which impressed and amused her. Thanks to a contact of Bren's father, Carraday even had an offer of work apparently: admin with a property company which would help with all the paperwork to let them into the country.

"I see. Could you possibly reach me that blue book down? That's the one. Thanks. Yes, how amazing. You didn't go but kept wondering, what if you had."

"Exactly so."

"Of course, with the web one can easily 'nearly' live somewhere else these days. All it takes is wi-fi I suppose." She flicked through the book, found the section she needed.

"Ah yes, the wiffy. I discovering my laptop one day on my walking about, in a briefcase hid in a bush by the reservoir."

"You found it?" Freya looked up from scanning *Small Business Planning in 15 Mins*. Mister Carraday stepped towards her, his breath hot and tangy. Freya was still wearing her reading glasses so found herself confronted by every detail of his face in unexpected detail, the childish intensity of those green eyes despite the wrinkled skin around them. He wore a lapel badge, she noticed now: a tiny silver kangaroo.

"I took the laptop home and finding there free Internet seeping through the walls – from the neighbours. No password require. Data wafting about in the airwave for me to be tapping. Deep listening needed. I convinced it meant."

"Like Collaborative Consumption – sharing resources. But without the collaboration. The laptop, you didn't think you ought to return it?"

"The thing was brand new. Been stolen and dumped, I assuming. Anyhow. Through the wiffy I decide I could move in my mind. I research more and more about where we nearly live. I investigate property which I might rent if I residing there, I read online – of the staff in the bookshop where I thinking I best like to work. I put a comment on the website, then people were commenting back, thinking I was actually there. They wanted to meet, to 'hang out' at what they call The Footie – or at The Waterfront. When floods hit Brisbane, I even received offers from individuals to put me up – they were worried my home might be flooded. They were imagining me under the water." He made frantic swimming movements with his arms. Freya looked round the library to see many grumpy heads turned towards them. And noticed he'd been speaking in plain English, that curious accent slipping somewhat.

"Perhaps keep your voice down, Mister Carraday? So you say… you told lies?" Carraday looked at her sharply, then stared down at the ground. She could see he was stung by the question. He whispered,

"I don't look at it like that, Mrs Seward. I not want to deceiving anyone. I not thinking anyone be bothered about me."

"Sounds like lying to me, Prof." Freya glanced at her phone. "Hell, is that the time?" She slammed the book shut, pushed it back onto the shelf and set off for the bank, trying to remember the speech she had planned for the business advisor.

From THE LITTLE BOOK OF NEARLY

Find a book you own but haven't read.
Recollect what you did instead.
Imagine what's in it.
Write what you nearly read.

AS A TREE

As the Nearlyologist's lifestyle choices highlight, the web makes it possible to create one's own unique cultural context. We can pick and mix, read a daily newspaper from Korea, listen to American radio, keep in touch with Indian film, build a network of friends around the world who share our niche interests. Mister Carraday has created his own land in which to live. So do we all – but mine may look slightly more like the world outside my window than his does.

What's more it's never been easier to reinvent ourselves over and over, and we can keep each reinvention running concurrently. Seward Associates can coach you as you create your personal social media action plan. Who do you really want to be and how can you stay in touch with your nearly selves?

Freya hummed along to Laura Marling on her headphones, tapped out the beat, hit 'publish' and the article was posted to her blog, potentially viewable by tens of millions anywhere in the world, actually clicked on by seldom more than five per day the analytics said, but, oh well. Four years ago a service like she was offering would have packed them in. No longer. No one had budgets that they actively needed to spend on consultancy any more. On the other hand, it was worth a stab. Since she'd started posting about Carraday on her Facebook page, hit rates had been increasing steadily. But then she'd called him a liar and he'd disappeared. Now she stood up, closed the laptop, slipped it into her new *Futurising Social Networks* tote bag, took her jacket off the back of the chair. Jamie popped his head around the door, did a double-take when he noticed her, seemed to consider slipping away then changed his mind, limped across the kitchen and clicked on the kettle. They nodded blandly at each other.

"Going out?"

"I'm off to the library. Looking for the Nearly Man. What are you up to?"

"Oh – you know."

"No I don't, that's why I asked."

"Pottering, sorting stuff out."

"What was that racket earlier on?" Freya moved around the room lifting stacks of papers, books and discarded jumpers in search of her phone.

"Playing some old cassettes."

"Very loud. Couldn't hear myself think."

"You should have come upstairs and told me. I was trying to find a recording of the old band. Martin says he's got one. He rang to invite us round for a meal on Sunday."

"And you said yes without checking with me." Freya felt her tired hackles rise. God, she wished she could stop herself, knew how hurt he'd been by the redundancy, but a switch had been turned off in her, sympathy replaced by constant irritation, an allergic Jamie rash she couldn't help but scratch at. "So you two can wallow in nostalgia. And have you sorted out any kind of paid work at all?"

"I've been looking. Nothing around."

"Of course, you've exhausted every avenue. Applied for every job going in the Western world. Ah – there it is." She retrieved the mobile from under a box of Corn Flakes.

"Nothing in my line."

"Your line. Whatever that is." Jamie opened his mouth to curse at her but stopped himself, busied himself instead with drink making. Freya popped the white pods of

62

her headphones back in her ears, watched her husband pour and stir his instant coffee as Laura Marling sang of England covered in snow. What had become of him? That lovely, shaggy older man of hers turned into a baldy-headed potato, spectacles the nearest thing to a distinctive feature. She sighed, swung her bag onto her shoulder, checked her pockets for her purse. Next time she looked up, Jamie was gone. She swallowed a final mouthful of her rooibos tea, walked out of the house, slipped her snarling mind off its leash to let it calm down, felt it scampering back to thoughts of Dan and what might have happened if he'd been the man clunking about in the box room upstairs playing loud music and she'd gone up to tell him to turn it down.

SNOW

Suddenly the air hissed with tension. Across the dinner table Martin glared at his wife, while Jamie and Freya stared down at the remains of Sunday lunch and fiddled with their wine glasses.

"How can you sit there and say you 'nearly' didn't want our child?" said Martin.

"I was frightened of the responsibility. And of losing my life again."

"How can you say that?"

"Because I've already destroyed one family."

"Jesus, Connie..."

"Well I have. And now I'm turning into a monster all over again."

That child, Stanley, aged two and a half, squirmed onto Freya's lap and announced into the silence, "I'm nearly as big as the biggest snowman." Martin stood to clear away the dinner plates this sunny afternoon and Connie rose up and yelled at her twin daughters to come in from the garden and bloody well eat something.

"Why, yes you are, Stan," laughed Freya. "Nearly bigger than that even." The small boy looked delighted. Conversation over Martin's spatchcocked chicken with roast vegetables had been flowing freely, especially once Freya raised her new interest which led to a string of anecdotes. Who knew that Martin was once all set to leave teaching and re-train as a therapist, but forgot to post the application and missed the deadline by a day? Or that Freya nearly died aged twelve when the weather turned nasty on a sponsored climb up Ben Nevis? But then came Connie's confession and this terrible eruption of argument during the homemade cheesecake and coffee.

"Nearly as big as a... skyscraper! A whale! A camel!" Freya enthused, breaking the tension. The little boy gaped in awe at the thought of such bigness, then got bored, wriggled free again to totter across to his box of toys. "Well I think it's lovely to be around your kids. I mean, Stanley *and* the girls," she exclaimed while Jamie stood up from the table and went to the bookshelves and browsed through Martin's new selection of vintage vinyl.

"You're welcome to take one away with you. A child, not a record. As a going-home present." Connie was Martin's second wife, and Freya, a good friend of Helen the Ex, and of Rosalind, one of his string of girlfriends in between, wasn't surprised to see cracks appearing.

"Maybe not this time, ta, Connie. I miss the mess and racket though."

"How's Pip's new show going?" asked Martin. He'd known Pippa all her life, was at The Rainbow Garden on the night Freya's waters broke, helped with babysitting, homework, advice on moods and traumas over the years. Through all the complications of his emotional life, he'd stayed in touch with his godless god-daughter.

"All good. She said to send you heaps of love," Freya replied quietly.

"Of course I wasn't saying I didn't want to have Stan – or the twins," said Connie, suddenly on the verge of tears.

"That's a relief, then. Because you're stuck with us now, darling. You can't put Stan and me back in the box and ask Apple for an upgrade. What you see is what you bloody get." Martin attempted a squeeze of Connie's waist, but his wife twisted away and looked to Freya.

"I'm sorry. I don't know what's wrong with me."

Martin tried to change the subject. "I found something for you guys." He took an old cassette tape out of his pocket and crouched down beside his son. "Hey Stanley, will you give this to… him over there?" Stan wobbled across the room, proudly holding out the plastic case. Browsing through his friends' records, he felt Little Stan collide softly with his legs. Jamie ruffled the boy's hair and proudly the child held up something for him. "Is that for me? What a clever boy!" Jamie crouched down and held out his hand. Stan relaxed his sticky grip on the cassette: *The Longstockings Live.*

"Thank you, Stanno! Where did your Dad find this I wonder? Nearly the hit album of the early Eighties! We were good weren't we – why on earth didn't we stick at it?"

"Sales in the nine or ten of copies as I remember. You said you'd had the band on your mind, mate. It was in a box of junk that Connie wanted me to chuck."

"Horrible rattly plastic things. I remember running off copies on a music centre, making the little photocopied cardboard covers. Got anything to play it on?" But the newly purchased, refurbished record deck had no accompanying tape deck.

"I've transferred it to my iPad though. I was going to email it to you lot, Chunk, Spacey, the others." And a few clicks later they were listening to their younger selves sounding not quite as good as they remembered being. A cold blast of air as the twin girls, Bella and Izzy, thundered in to wolf down plates of fish fingers.

"Girls, this is something called punk music."

"New wave," Freya corrected.

"Played by these two, when they were young. And you weren't born. And I was only little," Connie said in the singsong tone of an irritated nursery school-teacher trying to sound jolly. The twins shrugged, devoured the rest of the cheesecake, slurped down gulps of apple juice, wiped their mouths and headed out for more football.

"Nope, not a flicker of interest from the young generation."

"Looking forward to Christmas, girls?" asked Freya. The departing twins grunted in unison.

"It's rough I know, but we could have gone places," Jamie said, positioning himself between the two black speaker boxes. "What a waste."

"Martin clicked his tablet and the Best of Ian Dury replaced The Longstockings. "Anyway, that's enough of that. We may not have been that good but at least we were loud." Jamie saw Martin glance at Connie, aware she felt excluded from the memories of old Rainbow Gardeners. Freya might not be pleased to hear the band either. The end had been pretty acrimonious, and led eventually to Martin and Helen moving out of the Garden; they split up soon after. The group were still friends. Just. Nothing but time had been applied to all those wounds. Anyway, the embarrassing moment was passed. Now Freya was energetically explaining to Martin her latest ideas for her business, hands describing the ups and downs of medium-term goals, eyes sparkling with long-term visions.

"I'm not sure Mart wants to hear your whole pitch now, dear."

"Really? Am I boring you, Martin? Because my husband thinks you might not care that his wife is trying to make something happen in the world."

"Of course not – carry on."

"Thank you, I will." She glared at Jamie and did. Connie sat down beside Jamie on the sofa. Hard not to think of her as a sort of Nearly: the second go at love. Here was his old mate with this attractive new woman, reprising the youthful state of new parenthood. But their divorce had been horrible. Connie was clearly stressed, and Mart looked knackered by life as an older dad to this beautiful, boisterous toddler, stepfather to rowdy girls.

"Music from when you were nearly popstars and in your commune together and it was all free love and drugs and revolution."

"Oh, we were a bit late for that. More new wave and consciousness raising. Free love was over – we were into challenging monogamy by then, which was similar, but far more painful," said Jamie.

"But did involve sex, right? Not Old Macdonald and nappy changing. Sorry. It's scary energies she's unlocking, your wife. I'm not sure I can cope with digging around in regrets and desires, not right now."

"And you're not a monster." Connie smelt of shower gel, wore a loose denim shirt, bracelets that jangled as she toyed with her long, probably not even dyed, red hair.

On the other side of the coffee table, Freya continued to outline her new business plan to Martin.

"Mister Carraday believes it's important for people to talk about what he calls our Nearlies. And I've been reading up on it: imagining different past and future paths is good for us. The neuroscientists say that. So I'm going to ask Mister Carraday if I can pay him to do one-to-one Nearly sessions with people, make Nearlyology part of my coaching offer."

"OK."

"Oh, but that look on your face: you think I've completely lost my marbles?"

"No. I think you could be onto something, really I do." Mart didn't sound entirely convinced. He had half an eye on Connie who scooped Stan up into her arms, lay back on the sofa and blew into the boy's neck. The boy squealed with pleasure then slithered free as his mum murmured to Jamie,

"A little bird told me about the free love you and Frey and the drummer got up to."

"Really?" He'd forgotten about that incident.

"I shouldn't have said. Sorry. Your secret's safe with me. So, Martin tells me you've retired?"

"Retired? No way. Taking a break. Not on the scrap heap yet."

Did Jamie see a warning glance from Martin to Connie? Freya interjected. "How's the web design going?"

"It isn't right now. And I am – was – a coder, not a designer. Not a creative bone in my body, not like you lot."

"That's not true, darling," Martin interjected.

"I must pick your brains sometime, about my site," said Freya to Connie but she didn't respond.

"It is, darling, you know it. I'm useless. I'm horrible," Connie called across to her husband, eyes filling with tears.

"Jesus, Freya, you've upset Connie now. Why must you always be trying to get something for nothing?" Jamie burst out.

"Because we need money and you've lost your bloody job," Freya shouted with much more ferocity than anyone expected, including herself. Another silence which now Martin tried to fill.

"Please don't you two be unhappy, guys. You're the dream couple, you're the island the rest of us swim to when we're shipwrecked."

"We are who we are, that's all," said Freya.

"And who we nearly are," chimed in Connie, but nobody laughed.

"Probably more call for coders than play development officers, these days," said Jamie, trying to steer them back to normal conversation.

Connie looked like she really really really wanted to sound positive, but had to reply, "Probably."

It was the moment to ask, is that the time? What a lovely afternoon it's been. Such a delicious meal. Have a good Christmas. Thanks so much but we really should get going. Stanley rushed over to give a big hug to Freya, his arms tight around her, hot, snotty breath on her cheek as she lifted him. The foursome stood around in the hall feeling fond of each other again now, and concerned.

"That cheesecake! You must give me the recipe."

"Good luck with the business – and the job hunting or whatever."

"We mustn't leave it so long. Maybe we should try making music again?" said Jamie, and Martin nodded vaguely.

"Yeah. We'll have you over to ours in the new year," said Freya, setting Stanley down. Nobody quite wanted the afternoon to end now, despite all the tensions. Jamie remembering the Rainbow Days, when for all the quarrels and complications, a houseful of friends was like a ship of collective hope afloat in all the Thatcherite madness. Call a house meeting. Gather round. Discuss the possibilities. Agree on a course of action. Unite. Hold hands. Set sail.

REDCOAT

"Mister Carraday, I hope I didn't offend you the other day? Talking about not telling the truth? I haven't seen you since." She found him sitting on a bench in the park a week later, smoking of course. He looked a little more crumpled than usual, coughed.

"Been looking after the Mumma. She been more crook."

"Pot calling the kettle black rather, about lying," Freya apologised. "When I was a girl I told whoppers. Persuaded my whole class and my teacher I was Swedish once. You know the Pippi Longstocking books? No? I so loved those. In my head I was Freya Redcoat, super sleuth.

When Mrs Harris asked where my name came from, I didn't like to admit my dopey parents found it in some hippie book about legends and goddesses. So I said I grew up on a Swedish island with my uncle Sven. I mean I looked so utterly un-Scandinavian, but she believed me for ages." Freya was shy and gawky, one who lost her toys and other belongings and got left behind. Her mum called out to her, long-suffering, amused, protective, "Oh – FREYah!" And Freya felt stupid, annoyed, loved. Freya Redcoat was another creature altogether, tall and strong as a tree. She was Pippi's lost sister. A different shape and colouring, a different country but the same sparkiness, same superhuman strength and lack of fear. Freya drew pictures of her, crayoned in the red. And lived with Pippi in the hot, guilty shelter of her lies.

"I'm glad I spotted you here, Professor. I've been wanting to talk to you. About us maybe working together?" It was amazing how Carraday's obsession had melded with Freya's digital interests. On her blog she was writing with a new passion about how relevant Nearlyology seemed to her. Back at home her husband locked himself away in his room and did God knows what. Freya however hatched plans. Thanks to Freya's blog, the reputation of Carraday was growing. She enjoyed fleshing out the Nearlyologist's philosophy in her posts which explored how people managed the various virtual lives they led online. Friends and colleagues, intrigued by what they read, were starting to call in to the library to take a look at him, some adding to his store of handwritten cards. Rosalind thought he was 'kinda weird', which was a bit rich coming from her, but others were intrigued by Freya's protegé.

"How would you feel about me bringing you people to talk to about their Nearlies?" asked Freya. Carraday frowned. "I mean, they'd talk and you could listen." He frowned more. "I could pay you." He frowned less. "Not a great deal. But I'd find clients who might gain from sharing with you. I'd offer it as part of a coaching package, pay you a percentage." To her surprise Carraday broke into that bewitching smile of his.

"Everybody need to speak out their Nearlies," Carraday replied. "Help them dispelling the hissing all around."

From THE LITTLE BOOK OF NEARLY

Draw a map of your life that includes your nearlies.
You might make a timeline of the main events in your life.
Add in things that nearly happened,
show how big these nearly things were for you
and how long they lingered in your life.
Find the right person to tell.

DRIZZLED THAT

Freya arranged to meet Connie at the Café Del Mondo. With its horrible coffee but free-flowing wi-fi, this was the nearest there was to a hangout for the local digerati. The Del Mondo was now owned by the widow of a cholesterol-overloaded businessman. She had decided in his memory to fulfil their lifelong dream of setting up a traditional coffee house. Freya knew this because she'd been employed to write the copy for the website, reprinted on the menu which she re-read as a diversion from finishing her post. The clean, not quite white walls (linen or mushroom or mist white or some such) were covered in photographs printed on canvas of the owner and her departed husband in exotic locations. Pictured drinking bright cocktails through straws with beaming fellow travellers, they walked in swimwear across sunset beaches, rode on horseback through forests. Along with the free wi-fi, the café had a Facebook page and Twitter account with perky updates about the new flavour of muffin, menus on clipboards featuring the touching narrative of the company alongside the prices of flat whites and ciabattas, bruised this and drizzled that. It was what residents had always said the area needed. Except it wasn't very good. Freya itched to write a strategy to help it thrive.

Every day and always for a different reason the wi-fi didn't work, the over-described ingredients of the salads were temporarily unavailable and the underpaid Italian waitresses, one friendly and plump, the other shapely and sullen, were too harassed to care that your cheese and ham croissant had been melted in the microwave to blistering goo. The café did have high chairs, unisex baby-changing facilities, everything Freya had campaigned for as a young mother – and now cursed as a freelancer trying to work amidst the racket of toddlers and their hyperactive parents who cooed at their young, trilled into their mobiles and nattered with each other about mortgages and gluten intolerance. However the café also housed a community noticeboard with adverts for Shiatsu and Cleaners and Psychotherapy where Freya had pinned up one of her new flyers.

Freya Seward Associates
Personal & Business Coaching for the Digital Age
NEARLYOLOGY
Dr Freya Seward is on hand to help you
Turn your NEARLIES into Reality,
Create and Manage The Virtual Selves You Need To
Succeed
Plus
One To One Sessions with
Nearlyologist Professor G. Carraday
Explore your NEARLY LIVES and how they influence
you NOW

www.nearlyology.net

Connie burst into the café fizzing after her session with Carraday. "It was like totally amazing!" she reported to Freya. "In fact, I've booked another session for next week."

"So, what did you talk about?" But Connie refused to breathe a word.

**

"I nearly... drove away after crashing into someone's car. But then honesty got the better of me. And I'm glad I owned up because two years later the owner of the car I'd pranged interviewed me for a job."
"I nearly... ran off with a Kashmiri freedom fighter."
"I nearly grabbed the wings of freedom but failed :) Maybe next time."

**

SLEUTH

Making sure that security man wasn't on duty, Freya slipped into the library, hid behind the Local History display and peeped round the side of a screen of photocopied sepia pictures of Victorian shops to watch Carraday and Connie in the quiet corner between young adults, oversized non-fiction, the Business Hub and the community noticeboard. The two of them sat on moulded plastic orange chairs either side of an old metal table, its white formica top decorated with generations of childish initials gouged into the surface with biros, penknives and compasses, the graffiti hidden under Carraday's small, battered leather suitcase and stacks of Nearly Cards. Connie leant forward and spoke animatedly while Carraday sat still, looking her calmly in the eye. He didn't seem to be offering any actual advice, but Freya knew how cathartic it could be to describe significant non-events to the sombre Nearlyologist. At this safely private edge of a public space, Connie was letting her

73

nearlies spill. Nearly Czar Carraday smiled winningly from time to time, used Connie's name frequently and asked brief questions – too quietly for Freya to hear them, unfortunately – eliciting more precise details of the Nearlyincident. For a quarter of an hour Connie spoke with urgency and he listened. Then suddenly Carraday arose, scratched his chin, shook Connie's hand and left, sweeping magisterially out through the plate-glass doors which parted before him. This abrupt departure clearly surprised Connie but perhaps added to the therapeutic power of the event. While Connie sat alone mulling over whatever had been said, Freya Redcoat, super sleuth, watched from her hiding place, then followed Carraday out of the glass doors.

At first Freya assumed he was making a hands-free phone call, but no, Carraday was muttering to himself, walking round the little park. Now he stopped still and bending his arm at the elbow, began waving his upper body. What was he up to? It was like some kind of a ritual, a sort of dance. That was it: he was drawing letters in the air. And now he flung wide his arms, as if shaking water off them, and bent down, took a handful of paper fluff out of his coat pocket, sprinkled it on the grass.

"Oh wow," thought Freya, "my clients would love all that," then before Carraday could spot her, turned and set off for her office.

That afternoon, Penelope, a needy interior designer who'd befriended Freya when their children were at school together, called in to ask about coaching.

"I'm working with Professor Carraday now."

"Oh yes I read about this gentleman on your blog. Fascinating. Book me in." Then Penelope remembered that Charles was looking to pay someone to tweet about his design consultancy. "And I thought to myself, I wonder if the marvellous Freya Seward might be interested in that sort of thing?"

"Do tell him to call me. But did you know, Penelope, that at the end of each session, Carraday undertakes his own special form of meditation practice to discharge your negative nearlyness?"

"No. Really?"

"It's a blend of the ancient wisdom of Tai Chi and the latest thinking in neuro- psychodynamics."

"Oh. Really!" Penelope booked another session. "I'll email you a receipt and our online questionnaire." This had drop-down boxes to click on re. signs of increased sense of wellbeing / enhanced self-esteem / improved sleep patterns. It asked if clients a) saw the Nearlyologist as a private confessor, in which case anonymity was assured, or if they b) shared Nearly stories with partners/children/friends, if so their Nearly could be posted for no extra charge on the new-look website currently being designed *pro bono* but rather slowly by Connie. Delete as applicable.

**

"I nearly... took cocaine in an Ecuadorian prison but thought better of it."

"I nearly... didn't come back from my gap year, volunteering in the Caribbean."

"I nearly... had tea with the Queen Mother, at the Bishop's Palace, Wells, Somerset c 1978. My name had been picked out of a hat. The day before, in a close-run game of kiss chase, Ian Barrett had pushed me into the Homey Wall and broken my nose. Lip was too swollen to sip from a cup with royalty. I stayed at school like everybody else. I have been left with illusions of grandeur and an awareness of the power of attraction. Ian Barrett broke my nose and swole my lip because he wanted to kiss me."

**

EVERYWHEN OF KNOWING

In the Time of the Crazing, after the Unwedding
and the First Burning, Carraday felt-tip his body
as his imaginary forbears mark themselves of yore
with cuts and doodles on his arms, legs and chest,
and he dance by night in the wilderness end of the park
where lie the lager cans and condoms and shopping carts,
Boomer watching.
The new day dawn and Carraday still dancing,
morning arrive and no show Brenda,
but several young Mummas out promenading with their
buggy bound babies,
watching as the bigfella sweat and sweat.
They transfix by the magic of him and root to the spot there,
kids also mute and marvelling,
until Carraday grow so knackered
that he start to sob as he dance, hard then harder,
and the water of the sweat and the tears pour off him,
in droplets, rivulets,
then in streams, filling the puddles, then flooding the plain,
creating the pool soon to be Reservoir.
And the young Mummas rush screaming into the water
and turn into a gaggle of geese which whorl across
the surface of the reservoir and honk away
leaving their precious, squawking goslings behind.

Now in the Dozing, Carraday swim across the reservoir
of his own sweat and tears to an island where sit
that Seward lady still staring into the glowing face
of the oblong polished stone she consult on all things.
No word for it in normal speak: her faith in this amulet
to which she whisper, listen, find and leave messages
of elders and familiars, seek guidance on the way to go.
An everywhen of knowing, rooting and leading her.
The Hound Boomer scratch his phantom ear and shake
his body sending out a spray of water round him.

And Seward wipe the spray from her face
and said unto Gregory,
"Oh – hi there. Sorry, I was miles away.
You've come for your money?"

BITMUCHNESS

Sitting in the Del Mondo on a pink armchair at a refurbished school desk by a spiky yukka plant sipping a cold flat white, having checked her mobile for updates and messages, Freya emailed out her latest e-newsletter, totted up her outstanding debts, and sighed heavily. Next she fired off yet another urgent email to Zane. And became aware of Carraday facing her, leaning against the wall, standing on one leg.

"Oh, hi. Sorry, I was miles away. You've come for your money? How long have you been there?"

"Apologies for interrupt your working, Mrs Seward, but I see you in the window. I finish speaking with your friend."

Freya stood, took his arm. "Mister Carraday. Do join me." He refused a coffee but poured himself a tap water with ice and mint from a jug on the counter and sat while she chatted about the calls she'd been getting from potential clients thanks to him. She opened her purse and produced an envelope of notes.

"I thought paying your fee in cash would be simplest, as you're self-employed? And I've put in a little more than we agreed – you so deserve it." She was expecting one of those awful oh-no-i-couldn't-possibly-oh-but-i-insist-no-but-i-couldn't tussles, but instead he pocketed the notes promptly. "Excellent. I'm a terrier once I've got someone in my sights, Mister Carraday, I think they sign up for my workshops simply to shut me up."

"Oh no no Mrs Seward."

Freya knew she was the kind of woman some people describe as 'a bit much'. But why should she stop herself from making connections, butting in, getting suddenly cross about this, upset about that? She knew people could look strangely at her, and she didn't give a damn if they disliked her – Freya usually felt the same way about them. But sometimes it was more complicated, when she thought she was relaying a matter of interest or pointing out a flaw in their argument or suggesting a book they should read, and yet they looked... threatened? embarrassed? bored? overwhelmed? It was hard to tell. She was 'a bit much', and that made her angry. Men were defined far more actively, whether as fascinating experts or unspeakable bores. Well to hell with being merely acceptable. Freya had made a political decision some time back to embrace her bitmuchness, and now determined to be *a bit bloody more* and fight her way back into the black. Acceptable was not a word in Gregory Carraday's vocabulary. He seemed to find her so astounding, so unlike himself in every way, that he stared carefully at her when she spoke as if struggling to understand a foreign language. Freya liked that much better. He was looking at her in exactly this manner now.

"Actually I have another suggestion, Mister Carraday. I was wondering about us charging a higher fee for a full Nearlyology session, you know, to cover our time and marketing expenses. We could hold them at my office."

MOSTAMAZINGEXPERIENCE

The words tumbled from Jamie's lips like he'd been waiting for years to get them off his chest: "I nearly made it as a professional rock musician."

"Yes?"

"OK – I nearly played in a rock band which made a hit record, or rather, I did play in the band, which toured a bit after I left, and made a minor hit record – well, it got in the top 100 one week – but we had a baby instead."

"And?"

"Nearly spent months and months lugging amps about, doing soundchecks, playing the same songs over and over, doing drugs and drinking too much in the horrible changing room afterwards, wondering where the groupies were."

"So?"

"Instead we had a child. Most amazing experience of my life. Oh, it really was. And of course Freya was in the band too at first, she gave up the same dream, though I think more easily, she'd really had it with the rock and roll thing by then. Me too really... but."

"But?"

"Why am I telling you?"

Carraday opened his suitcase, pulled out a card and a biro, pushed then across the formica table.

"Please writing it down on this card please."

"I can't see what my wife sees in all this to be honest."

"Going to write it?"

"OK."

LOST TIM

Walking home afterwards, Jamie was overwhelmed with memories of that era, before he *was* Jamie, back before he was Jimmy even, when it seemed only a matter of time before a cool, edgy, new wave style of rock stardom was bound to engulf him. He still had, framed and hung by his desk, the souvenir of that time which he most cherished: a signed copy of the LP *Spike* by Elvis Costello, "To Jim with friendship & respect, Elvis". His notoriously grumpy hero had scribbled on the record cover in biro at the Exchange Club after a gig. A friend of a friend had known the manager of the venue, managed to blag them an invite to the afterparty where, by another series of coincidences they'd managed to sit in a corner with Elvis himself and briefly attract his irritable attention.

The thing was that at this time, before he became Jimmy, he was still known by his original name of Tim, but Elvis misheard him when the request for an autograph was hesitantly made. The message was so fulsome, friendly and impressive that Tim couldn't bring himself to mention the mistake, but nor could he stop himself displaying the cover proudly to his friends who couldn't not tease him mercilessly about the error. Inevitably Tim's nickname became Jim, then Jimmy, then when he moved town, he simply kept the nickname and changed his proper name. After all, 'Jimmy' was far more rock and roll than 'Timothy'.

As Co-ordinator of Play & Recreation for the Council, 'Jamie' had seemed more suitable somehow for the sign on his office door. In the office he would tell anecdotes of gigs and binges, making it clear he was at heart a musician only temporarily taking alternative employment for the sake of his family. Then realised Aditi was laughing about him in the canteen with the interns.

"Did you track down the elusive Zane?" Jamie asked Freya in the kitchen that night.

"Nobody I met at the Hub had heard of him or Webberations. But then it was full of tiny start-up companies that have only recently started up there. All a bit hipster beards and jam jars that place."

"I met your guy today."

"Zane?"

"No no, the Nearly man. At the library. What an interesting one."

"OK. Mister Carraday. Well well well, so what did you talk about?" Freya closed the lid of her laptop, turned to him, genuinely interested. And for a moment it was on the tip of his tongue. Oh, to let down his defences and allow this tsunami of emotional glunk to gush forth. Could he tell her how the ghost of his pop-self had haunted him over the years? Could he also tell her that his cock had gone soft and started hurting, that this was why he was avoiding sharing a bed with her? That he was terrified of losing his sexual feeling, of failing to give her pleasure, of becoming…well, the word that came to mind was 'unmanned'. Was it possible he could let spill, that they could talk like they once used to, discussing everything, staying up all night locked in wonderful, exploratory, healing conversation? Curling up together as the dawn light spread, united, utterly shared?

"Just nearly things and shit."

She reacted sharply, stung by his sarcasm.

"Yes, trust you to belittle him."

"Jesus, Fray, bonkers or what."

"He's not – he's helping to build my brand."

"Build your brand. Listen to yourself. You sound like my brother. With his brainstorming blather."

"God yes. Tyler." Of course, Jamie's stinking rich half-brother. They didn't see much of his mum's other son, whose posh father paid for boarding school and funding through Oxford, whereas Jamie went to the local Comp and Polytechnic, and to the football on a Saturday with his Dad.

"Burbling on about superbrands when we went for that meal."

"What *does* Tyler do exactly?"

"God knows. Capitalises. Realises. Invests in start-ups. Makes dodgy deals."

Freya was distracted, staring out of the window so hard that Jamie turned to see what she was looking at. A washing line? No – she was thinking, her head turned in the direction that denotes recollection.

"All that sanctimonious crap he came out with about his Charitable Foundation – so flaming proud of his funding good works. Tax dodge if you ask me."

"Have you heard from him lately?"

81

"Not since we drank too much of his amazing dessert wine and I told him exactly what the bankers could do with their bonuses."

"Which was very rude of you."

"You laughed at the time. All the way home in the cab."

"Which he paid for. It *was* rude. He was generous. Trying to do the right thing."

"My brother doing the right thing? Come off it!"

"He helped us buy this place."

"Don't get me started."

"I won't. I have things to do."

"Me too."

BUNYIPS RIPPING

After the Pissing Off
when Dadda went AWOL and writ to say
him living downunder now with anotherwoman,
After Mumma howled and swore in the nights and lostit
re. mothering and such. he go off playabout by the reservoir
Dadda posting back 1 plastic boomerang 1 rubber koala
1 Ladybird Book: *Flight One: Australia*
about 2 English kids on a trip meeting bushmen &
Aboriginals *wise in their primitive ways.*
Keeping all under the bed with the Eagle & Fiesta &
ManMyth&MagicMagazine
wherein instructions for the curse he made for
Mister fiddler Holdern:
Leg of chicken found in fridge, slit open,
scrap of schoolbook fingered by said teacher slipped inside,
nails hammered through from dad's old tool kit
Keep in a box and let it rot till flies and stinking.
Then bury in the park and piss on it.
And left to roamabout the park alone,
where Carraday found Boomer, his dog, pal and bunyip,

the Nearlyvoice he hear speak as he wander &
hide at the heart of him best secret friend.

SWAYED DELICIOUSLY

Carraday and Freya sat on a bench by the reservoir where
they'd walked to from the library this afternoon, much
further afield than usual, it being such an unexpectedly
beautiful day, warm but fresh, Freya explaining the jist of
her recent blog posts while Carraday smiled and nodded.
Now, at the melancholy edge of evening, Freya sighed and
stretched and finished recapping.

"So, when people truly embrace their Nearlyselves,
you believe they find within an inner voice expressing who
they nearly are – am I right?" she asked.

"All the Nearly energy stop fizzing in ears and
clogging up the Mamma's brains."

"Yes, I think I get it." They sat in silence soaking
up the dying light. Freya sighed, told him how over
Christmas arguments had kept breaking out between her
and her husband and how difficult it was in a long-term
relationship to separate out what was whose fault, as each
was by then part of the other. And she kept thinking of
what next. Carraday said, "Maybe when two people
spending a lot of time together the dust of nearly
occurrences hovering round each of us beginning to mingle."

"And they find themselves sharing inner voices?"
Carraday smiled. Then she stood up, reached down to pull
him up too, but he slipped on the mud and she gripped his
arm to steady him, then they began walking back towards
the street-lights of the road. Freya leant her head for a
moment against his shoulder.

"What I don't understand is how you can be aware
of these other selves without wanting to do something about
them. If I feel I should have made a different choice, I think

I should take that choice now, or at least do something to shake off the regret."

"What matters is the stilling of the buzzing," said Carraday.

"Very true," said Frey.

From THE LITTLE BOOK OF NEARLY

All stand together in a circle.
Introduce yourselves to each other
as the people you nearly became.

SHAKE OFF

"You invited Tyler?!"

"He's loaded, he buys art. Rosalind needs money. No brainer."

"He's my sodding brother. And I hate the guy."

"Carry this will you?"

"It's heavy. What's in it?"

"Leaflets. Advertising my coaching services."

"Artists can't afford services."

"No, but art lovers can. Like your brother and his posh chums."

"Half-brother."

Jamie lifted the box onto his shoulder.

"I can't stay late. I've got an appointment in the morning."

"Job interview?"

"No."

"Didn't think so. Come on – we'll be late."

"You invited Tyler – how could you."

Now both her husband and his half-brother seemed transfixed by the sight of willowy Rosalind in her M&S bra and knickers. Her male collaborator had an amazing body, graceful and muscular. They were in a studio of grubby white walls and brick. Stripped to their undies and coated in red paint, the two artists ran at each other shouting gibberish, slammed together, embraced and then pulled away, backed off and charged again, over and over. It was rather powerful, in a chilly sort of way. After the performance the artists put on gowns while their audience sipped cheap red wine from paper cups and sat on the floor ready for the Q&A session.

"Is Marina Abramović an influence?" asked an audience member.

"For us this piece is intensely personal. An act of magical ritual," explained Van, Rosalind's bare-chested associate. There was a general nodding of heads.

"Though not actually magical," Rosalind pointed out.

"No, not actually."

"But we see our practice as going beyond the confines of the conventional art world."

"Hi, Rosa, as you know, I'm Freya Seward. Management coach and consultant. I have a question. I work with many artists on business plans and digital strategies."

"And your question?" asked Van.

"There's more information about what I do in this flyer if anyone here might be interested. My rates are very competitive. But what I wanted to ask was, might you two see yourselves as 'Nearly artists'? Insofar as you are working outside the confines of the conventional arts world?"

"You mean like Outsider artists?" Rosalind answered. "Are we outsiders? Well, yes – except he went to art college and we received an Arts Council grant."

"But apart from that. As a coach I often work to help creatives to feel less isolated, less like outsiders, to build their self-esteem and market themselves more..."

"Tyler Jackson. Hello. My question is: what's the relationship between the prints on the wall and the performance?"

"She made them by rubbing paint on her body then rolling on paper," replied Van.

"The prints are for sale. The performance isn't," said Rosa.

"So – a souvenir of the experience?"

"Yes. And a way of earning some actual money."

After the Q&A Freya whizzed round the room handing out her leaflets, trying her best to network, but these artists were a sullen bunch and no buyers had shown up, apart from Tyler, who bought a print after asking Rosa which part of her body exactly she'd painted it with.

"Outsider Art – what's that about?" asked Jamie as he waved at Tyler's departing Uber and they and the other art lovers processed out of the old factory turned into studio spaces.

"Art Brut. Work made by mental patients and eccentric recluses. Much collected these days."

"Weird shit by weirdos?"

"Type thing. Yep. If you want to be offensive."

"I enjoyed that, actually. Apart from you doing your Dragon's Den pitch. Reminded me of us in a way," said Jamie.

"Really?"

"When we were both thinner and brighter and better looking."

"Hah."

There was a compliment in there somewhere, gift-wrapped in barbed wire. But Jamie was so crabby these days, nipping and scuttling away, back into his shell.

"Reminded me of those intense all-night discussions we had, about politics and bodies and power, the analysing of everything," said Jamie. And the event did catch something of the early years of their relationship, the cycle of arguments and reconciliation, patches of pure happiness like she'd never experienced with anyone else, shouting matches, belly laughs, orgasms, kicks in the emotional gut. They fought and fused and created a baby together and Pippa wrenched herself out from her mother's body into the world to be part of the scrum, the howling and cooing, the battles and peace-making. All in all she'd bloody loved being a mother. The stroppy punk diva transformed into radical Earth mother, then, to her amazement, into a highly efficient manager of lifts to school and packed lunches and adolescent advice. So how come she'd managed so effectively to bugger up her own career? The house had felt so big and hollow, at Christmas especially, and since the conference Freya had in her mind this Dan bloke and another kind of existence, a new beginning, so close she could taste it and because of this, wanted to run straight past Jamie and away. Others could surround themselves in traces of their nearly lives, but Freya wanted things for now and for real.

"They were exhausting times, weren't they," said Freya as they walked home in the rain, she hugging the leftover leaflets to her chest to keep them dry.

"Yes, but exciting too, all that communication."

"So exhausting, though."

"And on the subject of communicating. I meant to say: I'm going to the hospital tomorrow." He turned towards her, but she was already across the road, pushing flyers through the letterbox of the dry cleaners opposite.

LESS FRAZZLED

Carraday back in the Dozing snooze by the reservoir
under the branches of a tree.
He awake and look up at the leaves which
dance in the autumn light
and the lithe limbs of the branches which swayed

deliciously like arms above him.
The sky peep through the leaves like the most entrancing
eyes and the brown leaves
shine like soft hair and the branches dance and turning into
a beautiful woman
who climbed down from the sky soft, naked and bronzed
and a bit like Mrs Freya Seward
though maybe slightly less frazzled looking.

FLAT ON YOU

In a white airy room with a spectacular view over the cityscape, next to a sickly hot waiting room of anxious men in plastic chairs, after lowering his trousers and leaning back on a daybed covered with paper to have his genitals examined, Jamie now sat glumly listening to the polite Sri Lankan consultant calmly say, "It's not so serious, sir. Please do not worry yourself unnecessarily. There is a percentage chance it will improve."

The Doctor explained that Jamie had something called Hinchcliffe's Condition, whereby plaque or scar tissue forms in the penis, causing this strange bending.

"OK. Great... But what percentage?"

"Within six months around 30% of gentlemen recover completely. Their organs unbend, sex lives return to whatever normal was before." He waved a hand emphatically, then let it fall. "30% stabilise. In other words the pain and bending stop, what sensations that exist remain. And in 30% of cases there can be some further deterioration."

"And the other 10%?"

"Deteriorate further still."

"I see," said Jamie glumly, glancing out of the window but seeing three and a half different futures fired, like heat-seeking missiles, towards his groin.

"Actually that's not quite correct – this percentile includes a variety of extreme symptoms: some experience more penile bending with associated pain. Depression is common, suicidal thoughts etcetera. Yet others who completely lose libido report a blissful sense of relief – they feel they've rediscovered other aspects of life and relationships. Apparently. Another response can be obsessive and morbid nostalgia for past romantic and sexual highlights. Some report an improvement of their sexual relations, even when only achieving stabilisation."

"I see."

The Doctor cleared his throat, chuckled. "A paper by the Hinchcliffe Society described it as 'genital roulette' which I thought highly amusing. But no, don't worry, it's only Hinchcliffe's. There's no sign of anything more serious."

"More serious than having your prick getting twisted up and your libido going flat on you?"

"I mean, sir, it's probably not cancerous."

"Ah yes, well." Consultant and patient sat quietly in silence for a moment or two as all this sank in. Jamie's hair had fallen out in his mid-forties and he hadn't been expecting that either. This was more proof of his mortality, of the randomness of fate. If he could be one of the ?% of those men who develop baldness early, then there was no doubt that he could also be one of the .00?% struck down by any other kind of misfortune, however statistically rare. It could be him who was hit by lightning, the one who might find the lump in his lymph glands, feel his heart give out at the bus stop, step into the road at the precise instant the drunken motorcyclist was speeding by. He was already a member of the one in seven club of men who suffered from something like this.

"Although in your case the plaque is unusually extensive so I think an MRI scan would be advisable."

"OK."

"Although having said that, if it was cancer to be honest you would most probably be dead by now."

"Ah."

The consultant smiled again, weakly. Gone were the days when Doctors gave you pills to make you right as rain. Doctor Gunawardena was, as they say, not one to beat about the bush. "No cure I fear. For now. There is surgery in severe cases, if the bending makes intercourse impossible."

"OK."

"The Society advocates a regime of meditation and self-expression. But first I think losing weight, more exercise would definitely help."

Jamie's fatness had crept up on him slowly, coated him gradually in blubber, changing him utterly from bloke with a bit of a belly to bald, fat guy with glasses. One who sweated if he ran, who groaned when he stood up and, when he sat down, first checked out the chair to be sure it would take his bulk without getting his arse wedged between its arms. He sighed. Of course losing weight would help, and every morning he swore to do something about it, then ate three slices of toast and jam.

"Look I don't mind really what shape it is. Well, I do, but that's not the main thing. I mean, I think my wife and I could probably cope with that if we actually tried... If we did... I just... well, to start with I want my sexual feeling back."

Taken aback by this self-disclosure, the Doctor promptly issued further facts.

"Traction devices exist but these can be uncomfortable. Surgery straightens it but shortens it too. And usually results in some further diminishing of sensitivity."

"Well there's no point in making it straighter if I've lost the desire to... to put it *in* anybody."

"I understand, sir." He paused, looked nervously at Jamie. "We believe about 7% of men suffer from this kind of condition, though many don't report it."

"Good to hear the facts, but..."

"Viagra can be of help." The Doctor was speaking faster and faster.

"Doctor, you're a specialist in, you know..."

"Erectile Dysfunction. Yes."

"I keep thinking: isn't it weird how sexuality all boils down to one body part and what makes it tingle."

"Mmm," said the Doctor, scribbling a note, uneasy at such intimacy. "Perhaps you might gain from joining the conversation on the Society's online forum."

"Yes maybe, but what I mean is: erections – so entangled with the other reasons we may not be...getting it on – or up. I mean, a good friend of mine... Amazing how many relationships don't include any sex at all. And it's hard to separate what's the loss of your partner's sexual attractiveness, what's one's own level of desire – don't you think?" When Jamie first met Freya he fancied her, he spoke to her, he imagined sex with her, he flirted with her, they had sex, he loved her and they made a baby. Now that lovely, smooth-flowing continuum had been replaced by all these jagged feelings for a woman whose body had aged and changed, whom he slept beside and sometimes – though not lately – reached out to with his own wrinkled blob of a body, senses bloated and blunted by time.

"Lack of erection means the nerve endings do not respond to stimuli. It is not possible to feel the sensations without the erection. However massage and such can provide a different kind of physical intimacy." The Doctor was gabbling now.

Desire always seemed such a complex, dangerous, wonderful thing to Jamie, the shapes and kinks and personalities that grabbed him, made the blood quicken, flesh begin to stiffen. Rosalind in her bra and knickers doing performance art had churned him up too; all kinds of oceanic feelings stirred long before anything physical might actually occur. But now...

"Does my whole sense of my sexuality, of myself as a sexual being hinge on one bit of body getting hard? Is that really it, Doc?"

"As I said, no cause for concern. Not too much cause. Hopefully. Wise to check these things out. But please..."

"Don't worry? Yeah I know."

The doctor opened his desk drawer, rummaged till he found a photocopied sheet which he thrust into Jamie's hand, then stood up and nodded.

"There's a trial we're undertaking with the Hinchcliffe Society. You might like to join. It's all explained in this leaflet."

"Perhaps, but what's involved?"

"Contact details and FAQs are all in there, sir. Good day." The consultation was over.

ON NEARLYREADING

Do you read as many novels as you used to? Do you really? Or is the truth that you'd prefer to nearly read books than actually read them? The dream space we enter when we spend time in a bookshop or library helps us think in new ways, the idea of reading is delicious and enticing. The reality of being stuck in one person's fictional world for the duration of a whole novel is a major investment of time and attention and can prove frustrating. We nod off after a couple of pages each night; hurl it across the room then put it back on the shelf to warp and fade in the sunlight. But visiting bookshops, festivals and libraries, like hanging out in galleries, makes us feel brighter, more creative, opens up our ideas and appreciation of life whatever we may or may not buy and read there.

Booklover friends wax lyrical about the joys of hanging out in bookshops new and secondhand and howled with outrage when the local library was threatened with closure and our only bookshop closed its doors. But we know these shops close because although people like browsing in public, they prefer to buy their books online, or download them direct to their devices. (Oh yes, and how many friends said not so long ago they'd never give up paper books to read on screen? Now they go on all the time about how much they love their Kindles. And do they admit they've changed? Do they heck!)

Nearlyreading Workshops will help you look at how you can keep in touch with books and feel the inspiration and creativity they give you without spending too much time actually reading. Learn how best to skim and surf, to find the places that expand your mind just by being there.

Freya hit 'post'. She reckoned there'd be takers for this. Surely. All those book groups she knew about where they failed to read a book each month then talked about kids and house prices instead. Nearly reading could be the next big thing. And she was fed up with all the nostalgic twaddle Jamie came out with about the old days, reminiscing about vinyl and typewriters. It made her think of Dan and how he'd spoken at that conference about the potential of the future and conjured up a wired world which felt so free of all the drab clutter of now. Unlike at Rosalind's performance, where she'd handed a leaflet to a tetchy young woman who moaned on about the Internet as if it wasn't the most astounding means of information and ideas exchange imaginable but nothing more than a cunning device invented to stop her having more time for her art and hot yoga. Freya phoned Rosalind the morning after to apologise.

"I enjoyed your performance, Ros. Sorry I got cross with that friend of yours after."

"She's a crap painter and a complete cow. No worries, sister. Did you find any customers among the artistes?"

"Nope. It's bloody hard trying to get the business rebooted, if I could only find a way of packaging it up right."

"Hot Nearlyology?"

PLASTIC SHIPWRECKS

There was a man at a window waving wildly at him. It was late afternoon, the day fading to sorrowful grey, electric light illuminating rooms like they were Victorian peep shows. The bus had pulled up at temporary lights due to roadworks, and Jamie realised he was staring directly into what had until recently been his office. That guy from accounts looking up at the top deck of a passing bus to spot his old associate. Nice bloke, family originally from Jamaica, not sure of his name, but they'd often chat when they met in the sandwich shop round the corner. Benjamin? Who'd confided in him once that his daughter hung out with a guy he loathed, a bully and a manipulator, but she was besotted. Now that's a dad's worst nightmare.

Was it Benjamin? Benedict. Something like that – now doing a mime: wipe brow, look at clock, sigh, shrug, hammer at invisible keyboard, look at clock again. Jamie smiled supportively; he could see the corridor leading to the room which until recently had his name and job title so clearly printed on a sign on its door. Might still be there. Although by now some restructuring would be underway with divisions being moved about to blur the fact that so many jobs had gone.

The lights changed, the engine shuddered back to life, he waved goodbye to his ex-colleague who gave him a thumbs up. A few minutes later, Jamie stepped off the bus into a cluster of schoolgirls who shrieked and chattered, swirling round him like goldfish round a plastic shipwreck. He watched them as they racketed away, a pair of chunky prefects holding polystyrene boxes of chicken shouting at another pair, slim, brown and veiled. A busty white girl swished her long blonde hair back and screeched with laughter as she took their picture on her phone. He was from another age and dimension, invisible as a ghost.

What did Jamie need a working cock for anyway? Why did this condition of his feel so shameful and yes, disabling? Like he needed a big stiff prick he could produce from his baggy chinos any time that it might suddenly be needed by a passing female who eyed him up and demanded, "I'll have you – here, now." It was almost funny – no, pathetic – this predator whose voice still whispered somewhere in his head, like some lecherous pub bore. And why couldn't he speak about this to Freya? Weren't they the great believers in sharing their feelings, opening up and letting go? There hadn't been much of that lately. But these still seemed demeaning kinds of feelings, not the safely sensitive sort.

Arriving home in a haze of dejection, Jamie found a van parked in the drive, Freya standing with the deliveryman at the door signing her name on the little grey screen of the device the guy carried.

ALL GO

"Where have you been?" asked Freya as she carted a box through to the kitchen and plonked it on the table, took her keys from her pocket and used them to slice through the gaffer tape. He so nearly told her.

"Oh – nowhere."

"Ah – your favourite place then." Freya hated herself for saying it, though it thrilled her too. With both hands she ripped open the box then took out one of the new leaflets she'd ordered, checked it over, looked pleased,

"Hah. So how's your sell-out to capitalism going?"

"We're a social enterprise, you prick. Mister Carraday is proving a much more positive business partner than you'd ever be. We're planning to run workshops." Pushing past him, Freya went back for the second box. Jamie stood in the doorway so Freya pushed past him again, dropped the second box on the table, keyed it open and tipped out bags of 'I nearly' badges.

"Workshops. Wow – really?"

"Really." Opening one of the re-sealable bags, she tipped out a badge and pinned it to her blouse, brushed it proudly with her fingers. "We'll help people tackle their writer's block, look at self-publishing options, blogging, Twitter, then I get them to pay me to set up their blogs and e-books." Freya's eyes sparkled.

"Good scam."

"Well, thanks for the positive encouragement of my entrepreneurialism." The light dimmed.

"Look all I meant..."

"You put me down about anything I do to generate income for this household." They stood either side of the kitchen table now, letting fly.

"That's not true."

"I'm sick of it, Jamie. While you sit upstairs doing damn all."

"I'm sorting out my study."

"Ah yes, well."

"After all those years working I deserve some bloody creative space."

"Like I wasn't bloody working?!" They fought with a bitterness now that frightened them both. Tempers held in check by the need to preserve familial calm could, with the house child-free, let fly. Stunned silence. The room humming – fizzing with energy on the edge of detonation.

"OK. You want some bloody creative space. Why don't I move out?"

"Why bloody don't you."

"I'm sorry, I know you're down, Jamie, but I can't reach you and it's draining all my energy. I've had enough." Freya had said these words in her head plenty of times over the past few weeks. She hadn't expected to actually speak them. Nor for Jamie to agree.

"Me too."

"Well then."

"Are you seeing someone else? That goddam nearlyman?"

"No, no – not him. I mean I see him but not... Not anyone. I just... I don't know if I love you any more." As soon as it was spoken, this became for both of them the hideous, inevitable truth.

"I don't know what I feel. But something's changed, that's for sure," he said. Within an hour she'd packed a bag and left.

IN THE DOZING

In the Dozing air fill with microscopic traces of every
nearly moment, every missed opportunity,
every shattered dream.
These specs blow like clouds of dust into every corner
of the Nearlyverse, they clog the planet's heating ducts
melting glaciers and such, they fall like dandruff
on the shoulders of the lost, then rise, flocks and swarms
of the tiniest specks, rise higher ever higher, up to the stars,
up to the very lid of the cosmos
where they accumulate, become the dark matter
that binding time and space together,
they stick in the throat of the great creator
and make him cough like Carraday coughing now
as he stub his roll-up out in his Garden
and push in his trowel, dig a hole in the cold, wet earth
and take out of his pocket the scarf Freya leave behind
at the library the last time they meeting there.
He wrap it tight around the wooden doll he make of her,
slice of broomhandle whittled with pins for eyes and
hair of shaving brush, body coloured in the spots of
the nearly powder, a cavity cut in the body where he nail
a chunk of chicken from last night's balti,
pinprick of his blooddrip below,
then tie the scarf round tight with garden twine,
put the wrapped shape to his nose and inhale,
drop it into the hole and cover it with soil.

THE INDISPUTABLE

In the title sequence of that old kids' cartoon show, Top Cat, the one whose close friends used to call him TC appears to be reclining in the back of a chauffeur-driven limousine. It draws up outside a swanky hotel, but when the car turns round you realise he's actually sat on the outside, perched on the car's chassis. TC hops off, tips the porter with a note on a string which he uses to yank the money straight back out of the guy's pocket, then goes to sit on the terrace. But we see Top Cat's hopped over the fence onto the pavement and is scoffing sandwiches from a lunchbox he's taken from builders at work, hooking the tin with his cane from a hole in the road. As a girl Freya always loved that bit.

And these days why go to the trouble and expense of an office in London when she can nearly have one wherever most impresses whomsoever she's meeting with? A funky art space in Hoxton? Posh office in Mayfair? Cool business hub in Covent Garden? Let's meet in a café nearby. She'll burst through the door looking frantic and apologise about having the builders in. Why not? All she really needs is a mobile and laptop and her office is anywhere. It's what she's been telling her clients to do for years, in a way.

Freya Seward arrived in this particular café in red lipstick and business-like black suit, wobbly on higher heels than she was used to, mobile pressed tight to her ear.

She glanced round the oak-panelled room and gave Tyler Jackson a brief smile, pointed at the phone, pulled a face implying frustration at these demanding clients, said. "OK. Laters." And pocketed the phone. Then: "I am so, so sorry, Tyler. Have you been waiting long?" Mwah. Mwah.

"So good to see you." He stood up to take her hand and air kiss her, smelling of leather and soap, essence of alpha, in his pristine dark suit, crisp shirt, snowy white hair. Something about the arc of the eyebrows, but that was the only family resemblance. When she and Jamie had last dined at his huge, pristine home, Tyler wore a checked shirt, with sharp, new chinos, formally informal, and he poured them a different wine for each course – even dessert – followed by a malt whisky which transformed her mouth into sunset in a field on the isle of Skye on a fresh, autumn evening, so it was hardly a surprise that by the end of the evening Jamie was slurring his words and making loud, blundering asides about tax evaders. Tyler smiled and rested his hand on Freya's bare shoulder when he topped up her coffee cup. He wasn't lecherous but so attentive that Freya's body ached in the taxi home as if she'd been massaged by the guy.

"You too. It's been ages." That night she'd basked in the couple's sumptuous plush which seemed such a pleasurable break from domestic austerity. Whereas it sent Jamie nuts.

"Last time was that delicious meal Diana cooked for us. Got a bit rowdy I remember. Jamie drank too much..."

Tyler Jackson flapped his hand to dispel any bad feelings. "Marvellous to see you. Di-di sends hugs by the way." Tyler looked around the room. "But is this mysterious organisation of yours based around here?" He glanced at his watch then brought his attention back to her. "I'm all ears." His ears, she noticed, were large and hairy.

"Well, I looked at premises round the corner..." As she spoke he turned his head away, apparently bored again. It's a disconcerting trait. Probably designed to wrong-foot employees and clients. Very effective.

"Expensive part of town." He was smirking.

"Absolutely. Actually one of our potential board members has his HQ here and might be keen to donate us a couple of rooms. Amazingly kind."

"I'm impressed. And well worth it, I assure you: a central location. Important for credibility. Oh, but Freya – we were so sorry to hear about you and Jamie."

"The redundancy was a big blow, but now he's cut himself off from me. He's changed, your brother. Perhaps we both have."

"I should talk to him."

"Maybe. If you do, it's probably best not to tell him you and I are in touch. You know how he gets."

"I know Timmy resents me, or Jamie or whatever he calls himself now. My absent father spoiled me from afar. Guilt money of course. But I was so jealous of my brother having a 'proper' family. And then a beautiful wife of course." Bordering on cheesiness this flattery, and yet he kind of made it work.

Tyler turned away again so she was left beaming at mottled, stubbled cheek. Then he looked back sternly, the piercing interrogator. "A wife who it seems might be needing some financial input. You're planning an application to our little Foundation?"

"I remembered what you'd said that night. About supporting start-ups. I've been working on a business plan to provide consultancy on social media marketing to women working from home, building a community online and through book groups and socials, with one-to-one sessions on..."

"Well good luck with that. I've invested in a few new companies lately, for my sins. But Freya, we're trying to break into some new territories overseas. Our advisors say we'd gain from charitable giving in the area of re-training around digital well-being. It's your community activities that caught my eye."

"OK." Disconcerting indeed. Freya had her pitch all planned – her shiny new concept aimed at a well-heeled and growing sector. Instinctively she grabbed at her bag, fished through it as if in search of glasses or a mobile, whereas actually she was regrouping, marshalling new arguments, seeking inspiration – ah, but at least found a biro and notebook she could open and write in big letters: Nearly.

"You mean my work with the hard to reach?" Those drop-in sessions for people so socially excluded they failed to drop-in. The hard to reach proving un-bloody-reachable. "That work has been in abeyance recently." Was that the right word? Abeyance sounded OK. "But I'm confident we'll get support from major trusts soon." Just need to write an application.

Tyler nodded, waved over the waitress to take Freya's order and another cappuccino for himself, and a croissant too perhaps. Shouldn't really but they do look delicious.

"As you know Freya, my foundation is terribly small fry. Not in a position to give major funds. Competition is fierce of course. But, look, to be honest we've had some bad press lately. Redundancies we had to make. We're keen to do something for the jobless, the people we've replaced with technology. I copied your email to some of my management team and they were struck by the unusual nature of your... Well, tell me again about that community thing you were going on about the night you phoned."

A deep breath. Wow. That. Yes.

"We're exploring imaginary possibilities among the young unemployed." Here's the thing about fundraising – take notes, this tip gleaned from a course which cost Freya's employers a good few bob some years ago, but paid dividends. When pitching for money don't start by trying to tell them what's wonderful about the project you run. Begin by describing the problem, and it needs to be precisely the one the funding body exists to deal with, at the top of its current list of priorities. Describe this problem lavishly, emotionally. Linger on its profundity and awfulness. Then present your project as the ideal solution. This is not difficult. Open the heart to open the mind to open the cheque book. And she'd been thinking about this idea in Rosa's bath last night.

"Young unemployed youth. No prospects, no role models, not enough learning. What they do have are mobiles which connect them with a digital universe, and they have imagination. How can we help them broaden their horizons, raise their spirits, empower them for the future? What they need is an opportunity to reinvent themselves, to imagine a better life…" It was a physical thrill pitching like this. Freya's face glowed, her eyes shone.

"The other day at the library where we run sessions, Mister Carraday and I were interviewing a young man, brought up in care, abused at home, failed by his school and local authority. Now he thinks of himself as a kind of nearly doctor. He surfs the web for podcasts and downloads to help him broaden his knowledge of the field he nearly works in."

"But he'll never get to be a doctor. I mean that sort? Let's be honest. And certainly not without years of training."

"No, but he could work in a chemist, as a hospital porter, as a volunteer for a health charity. He's broadened his horizons. And developed a hobby to sustain him through unemployment."

"Fascinating. And your 'Nearlyologist'?"

"Mister Carraday has… been working for years on an extensive databank containing stories from potentially thousands of people. He believes it's hugely therapeutic to share these hopes and disappointments and missed pathways."

"I can imagine."

"We've been running one-to-ones in the local library, but it needs scaling up. Needs to be turned into a digital resource and that takes finance to create."

And all of this was a whisker away from being true, would soon become so. The young man, Abdul, a regular in the library, lived in a hostel nearby and sat for hours in a corner of Central Lending, surrounded by plastic bags containing his bedding, clothes and papers. Freya had chatted to him, taken him to meet Carraday and they'd talked about how he could use the free computers to follow up his interest in healthcare, including Abdul's theory that anti-depressants are used in making communion wafers to entice more people into the Catholic Church. It was a start. A pilot stage would be necessary. Research and development. Merely a timing issue, the gap between planning and actualisation; to bridge this, some kind of funds were more than urgently needed, now Freya and Jamie had actually split. And Tyler was loaded after all.

"You really think it's over?" This news like the tremor of an earthquake was reverberating through their families and friends, rattling the crockery, exposing cracks in unexpected places, her angry outburst and exit leading to phone calls and emails, side-taking and name-calling. On the night when she left Jamie, Freya had driven round to Rosalind's, cried a lot, said she ought to go back home and patch things up. But by then she'd drunk too much of Rosalind's duty-free Bunderberg rum, and the next day she woke up with a headache and an extraordinary feeling of weightlessness, the thrill of free-falling into a clean, white void. Like drowning, like flying.

The few times they'd met since, when Freya went back to the house to collect things, she and Jamie ended up shouting at each other, mostly about money. For now Jamie had some redundancy cash, but already he'd mentioned the other savings he thought were in reserve to fall back on, and how at least that meant the house wouldn't have to be sold or anything.

"For someone who hates figures, you're getting pretty keen on money," Freya raged. "No wonder I've felt so stifled in our marriage." Now she was too cross with Jamie to worry about the rights and wrongs of contacting his loathed half-brother Tyler whom she was beginning to think her husband had always been unfair towards. After all, Jamie was always his mum's favourite.

"This Carraday fellow: people do love a guru figure," said Tyler.

"Like I said, the social media project's been a bit dormant lately." Dormant. That was the word. "We started life providing digital training to the young unemployed, but the funding dried up. Our charitable aims maybe ought to be changed with the Charities Commission. You'll probably want to wait before making any donation."

"Well..."

"No problem whatsoever. I mean, it is a bit difficult right now, cash flow and all, a bit of pressure on the business account."

"Oh, I think we can make an exception for you, Freya dear. I quite understand. And the grant?"

"Will be spent on our educational work. Nearlyness among the young unemployed and other target groups, how imagining a career can help them to find one."

"Fascinating, absolutely fascinating." And then he yawned, stretched, looked around for a waitress.

"So I'm sorry you've not met any of the rest of the team. They were all so keen to meet our – potentially – generous benefactor."

Tyler Jackson radiated affluence and the ineptness of the super-confident. Fragrantly laundered, pink as a piglet, he looked her in the eyes. Freya touched the neck of her blouse.

"Ah well – another time perhaps, Freya my dear. And if you see that dumb half-brother of mine tell him from me he's a mug to let you go." Tyler patted her wrist supportively. "And by the way, I'm sure we can find you some top-flight trustees for your charity. Well-connected, business acumen. Also my accounts people could help out pro bono."

"Oh wow – book-keeping is not my forte."

Another wave of Tyler's hand and the terrible weight of financial management seemed lifted from her shoulders like a heavy coat whisked off to the cloakroom.

"But look here, there is something else I want to ask you, Freya." He pressed his hands together in mock prayer. "My company does lots of work in the Middle East, United Arab Emirates, scoping projects. There's a business and education expo out there in a few weeks and we're hoping to have a presence. We are keen to stress the potential of digital marketing tools, social media etcetera etcetera. Need a bit of a gimmick to attract some attention – and someone who's up to speed on all that malarkey to run some workshops. "

"I couldn't pretend to be an expert."

"Oh, but you 'get it' don't you, and so many of our people – well, it's a small team, most of them my age, and older. Digital dinosaurs. All men too I fear. We need someone to present a different face."

"Seward Associates is all about presenting different faces."

"Marvellous. That's the ticket." Tyler Jackson glanced at his big shiny watch, slipped a tenner and a wink to the waitress to cover the coffees and croissant, and slid away like a paunchy, slightly arthritic pink shark, out into the shallows of Regent Street. Freya gathered her things into her bag, swapped her high heels for trainers in the ladies' loo, washed her hands in hot water and fragrant liquid soap from the glass dispensers, dried herself carefully on one of their fresh, white cotton flannels which she quickly pocketed, checked no one else was in the Ladies, then whooped and punched the air.

PLAYWORKER'S DAUGHTER

Arriving early, Jamie stood in the gallery bookshop nervously flicking through a hefty hardback catalogue of a show about that Outsider Art while trying to find the right words to say to his daughter. He glanced at himself in the glass wall of the store to make sure his lips weren't moving, so strong was the stream of words boiling in him, bubbling with hurt, self-justification, guilt, fury. He was determined

105

to be someone who chose to hang out in art galleries. But knew in his gut this was Freya territory. He was one lost fish adrift amidst the shoals in this cultural aquarium.

A touch on the arm and there were Pippa and Sophie beside him. Father and daughter hugged tearfully amidst the Hockney calendars and Matisse tee-shirts while her girlfriend hovered. Jamie hadn't been surprised, had felt more proud than shocked, when Pip announced her feelings for best friend Roxanne, but was fearful that daughter would turn against Dad in the process of coming out. The thing with Roxanne didn't last, but now she seemed deeply happy with Sophie, fellow member of the puppet theatre company which toured shows round children's festivals and parties but aspired to do serious work at what they called the bleeding edge of contemporary puppetry. Jamie had joked with Martin that he had no problem with Pippa being gay, but why couldn't she, the Playworker's Daughter, be attracted to a lesbian plumber or banker or someone with a skill a bit more useful and lucrative?

"I'll see you back here in an hour, Pip? I'd love to do art with you two, but I have a meeting I need to get to, Jamie. Sorry." They brushed cheeks and Sophie, a thoughtful woman who wore a pink knitted hat, big coat and a friendly but anxious expression, slid tactfully away.

"It's difficult to know what to say to you, Pippa."

"Mum phoned me. But it doesn't make much sense yet. I'm still confused about what's going on with you two, Dad."

"Me as well, my love. But you know, long-term relationships – it's complicated."

"You're a married couple not a Facebook status. What do you think of this tee-shirt?" Once Jamie had paid for it, they left the shop and wandered through rooms of the permanent collection, chatting and pointing out paintings they liked.

"What is it that's so complicated?"

"I don't know. I don't know how to talk about it really."

"Oh Dad. You sound so adolescent. We're family – you can be completely open and honest with me."

"About our sex life or lack of it?"

"OK – no. Maybe not that bit."

"About our arguments and my deep sense of worthlessness?"

"Yes. Well. Maybe someone else is better. Do you, like, have any friends?"

"Of course."

"I mean other than Martin."

"Um..."

"I mean I love Martin to bits, but he's not proved much good at long-term relationships so far."

"No. Perhaps not."

"Hey – look at this: 'Nude Woman In A Red Armchair'; looks a bit like Sophie."

"Sophie's not quite that curvy!"

"Cover me from that attendant while I take a picture. I might make a puppet version for her birthday. Mum says losing your job made you impossible to talk to. You bottled things up and got miserable. She's in overdrive now, setting up this bloody Nearly thing, fundraising like crazy. Mind you, she seems pretty miserable living at Rosa's."

"Oh well that's encouraging: she's miserable about something."

"Jesus Dad, have I gone to all this trouble growing up and coming out only to have my folks turn into stroppy teenagers?"

"Sorry Pip."

"I go round to see Mum for advice about my career and end up pissed and stoned listening to her and Rosalind reminiscing about their experiences with hallucinogens. My Dad meets me at art spaces and tells me about his sex life."

"About his lack of one. Nearly tells you."

"That bloody word again! Why couldn't you two get an allotment or buy a puppy like other people's mums and dads?" They left the gallery and made for the escalator down to the ground floor.

"It must be hard for you, love."

"Yeah. Anyway, I actually do need to talk to you about me for a change: whether you and Mum might lend us some money to help us set up the puppet theatre. I know it's not a good time but, any of that baby boomer fortune you might be able to share with your progeny?" She was affectionate but serious, an edge of annoyance in her voice. His daughter had a life of her own which she wanted to concentrate on without being upstaged by her parents, fond of them as she might be.

"Your mum's the one to talk to about that, though. As you well know, I'm phobic about money."

Pip scowled, welled up with tears.

"You've left home now, Dad. Time to learn to stand on your own two feet." She turned and ran to the down escalator, disappeared into the crowd.

"Pippa...!"

LISTEN UP

Freya Redcoat, super sleuth, today in new wellington boots splish-splashes through mud on the tail of the villain who came in the night and tried to steal her treasure. She's following the tracks of his shoes, footprints waterlogged, fading fast, but can still see traces and hurry after them, further into the marsh. Dangerous territory this. Creaks and moans of wind in the trees. And too late she hears him, feels his rough hand clamping down on her face as she's lifted up into the air, legs thrashing, but he grips her tight. Redcoat bites back, sinking her teeth into his money grubbing fingers. He growls and drops her and she flees, quick as a flicker, into the reeds. Hears him cursing and cursing. She presses herself down onto the cold, soggy earth, plucks a blade of grass and expertly slots it between her fists to make a reed, then blows.

Freya jolted awake to the glare of her laptop shining; she began again to read the presentation she was planning. Good morning and welcome. I am Freya Redcoat, founder and CEO. Here we offer the facility for members of the public to talk to our expert to help them achieve resolution. With funding earmarked to reinvigorate our high streets, the Nearlies are harvested, exhibited on the walls and posted online. Tee-shirts come in all sizes. I am Freya, digital guru, feminist icon, grown girl detective; it's a delight to be here with you today and by way of introduction let me say, I can multitask and touch-type, can Skype, tweet, twist, boogie and boggle, can install a Wordpress blog with widgets, can throw a horse over a sunset and into an ocean stinking of coriander seeds crushed with gemstones.

And I am on fire here this morning with you in serried rows and I pacing the stage like a lioness, my microphone clipped to my face and the hall ringing with my pithiness and sassiness. Listen up world. I'm the tip I'm the top, And I'm going to mint it with this. By next year you'll all have one, will sit on trains twiddling yours, will tell your friends you don't know how you'd get by without it. Articles will be writ and documentaries made about how it's rotting the mind, reshaping our frontal lobes, re-forging contemporary identity. OK so looking at it now, technologically it's not so complex. OK so it looks like a mirror. Ah, but see what you do? Put this mirror under your nose and look down so you feel like you're walking on the ceiling, in the sky. Step outside now and everything is giddy-some and difficult.

This gizmo is a tool to help us be in one place whilst imagining another, walking on real ground but seeing something else. Embracing your nearliness involves this kind of shift. No regrets, allowing yourself to be in more than one place at once, be more than one version of yourself simultaneously.

And even as Freya hears herself utter this guff she knows she's also dreaming, the front row containing a bizarre assemblage of celebs and old school friends looking nothing like themselves. She feels this elation the applause the warm fug of successfulness slipping away as she opens her eyes a crack and sees she's staring up at the ceiling on the sofa in Rosa's front room which smells of stale wine and cat litter. Above her stands Rosa in spotty pink nightie proffering a mug of tea which she slops down beside the mattress, then yawns and yanks open the curtains. Dammit, thinks Freya, I'm late.

From *THE LITTLE BOOK OF NEARLY*

Describe or draw some of the pictures you have in your mind
of things that didn't quite happen to you.
Use collage and colour.

Think of a place you nearly live.
In a safe place ask your partner to close their eyes,
then lead them across the room as you describe it to them.
When you've finished
both sit down and write.

THESE ASSOCIATIONS

In the dark immensity of the Turbine Hall Jamie searched for his daughter. How could he have been so thoughtless? Too bloody self-obsessed to respond to her needs. The space was packed with women looking a bit like Pip. There were no artworks on show in this cathedral of culture, but plenty of people Pippa's age milling about. He spotted her, talking to a woman, presumably a friend she'd bumped into. His daughter stared blankly at him, then stuck out her tongue – a sign that she wasn't too angry with him. But she carried on with her conversation. He stood at a distance, thinking how thin she looked, and yet comfortable in her skin. Actually that fringe is quite stylish, thought Jamie. A flurry of people rushed past suddenly, and the young woman talking to Pippa broke off to join them, running suddenly away.

"Who was that?"

"No idea, Dad." They became aware that a flock of people were milling about amongst the tourists and school groups. It was hard to tell who was or wasn't part of the group, some kind of a performance or installation presumably. Most were young and athletic, gazelles in tight jeans and thick trainers, pounding on the polished concrete floor, but there were others too: an old bearded man like Father Christmas, a skinny guy with long hair, glasses and baggy yellow shorts, a wiry white-haired woman... all chasing each other round in circles, playing some kind of secret game of chase amidst the punters.

"Sorry, Pip. Of course we'll lend you the money. I'll talk to your mum." Father and daughter walked arm in arm further into the hall which sloped down like a car park forecourt into the dark, heard the squeak of soles and exhalations of breath, intimate grunts of exertion as this tribe moved, playing a variation on tag. Pippa broke away from her father to join the game. He watched her running, circling around the girl who'd approached her. He wanted to join this swarm himself but felt too self-conscious. Suddenly the whole lot of them came to a halt. The lights cut out and in the dark the flock began to chant. Dozens of voices in unison, a cloud of strange song. Jamie and his daughter walked amongst them, able to view the figures like they were living sculptures, observing how each person chose to arrange their limbs and place themselves in relation to each other. Jamie tried to catch the meaning of the words being sung in sonorous harmony, then in percussive shouts, but couldn't quite make them out.

No one gave a command but at a preordained moment the flock dispersed, began running with all their might up the huge grey concrete expanse. The happening appeared to be over. But as Jamie and Pip prepared to leave, the flock careered thunderously back past them, down to the shadowy back of the hall, then a few seconds later, slightly more slowly ran up again, a wave of movers, of all ages and nations, younger, older, fatter, lamer, each at their own full pelt, then very gradually slowing, slowing to become a silent, stately procession of meditators, with which Jamie and Pippa found themselves walking, beside small children who copied the participants earnestly and with delight, joining in their inexplicable labour as they started now to hum and together processed towards the body of the hall where watchers on the bridge looked down. And all the time individual members of the herd would separate themselves off to attach themselves to a watcher and start to tell them something, some kind of story.

A young man materialised out of the gloom, breathless from running, and launched into an anecdote. "I used to work in the city and took the same train every morning. One day trains were cancelled due to snow and I got chatting to a woman on the platform about it. For a year after that we'd bump into each other every few days and chat for a few minutes until the train arrived. I was engaged to be married and she was having work problems, so our conversations were short but intimate. As my wedding day approached I realised that my chats with this stranger were more important than any I had with my fiancé. We understood each other like we'd been married for years. I imagined telling her this. I imagined us staying on the train and getting off together to start a new life. But something must have changed about her work routine. She didn't appear on the platform for a while. As the weeks passed I realised I'd never see her again. The first time we met I'd asked her name, but soon forgot it and was too embarrassed to ever ask again. So I had absolutely no way to trace her."

"Is that a true story?" Jamie asked.

"It is, isn't it," Pippa said to the man. "Did you get married?" The young man touched his fingers to his lips and slipped away into the dark. Now a flame-haired young woman appeared at their side, startlingly beautiful, talking rapidly in an Eastern European accent about her bizarre dreams and their symbolism. To Jamie's amazement, Pippa started describing some of her nightmares in reply. They spoke intensely, openly. After a few minutes the girl also smiled and ran off. A woman with short blonde hair peeled away from the crowd and began speaking to Jamie, talking about her struggle with alcoholism when she was a student in Stockholm. They started chatting about the differences between Swedish and English culture, and Jamie reminisced about their holiday in search of Freya's semi-imaginary roots.

"We found Swedish drivers stuck to the speed limit because they took it for granted that restrictions were wisely imposed for public safety. Whereas British drivers wait till they're out of sight of CCTV then speed like mad." The stranger laughed, touched his arm, slid away. And the group stilled again, configured across the immensity of the space, sitting or standing in clusters, and softly they chanted again in unison, something about creating a new ground even in the technological age. Another hand tapped Jamie on the shoulder, but this was Pippa's. Now she pointed at her watch,

"Hey Dad, I'm sorry too, OK? It's me getting emotional. I ought to go and find Sophe. But that was amazing. Love you." She squeezed him tight. How wonderful to be held. He'd taken it for granted that his daughter would take her mother's side for sisterly or daughterly reasons. Now she gave him one last kiss and was gone into the crowd.

After they parted he looped back to the Turbine Hall, fighting back tears. He sat on the cold, hard floor in the huge, dark room, watching the flock, wondering if another thrilling stranger might appear at his side and swap intimacies. They all rushed past.

Now as he looked up into the immensity of that echoing space he found himself humming. A shoot of fresh, green song sprouted in his head and swayed there, refusing to settle until he'd stood up and walked through the movers, up the hall and out into the sunshine by the Thames, had pulled out his mobile, pressed on the screen with his thumb to open an app for taking voice notes that he'd downloaded, and very quietly sang to it a fragment of words and melody. On the way home he texted Freya:

> How much do we have in our savings? Daughter needs dosh.

THE SINGLEHOOD

"You're welcome to stay as long as you like, Frey."

"You're a lifesaver."

"Really. No pressure," said Rosalind.

"Thanks so much."

"To be honest it could save my life right now too, if you could pay some of yer ill-gotten gains towards my rent."

"OK. Sure. But it might be a little while before I can get my hands on cash."

"Whenever. I owe the studio for the wine, you see, and the grant we got was pathetic."

"Jamie's very uptight about our finances right now. And Pippa's looking for a loan for her puppet company. But I am waiting to hear about a funding application."

"I mean I wouldn't charge you if I didn't know you were such a big shot consultant these days. But boy o boy am I skint."

"And I've had to pay out for new flyers and badges and everything. But it won't be long."

"Jamie's acting like a shit, Frey. But that old library guy truly creeps me out. Bet he wants to get into your knickers." For one whose artistic work was so experimental, Rosalind's views on relationships were somewhat conventional.

"Carraday's an eccentric, but in his way he's a very serious thinker, Rosa. Anyway we're both too old for him to be thinking of being in any relation to my underwear surely. And Jamie may be lots of things, but he's not a shit."

"You sure you're better off out of that marriage, then? Better watch out on the mean streets of singlehood, lady." Rosalind was from Melbourne, younger than Freya; she dressed like a punky Frida Kahlo. Men were fascinated by her, frightened of her, froze in her presence like rabbits caught in headlights. Freya's first impressions as an older woman of what Rosa called 'The Singlehood' were that men looked straight through her to the slender younger women the planet seemed crammed with. The wolves took one passing look and moved on further into the woods. But that was OK – time to herself was what she'd told Jamie she needed, and it was what she was getting.

"His phony Aussie thing pisses me off too. He never looks me in the eye.

Rosalind's latest project involved painting herself in the styles of other artists and photographing the results. Her partially naked body had been going viral. This morning she still had traces of Yves Klein blue around her eyes despite a shower and much scrubbing as she sat in her dressing gown at the kitchen table, hair up in a towel turban, nursing a glass of green liquid, apparently a great natural hangover cure. Freya sprawled across the sofa-bed and sighed deeply.

"Actually Ros, The Singlehood is wearing me out. You're younger than me. I'm used to evenings spent gawping at Master Chef on the telly then going to bed early.

Now every night's a blooming magical mystery tour of drinks and events and meals and clubbing. I don't know where you get the energy."

"I drink the blood of virgins, Frey." She scratched her armpit, sniffed her fingers. "Fat lot of good it does me. Where am I going to find a babymaker before the biological clock cuts out?"

"What about the artist you were rolling around with the other day?"

Rosalind jabbed her fingers down her throat. "Talented artist. Utter tosser."

"Are you sure you want a baby? You don't exactly radiate the maternal."

"I'm defending myself, girl. Reckon I could do it given the chance. It changed you didn't it?"

"Way back when. But I wanted to change."

"Nappies – broken nights – shitty nappies – yeah – bring it on!"

"Jamie was a pretty good dad, I have to say that for him. If a bit smug about it sometimes."

"Ah you're so lucky – I mean were so – I mean, lucky then and better off now. I mean... O to hell with it. Where shall we go tonight?"

"Must we go anywhere?"

"We could stay in. I've got that acid."

"That wasn't what I meant."

"You don't fancy tripping then?"

"Like I said to Pippa, I took LSD years ago and found it sort of mind expanding, but not since I became a mum. And I'm not sure we should have had that conversation with my daughter."

"Pip's an adult, she can handle it. You should try it again."

"No thank you."

"You should nearly try it, shouldn't you – keep it in reach for whenever you need to expand your mind. I can sort that out."

116

"Makes me weary thinking about it." Tempting though.

"I don't want to do it alone, and I thought an old hippie like you would jump at the chance to try it again. Wasn't there a boutique on the King's Road called Granny Takes a Trip?"

"I'm not that bloody old!"

Rosalind was up for anything, dropped hints she'd tried all kinds of kinky polyamorous and bisexual acts, had fought off the gropings of uncles and employers then launched herself into what she called her Slaghood. During this time she'd shacked up with Martin for a while. Freya first met Rosa half way up the stairs at a house party; they had a furious argument about whether Kylie Minogue was a shit role model for girls, shared a spliff and bonded over a mutual love of Aretha Franklin. It had impressed Freya that this young woman seemed to cope with the perils and pleasures of promiscuity without the protection of political ideology which Freya in her wild youth had to defend herself against damage to self-esteem. And now Rosalind's romantic aims were utterly conventional; she longed for a white wedding to a nice wealthy man who would help her make babies which she'd cherish and cook for in monogamous bliss. Freya had always assumed her stated aims were ironic but now she wasn't too sure.

"You're looking for Mister Right?"

"Mister Right for The Time Being. Can't imagine sticking with one guy forever."

"Mister Well OK He'll Do For Now."

"Something like that."

"I don't understand your generation's concept of serial monogamy."

"Why so? You were with Jamie for aeons."

"In my day we believed we could have as many kinds of sexual relationships as emotional ones, that being

117

constant to someone was about more than whether or not you slept with anyone else."

"Sounds like a minefield – a love rat's charter to me, Frey. Simpler to deal with the bastards one at a time."

"Then find you've lost the one you really love? And feel betrayed over and over? Or be branded a betrayer simply for acting on desires we all know we have." Rosalind took for granted a world of Internet dating, downloadable apps that could point you at swipe of screen to the next available consensual shag, and yet longed for valentines and white weddings. Despite all her youthful political promiscuity, Freya's generation had been fundamentally romantic about love, believed the real thing was hard to find and worth holding onto through the ups and downs, the compromises and strayings. She admired Rosa's ability to decide first what she wanted from life, then secondly to seek a partner to do it with. And yet it shocked her too, this cool assumption of the probability of separation: a mix tape of happy scenes from different romcoms all spliced together. Splitting with Jamie felt like a defeat and a waste as well as a kind of liberation. The Analogue Scarcity Model Versus Digital Sexual Abundance? There was a blog post to be written on this.

"All I want is a baby. Close your eyes," Rosalind said. Freya was led, shut-eyed across the room and into the hallway. She heard the squeak of a drawer being pulled open, then: "Open now." And Freya was looking down into the cupboard in the hall where babies' booties and titchy socks and sandals, babygros and nighties were laid out.

"I've been buying them from charity shops," said Ros quietly.

Freya laughed, assuming this was part of some ironic art practice exploring notions of maternity, but then saw how seriously her friend knelt there, unfolding and refolding her layette. To cover her amusement, Freya began reminiscing about Pippa's early years, the joys and horrors of tantrums at the gates of school. "…And once we searched the whole house for a lost lizard which Pip had brought home from school, and that night Jamie spotted it crawling up the pillow towards her hair as he tried to soothe her to sleep, so he had to scoop it up with one hand while stroking her forehead with the other."

"Gross." The anecdote received nothing but a blank stare from Rosalind. Apparently the desire for a baby wasn't the same as an interest in actual children, not yet. Freya missed her husband fiercely then. She couldn't stay long at Rosalind's, she realised now. But a moment later she was equally fiercely happy, inhabiting this new present in which everything seemed so fresh, direct, harshly simple.

BIRDLIBRARYWOMAN

In the dawn light outside the library a woman, exercising,
writes words in the air with her whole body twisting and
swooping, flailing then posing. Centred like she's
holding a bowl she must not spill
containing the most precious of juices.
Pigeons flock round a tree, wings like pages rustling
this Birdlibrarywoman another one helping
dispelling the Nearly.

Carraday been roamabout all night long
after Mumma bedded down and drugged up
till sunrise and lifting and porridge making.
Pulled on his greatcoat and laced up the big boots, put on
his outback hat, quiet open the door and click shut
behind as the chill come to surround him.
down the street, in his pocket the Nearly Jar,
lid off so he scoop out the fluff and sprinkle it
in pinches so nobody ever knows,
a few more particles that drift about the place, nondescript.
Down to the reservoir and along to the edge

of the school he got sent to and hated,
later working did oddjobs there,
painting and hammering, cleaning and clearing
until they got shot of him.
His strangeways starting out way back back asakid
with switching his bedroom light off on off on off on off on
to scare the nightmares away when dadda still there
muffled shouts the sweet smell of his Woodbine smoke
and thumps of him downstairs threating Mumma
and Gregory write the rudest words
slip them between the floorboards where they must still sit
or turn to dust like we all will someday.
And muchmuchlaterlater Brenda,
the Headmaster's wayward daughter,
a charm doll of rope, card and barbed wire
buried in the school yard to win her.
Though later she vamoosh to Tasmania
The school gym set alight and burning up
and Boomer saying sweet revenge
for the vagrants and downtrod packed off in ships
by the British Crown to hell & the outback
to slaughter indigenous.

Mrs Birdlibrarywoman, spirit of the building who must
each morning dance the books and the birds alive,
hum open the bookplace which he seeing in the Dozing
lumbering here with its belly full of learning,
a giant armadillo of cleverness which the people venerate
and treasure so much that the men from the centre
come once and shoot it with drug darts, then tie it down
while it sleeping, shackle and dope it up good so it learning
turned cold and olden, veins clogging with blutac tangling
with sellotape, needing the dancer each day to
unstick and revivify
till the glass doors open or else needing Carraday maybe
to burn back to life.

120

EXTEND LIFE

On the morning when Tyler Jackson's cheque arrived the two flat-mates were slobbing around Rosalind's kitchen in their pyjamas, like pre-teens at a sleepover. Throughout the night Freya had heard the sounds of Rosalind at work in the boxroom she'd turned into her studio, and was woken early by her friend crashing into the room to ask her to take pictures on her phone of some of the paintings she'd been making, using her feet as brushes.

"They look a bit like those paintings elephants do."

"Surely not that good. But I like 'em."

"They must have been fun to paint."

"Yeah, like playing in mud."

The letterbox clattered as it swung open and envelopes flopped onto the mat in the hall. When Freya opened the Coutts Bank cheque from Jackson's foundation, the figure handwritten in fountain pen, she waved it over her head like a placard and they cracked jokes about holidays in the Bahamas. They took a selfie of the two of them gripping each corner of the paper and smiling at the camera like in those pictures of giant cheques being handed out to good causes.

"Better not put that one on Instagram." Freya folded it in half and tucked the cheque into her purse, showered and, dressed in her professional black dress and tailored red jacket, set off to the bank. But once outside she instead walked in the streets around Rosalind's place telling herself over and over how wonderful it was that she was now able to pay off her debt and put the rest back into the savings account before Jamie noticed it was missing. He was hopeless at anything to do with numbers, seemed to think checking his bank statement was somehow a reactionary act, but surely he'd take a look sometime soon, now he wasn't earning and didn't have Freya around to do all that malarkey. In a drizzling car park she stood rooted to the spot, on the verge of a change of heart, picturing an ergonomic and stylish desk and office chair, slick rebranded website, part-time assistant and shining new state of the art laptop, her drab office transformed into a centre for Nearlyology.

Freya marched to her branch on the high street to present the fat cheque feeling the proud disappointment of being about to do the right thing.

Two hours later Freya unlocked the front door. Rosalind called to her. "You all paid up, Frey? Sucker! That puts paid to our world tour! At least you can sleep the sleep of the just." Walking through to the kitchen, Freya found Rosalind cross-legged on the floor in the kitchen wearing a tee-shirt and nothing else, doing her kind of mindfulness meditation, a cup of tea in hand and an e-cigarette in her mouth. "Don't look at me like that Frey. It's not bad for me, is it. Helps me concentrate on my breathing." She took another e-toke. "Peppermint flavour. Good for the lungs."

"Oh yes, like menthol ciggies used to be. 'Cool as a mountain stream'."

What Freya didn't tell Rosalind was that she'd stopped once again on her march to the bank. She'd stood outside the office she could no longer afford, pictured it with improved access to the high street, repainted with proper signage. She turned and marched back to the bank but with a different action plan developing in her mind:
to put the money into the business account not their joint account,
to spend it not quite on the new activities she'd outlined somewhat vaguely in her letter to Tyler Jackson, but on giving Ros something for the use of her sofa, catching up with the office rent, paying off the bank as she'd intended, and well, not paying back the joint savings just yet, but spending the rest on another relaunch of her business, a new website to be built by Connie, a new strategy based around Carraday and Nearlyology, which this time, surely, would bring clear, fresh streams of liquidity to pour back into the dry sandflats of the family finances.

From THE LITTLE BOOK OF NEARLY

How many whiskers were you away from it happening?
How much nearlyincidence did it generate?
I mean, how deeply did it nearly happen to you?

EMINGTON

Of course Tyler phoned a few days later to ask when she was moving into new central premises.

"I cannot thank your foundation enough for the cheque. There has been a slight change of plans, though. Tyler, do you think the Trust will mind if we delay the move to the new office and spend some of the budget on temporary admin assistance for me? We won't commit to appointing permanent staff, but bring someone in on a short-term contract. I have someone in mind for the position."

"No problem at all, in fact the board looks very favourably on organisations capable of revising their strategy in the light of changing circumstances. Good on you, girl."

It made sense to pay herself to do the admin. On her blog Freya created a Virtual Editor by the name of R. Emington, named after an old manual typewriter which Rosalind kept on a shelf in the lounge as an objet d'art. The typewriter, made in 1922, was a heavy, square block of painted metal and intricate mechanisms stamped with the slogan, "To Save Time Is To Extend Life". Freya pictured her new assistant Rauri saving her time, sorting dull admin and complex finances, offering tea, sympathy and technical support. He looked a little like Dan, but squarer, reliable and dogged. Shame she couldn't really afford someone like him, but she signed emails with his name and even set him up with a twitter account.

"Looking forward to meeting the famous Rauri!" wrote Tyler Jackson when he heard of the appointment. Freya emailed back: "I should have said that Rauri works from his home in Wales. Will try to get you two together next time he's in London, but it may be a while." Next she thought out a complicated backstory to explain how her Irish assistant had ended up living in Machynlleth, because he liked hiking and the nearby Centre for Alternative Technology. Then Freya felt sad as well as guilty, like she'd sacked someone or had a good colleague resign. She'd liked sharing her office with the imaginary Rauri, and though she continued to credit this imaginary assistant on the website, he had become a distant figure now.

It was Rosalind who came up with the idea of the Nearly Store. Her collective of artists had negotiated to run an exhibition in an old pharmacy on the High Street last Christmas and it went well: a good notice in the local paper and one national, not too much mess or noise, and a few sales. The owner was pleased with the publicity and the peppercorn rent he received; it was better than nothing and he'd not had a serious approach from a business in months.

"You could do a Pop-up Shop."

"Of course! And I don't need to find premises. My office – it used to be a shop – I can turn that back into one." Which meant she could tell Tyler about this exciting new space without mentioning that it was hers already.

On evenings when Freya pleaded exhaustion from nights on the town, the two friends stayed in and talked until late, accompanied by music she didn't recognise, twee, innocent tunes with twangling instruments and fey lyrics about meadows and handholding, Rosalind knocking back the wine and vaping, then sprawling on the floor next to Freya's sofabed in a lovely warm fug of friendship. Freya's stories were no longer the tidy, well-rehearsed anecdotes of the couple, but the stuff of the solo Quest for Fulfilment. Her life since the split had unfurled before her, a rich quilt embroidered with maps of past journeys and future possibilities, a splendid heraldic bird fanning its magnificent wings and preparing to soar.

Rosalind told Freya of her tomboyish childhood roaming free in the Melbourne suburbs with Labrador BamBam for company, her brush with anorexia, then wild teenage times clinging tight to men on Harley Davidsons, breaking away from a heavy drinking father and depressive mum to vroom through the outback for joints and tinnies under the ubiquitous antipodean sun.

"Makes my childhood sound a bit tame," said Freya, but that didn't stop her telling Rosalind how when she was young in chilly Britain, she loved to play shop. "I'd set out a few old toys on the wall outside our suburban Birmingham house and write signs with prices on. My friend Stacey and I picked the petals from flowers in our little garden and crushed them up with water to make perfumes and lotions. We were a café too, but the coffee was made with poster paint. I was boss because I had a toy cash register." She kept a stack of old newspapers and some paper bags her mum set aside from the rubbish and used these to wrap her produce for the customers, writing on the bags in ballooning crayon letters: 'Freya's Shop', because it was.

"I can't walk through town without spotting which shops thrive and which have closed down. I try to analyse why this café is always full and this one empty – maybe if they'd put a display of cakes in the window, rearrange the table layout, retrain the staff to actually be knowledgeable about the food they were serving. Or at least be friendlier. What is it makes this establishment such a pleasure to dawdle in, whereas that one across the road feels like a leech on your purse?"

"You're a proper little Queen of Shops aren't you," Rosalind laughed. "Are all the ladies going to be wearing your Nearly line of dresses next season? Backless, topless, frontless, bottomless. Or your fragrance: slight absence of woody notes and a subtle hint of sweet eff all."

Freya was overflowing with gratitude the day a bunch of friends showed up with buckets and brooms to wash and clear out her little office. They painted it white, put up shelves. Gregory Carraday also arrived with a toolkit and, to Freya's delight and amazement, proved very handy at the practical work, bringing with him an electric drill and the right-sized screws to fix a wonky light socket, meticulously applying masking tape between shelf and wall to ensure a crisp edge to the paintwork. When she complimented him he glowed, told her he'd been a painter and decorator for years, done plenty of odd jobs for his mum and customers in the neighbourhood, including the local the secondary school. On building sites too. He was a dark horse.

"We're all stores on social media," Freya opined to Ros in the early hours. "Setting out our digital wares: photos of the holidays, the kids, details of the price of our services, we're each of us a brand."

"Speak for yourself, Mrs FreyaCo. I'm not a number, I'm a human beeeeying."

"And a product in the Facebook store too. But what can we sell? Nobody buys anything these days, not from physical places."

"Yeah but they buy loads of bitty shit."

"The Nearly Store could have art on the walls, flog second-hand books, postcards, tee-shirts, badges – 'bitty shit'. Maybe Pip could make puppets for sale." Pip and Sophie's flat was packed with hanging marionettes, discarded glove puppets, heads, legs and arms left dangling. They freaked Freya out, these foam and wood caricatures which her daughter spent her evenings modelling, an ensemble of Nearly people with their bulging eyes, fake hair and gigantic limbs, characterful but inanimate. They could be very saleable, mind. "The real point of the Nearly Store is a place to hang out and share stories in. Which leads to punters for workshops and coaching." She was foreseeing one-to-one consultations involving flipcharts and takeaways. Late into the night Freya and Rosalind spun ideas for the shop, pictured it thriving and growing. Customers would queue round the block for their special events, whatever these might consist of. Chains of Nearly places would spread worldwide.

"It's all down to the marketing spend. If only I could raise some proper dosh so much would be possible. Maybe Tyler…"

"Enough of Tyler already," whispered Rosa, pressing a finger to her lips "Hush."

Another bottle of wine and the last of an old bottle of grappa later, realising night was over and a milky dawn had broken, they put shoes and coats on, stepped out into the cool, dewy, echoing street and walked awhile, both silent now, jazzed and fractured from sleeplessness, thoughts beyond articulation. They walked for an hour watching deliverymen arriving, shops opening their shutters, workers beginning to set off for buses or the station, or unlock their cars, rev up and zip away. Arriving back at the flat with warm, fluffy fresh bread from the bakery around the corner, they staggered to their beds and slept and slept and slept as the warm loaf cooled.

GUNK

"Oh and this is one of Stan when he was first learning to walk – look at that adorable wobble. Isn't he a peach." At The Oak, Martin sipping fizzy water, Connie a small glass of white wine, Jamie a pint of lager. Where once they'd have discussed Blair's war crimes and which was the best Dylan album ever, now Martin had his laptop out and was scrolling through scores of family snaps so quickly that they merged into a jerky silent movie of their son's first years. Stan flopped then crawled then toddled in and out of seas, around gardens, in and out of the arms of his doting parents, relations, friends and assorted strangers.

127

"But let's not overdo it, darling," Connie said. "You know how boring other people's kids' photos can be."

"Well you know I love yours," interjected Jamie. The couple stopped glaring at each other and beamed at him proudly.

"I saw your Pip round at her mother's the other day, and isn't that young woman a gem. A credit to you. So smart and sassy and seems so happy now she's *with* her girlfriend and everything." Connie's light chitchat tiptoed its way around the break-up and the coming out. She consulted her phone, downed the remains of a white wine spritzer and stood up. "Time to pick up the monster from Granny's. Jamie, so good to see you. Glad you're OK." Her intense stare and serious smile suggested he was now officially a problem in need of solution. "You two boys enjoy chewing the fat. I'll see you later." She tousled Martin's hair, blew Jamie a kiss, swung her bag over her shoulder and went, watched admiringly by both of them. Martin turned back to the screen.

"One more clip. Where is it? One of Connie and Stan in Crete with the girls... No – not that. Ah, this one?" It was only on the screen for a moment before Martin found the tiny x in the left-hand corner and clicked it away. But that definitely was not a video of family frolics on a Greek island. No, the image was a close-up of a woman's lips wrapped around a large, erect penis. And now it was gone and the few seconds had also passed when one might have responded to it spontaneously with a slight laugh or a gasp. Now they were suddenly suspended in a strange bubble of time during which both colluded in pretending they'd not seen what they had seen.

"He's growing up so quickly. And looks so much like Connie," Jamie babbled. He was pretty sure the woman wasn't Connie – or was that a wig? This made it a bit less embarrassing, and less interesting. Surely that couldn't be Martin? This was some anonymous piece of porn, a little animated gif file of mouth travelling up and down some bloke's shaft, over and over. Martin put the laptop into sleep mode, closed it and slid it into his shoulder bag on the seat beside him. "Anyway, that's enough screen for one day. Drink?" And he leapt up from the table as if he'd been electrocuted. "That's enough fizzy water, too. I'm going for a pint this time."

**

"I nearly...married a burglar. I didn't know he was at the time. There was just something off about him. I couldn't put my finger on it. But it had all happened so fast anyway, so I put a stop to it. Six weeks later I was burgled. My laptops, all the digital gadgets, and my car keys (and my car) all gone.

Then he phoned me and said 'I had a premonition, a feeling that something bad had happened' and he thought I didn't know. I changed my number."

"I nearly... got married. It seemed like a sensible grown up thing to do. We have been almost-married for ten years so it seemed like a good idea. We booked a date at the Registry Office. But that's all we did. As soon as we did, we both realised at the same moment that we never wanted to get married. We thought we might so we waited. We didn't invite anyone. We didn't plan anything. Mostly, we forgot about it and just had fun together instead. We lived our lives wrapped up in each other. We tried to list reasons to get married but couldn't think of any. So, we cancelled it. I tried to explain to the woman on the phone that we nearly wanted to get married but didn't really want to. She sounded sad. Her job was about helping people get married.

So, a week ago we nearly got married but we didn't. I had completely forgotten about that, until this moment. It all

129

seems a bit silly now. Good job we never told anyone else. So,
instead we shook hands and agreed to stick together, be kind
to each other and not mess this up.
This is not a sad story."

**

BELLOWED LOUDER

Jamie lost himself in watching the football on the screen in
the corner of the bar until Martin returned, talking already
as he plonked down the drinks and squeezed back into the
seat.

"I bumped into your missus the other day, outside
the library."

"With Swami Carraday?"

"Never met the bloke. She was chatting to a guy I
thought I recognised. Used to do odd jobs round the school
when Mum was still teaching. When the gym block got
burned down."

"Used to do what for your who? Can you speak up."

"Oh, never mind."

"What??"

"Nothing."

That background pub racket of talk and music and
the footy and beeping fruit machines: these two had once
been so comfortable conversing in the midst of all this. But
now the hum threatened to drown out their voices
completely, their hearing diminished with age. Each cupped
a hand around one ear, leant a little closer, bellowed louder.

"Talking of Freya, mate, can I say you are nuts
splitting with her. I mean you're my best friend and
everything, but I do actually like Freya much more. Always
so active that woman, always prepared to give things a go. I
find her very inspiring."

"She left me."

"Really? That's not quite what she told Connie."

"It was not my decision. She's the one who wanted out."

"Seriously mate, I hope you realise what you're throwing away." They returned to sipping their pints and eyeing the football.

"OK and what about *your* perfect relationship, 'mate'? How's Connie?"

"Fine on the surface. We're polite. Smile when we take selfies of ourselves with the kids. But that's it. Hardly touch when we're alone together."

"Oh dear."

"'Oh dear.' Is that it, O best mate of mine? Jamie, for someone I was in a Men's Group with for all those years raising our consciousnesses and challenging masculinity and what have you, we're still pretty crap at talking about feelings."

"Really? Oh. Yes. Maybe." He was taken aback.

"All those evenings round at The Rainbow Garden with Chunk and the others, sitting on cushions in circles." Martin sat back, crossed his arms, scanned the big TV.

"Of course." Jamie recollected bean bags and skinny young men struggling to articulate their inner angst. "But life moves on."

"We don't talk about any of that anymore, do we?"

"No. We don't." Jamie threw back his head, funnelled a handful of dry roasted peanuts into his mouth. "Thank God."

"Really? You don't think we ought to talk about anything difficult?" The peanuts were washed down with another mouthful of beer. "Like you said, we used to try to change the world."

"We made everything so difficult then. Life was all one big struggle."

"Whereas now – it's a breeze?" Chewing, sipping, eyeing up the football on the big telly, listening to the commentary over old pop hits. Jamie wiped his mouth on his hand.

"So you two – still no..?"

"I fancy her like mad, but she's turned right off me since Stan was born. And we don't know each other like you and Freya do. We don't have the history. That's what you're chucking away. I mean, I'm just saying, mate."

"Cheers for the advice, my friend. Based on your experience as insightful agony uncle." Best pals they liked to say they were, but the defences were never quite down, the jolly banter laced with competition.

Jamie said nothing. The racket drowned out the sigh of the elephant in the pub. He felt a wave of relief and a terrible weariness, his longing for disclosure overwhelmed by dread, wanting it all to crawl away. Also the urge to say something honest himself, but the seconds ticked by. He recalled his recent hospital visit, his diminished desire surveyed by the little man in a white coat.

"OK Martin, I was going to tell you, talking of secrets, I've got a bit of an embarrassing health thing myself..." The room roared at a goal.

"Hey," shouted Martin to the trio of students watching the match. "Who scored?" Jamie announced he was going for a slash, stood up and made his woozy way to the gents, ordered two more pints from the bar, stood staring at a poster about an 'Open' 'Mic' Night' starting soon, grumbled to himself about bad punctuation and the decline of civilisation, returned with the beers to find Martin sitting in the midst of the students talking goalkeepers and relegation fears.

"This is my mate Jamie. Mind if we join you? Dave, Ken and... Sabrina was it?"

And it was enjoyable actually, a chance to switch off, watching a match he cared nothing about, oohing and booing the players, listening to Mart yak on, revelling in being the pub bore, loving it when cheeky Sabrina dug him in the ribs and told him to shut his cake-hole, old man. After the game the two friends put their coats on, had a parting man-hug on the street corner.

"I appreciate it, mate."
"What?"
"The chance to talk."
"We didn't much."
"Yeah, but..."

From THE LITTLE BOOK OF NEARLY

Stand opposite your partner
Approach him/her
Encounter each other as close as you can
without quite touching.

JAMIE WHO

Stabbing at the house with his key, finding the lock, turning it and walking into the dark hall of his empty family home, Jamie slammed the door, didn't switch on the lights but fumbled his way through to the front room, sat on the sofa staring into the dark.

The family home was Jamie's nest of misery now. Since Freya left, he'd tried his best not to let the house descend into squalor. The takeaway boxes, the packets of mouldering sliced bread, the floors strewn with coats and clothes were cleared every few days in a blitz of activity, but still the reassurance of day-to-day domesticity was gone. Martin was right; it was time for Jamie to confront himself. He lived in a fart, a wank, a shit. He was one blobby body, clutching his laptop close at all times, relying on it to provide multiple layers of distraction from real life misery. Now he lived alone, yes, like Martin apparently he'd succumbed to dredging through porn sites on his computer, watching hot MILFs grinding and gasping absurdly in one window, the suited BBC newsreader on another tab, overlaid with an iTunes sound track of Radiohead, a half-written email open at the same time. Putting on headphones one evening to gawp at a skinny Eastern European couple copulating on a stained black leather sofa, he was surprise d to hear the theme tune from the Archers playing. The young man ejaculated on the young woman's face as Jill Archer stormed out of The Bull after an argument with Brian. He switched off iPlayer then, but the counterpoint only heightened his shame.

Sex obsessed him now. He searched his mind and laptop for fantasies powerful enough to arouse him again, struggled to lust after the rabble of humpers he found online. Orgasms were short and painful and followed inevitably by pain in his cock and waves of self-hatred through his whole body. His personality, like his sexuality, was crumbling to dust, or rather, rotting to a nasty viscous gunk. The homunculus of himself curled up on the sofa, ectoplasmic ghosts wafting out of him one by one.

> Jamie the happy married man, portly, fulfilled, comfy in the glove of their long-term love.

> Jamie who had gone for the Head of Department job at that point when no way would that loser Graham Stone have got it, so Jamie was the boss now telling people how tragic it was that they were being made redundant but the good news was his own position was secure.

> Jamie who had met that woman at a party in nineteeneightywhatever, gone home with her and become her lover weeks before she was discovered by Channel 4 and became a household name until her cocaine habit got out of hand and she ended up, a friend of a friend told him, living on a campsite in Cornwall selling ices to tourists in the summer, though maybe his influence would have kept her on the straight and narrow and in the process helped kickstart his career as a singer songwriter before their acrimonious but headline-grabbing bust-up.

> Jamie who said to his wife, don't be crazy, when she said she didn't love him, I'm down that's all, sorry I've been so hard to live with lately, and there's this Hinchliffe

thing we need to discuss, which is kind of embarrassing as well as frightening but not fatal and I love you so much and I think you could love me again too, Freya my beloved, and I'm sure we can be wonderful together again.

> Jamie who had worked much harder at school instead of hanging out with Chunk and co. then taken the Oxford exams and gone to the one pronounced Mordlin falling in with a bad crowd who'd lure him to the dark side of right-wing revelry and then into a ministerial post in the Government when he'd lobby for cuts in the play sector and in the process demand an inquiry into poor management of leisure departments country-wide specifically where talented staff were passed over in favour of line-towing wankers.

> Jamie who had worked much harder but dropped out of Uni to dedicate himself fully to the destruction of Capitalism, the building of a new world order of communal living, free love and liberation of the oppressed of the earth arising in tolerance and peace for all except line-towing middle management wankers of course who would be first up against the wall. Followed by the sodding Nearlyologists.

> Jamie who shouted and shouted at his wife when she said she didn't love him, had grabbed her round the throat and squeezed, hanging on as she thrashed about and wriggled then quivered then eventually went limp, dragging her into the garden and digging a hole next to the bed of nettles which was once his potato patch, shovelling earth on the body when Pippa popping round, screamed, called the police.

> Jamie who stood and roared for revenge in the dark room, pulled on his coat, raged back out into the night.

HOUSEWORK

"Shiver mi timbers! Gold doubloons!"

"Well, we'll do what we can to help, Pip love."

"No need to walk the plank then."

Freya had hurried round to the tiny one-room flatlet which Pip shared with Sophie. Mother and daughter perched on the edge of a double bed which filled most of the space. From hooks on the walls hung all kinds of marionettes and glove puppets in various states of construction. Pip waggled the strings of a pirate as she spoke.

"It might take a while to sell the house, though."

"You won't have to do that will you, Mum? I thought Dad said you had savings."

"Maybe."

"We'll have to cast a spell to stop that happening!" said Pip in her witchy voice, an uncanny impression of the Home Secretary.

"I know, darling. It's so full of memories – your childhood, our lives together. It would be unbearable."

"If anyone tried to move into my old room, I'd put them to sleep for a thousand years. Or turn them into toads."

"We'd be delighted to make puppets to sell in your shop, though," said Sophie squeezing into the room with three mugs of tea gripped in one hand, plate of biscuits in the other. "Wouldn't we, Pippa?"

"Of course. We'd do you a good price, Mum, but each one takes a lot of work." Pip, now completely adult and human sounding, hung the witch puppet next to the pirate, the crocodile and the mermaid, took a sip of tea. She still acted like a big kid sometimes, sulking now and speaking through the characters she'd surrounded herself with since the days of Teddy Eddy and Blabamus. "You could get the house valued though," this was The Crookodile speaking, "it must be worth a fa-fa-fortune!"

"We might have to, honey. Needs must. Thank you for recognising that. The Nearly Store's a big hit, but it's going to take a while to recoup the set-up costs."

"So Pippa's been telling you about our plan to set up a venue for the company – a proper little puppet theatre. Wouldn't it be great?"

"Sounds like a marvellous idea. You're sure you could attract an audience though?"

"We're planning a crowdfunding campaign too. Sophe's done a plan to show it'll make money in the long run. Dad thought you two might be able to contribute something to help us set up. Which was kind. I said I knew you were both broke so of course we weren't expecting much, but he said there were savings and he'd see what he could do."

Freya looked up at the gurning faces of her daughter's inanimate company of characters and a chill ran through her. "Like he said, your dad doesn't know anything about our finances. I'll look into it. Tell him to leave it to me."

"The thing is we kind of told them we could pay the deposit… Are you OK, Mum?"

Freya exhaled, pulled on the neck of her roll-neck sweater.

"It is a bit airless in here, darling."

ENTREPRENORRHEA

Mrs Seward she say to Carraday, these people get loads
from telling this. At the Nearly Store things hectic now, and
she handing him twenty pound notes weekly saying
thankyouthankyou
for the work it bringing when they buy her time
to help them with planningandactioning whatever that is.
The little store filling up with punters sometimes
as he sell them badges and tee-shirts and postcards
and little Nearly Books and she talk therapeuticals and
closures and all kind of hocuspocus,
spells to make people happy to give her money.
They look pleased as punch with the strategy they bought,

like a haircut, a blowjob, a skinnysoddinglatte.

Almost home from his late night opening
at the Nearly Store,
carrying a carton of milk in a blue plastic bag,
hears footsteps and his name shout loud behind him.
Carraday spins round to find MisterJamie
bearing down on him,
fat-bellied, sweaty, rotten sweetness of drink on his breath,
blurry and smeared with drunkenness and sorrow,
he grab Carraday by the arm.
"What have you done to her you bastard?"
"Let go of me please, sir!"
"You've filled her with all your crazy shit ideas."
This fella's grip not so tough.
"Me? I listening to her. She listens to me."
Pissed Jamie stepping back, tries to focus his eyes on
Carraday's but can't quite.
The words filter slow into his, but then howl in outrage.
"Right – you're saying I don't listen?
My wife and I never talk properly? You bastard."
"I didn't say that, sir."
"We were good before she met you."
"If you say so." Them rocking together in clench,
hugging almost.
Mister Jamie on the verge of a peacemaking,
eyeball to eyeball, but then he launch himself back
drunk into rage. A howl from his guts.
"You...how could... you..."
And he swinging his fist.
"Leave me alone, please."
He block the blow but MisterJamie not backing off.
His belly ramming into Carraday and some
half hearted scuffling ensue. Fat Jamie fella
breathing hard, kicking weakly at his ankles,
Carraday fending him off no trouble,

pushing back but without much urge to hurt neither. Heavy
breathing in the cold air of evening, some weird waltz
they dance, leaning together like exhausted boxers.
O but Boomer alive in his gut now hard and nasty, urging:
finish him, strangle this fat bag of wind and shit till the last
breathe of him fly. Then MisterJamie utter a deep dark cry
stumble flee flee away.

Carraday shaking all over. Unlocking his door slowly after
all that yell and strut. The cry ringing in him along
with those hatewords.
He petrified, livid, jangling with shock, but laughing too,
astounded not to suffer the kicking he expect.
Something concluding, like always used to happen.
Up the narrow stairs in the dark and open the door
to the flat. He find his Mumma in her chair, head back,
face skeletal, flesh translucent, like waxed paper.
O no.
No.
He tippyup close. Any sign of breathe?
He call her name. No reply. Again. Heart in his throat.
A step closerto touch her brow.

And she startle awake. Like rebooting in mid conversation.
"Did you have a good evening, son?
You must be sure you have fun.
I worry about you cooped up here with me."
The voice still melodious.
"I'm OK, Mumma."
He go to fetch her water for her pills and she call through.
"You sure? I don't think so. You need a break.
I been thinking."
"Thinking what, Mumma?"
"That no good baby sister of mine could take me off your
hands for a few days. They've got a spare room in their place
in – whatsit – Bournemouth, never think to invite me.
Tight buggers. I've been thinking I should give the witch

139

a call." Lancing her boil of annoyance, she ask him meekly
to help her to bed and Carraday do, lifting her out of the
chair, looping her arm through his,
walking with her slowly to her room, such a scrap of a body,
yet not easy to carry, help her onto the commode
where he stand at the door as she straining, then he lift out
the pot and go flush the stink away as she totter
herself to the bed which adjusting to rise and fall and
sit her up and even rub her back. And when he lift her
and lay her down on the sheet, tucking her in,
she brush his face with her dry, wrinkled fingers, say,
"You're such a good boy. Good night, love. I'll phone Nellie
in the morning." Reassuring still, her boy an old man
for chrissake. His own bed don't do no massaging him nor
shape itself to help him sleep. He lie in the night abuzz
from that man's anger and futility.

Maybe he should stop thinking to himself in this
stupid voice of his.
I mean he is perfectly capable of forming whole sentences
and does it all the time out loud.
It's only in his innermost he talk this way.
Grow up he cry out to himself in the dark dark night.
Grow up you thick shit dip stick stiff wick git git grow up
and get a life and stop hanging round here take your eyes
off me creep creepy Carraday.
Get lost. Then he back lost in the outback of his solitude
like when Bren scarpered and the nights
jagged with the loss of her
the notsex and unbabies, the handholding times all become
fantasy. Without his spells he be
starkstaring by now
or rather, starkstarier.

140

**

"I nearly… became a wing-walker in a flying circus."
"I nearly… was a mother 3 times before actually giving birth but time and circumstance did not allow. I often wonder what it would be like to have 4 children and not one."
"I nearly went to live in Sicily as I had a job as a teacher there. However I intentionally missed the train to arrive for the beginning of term and although I felt guilty because the staff were waiting for me at Palermo station, I knew it was the right decision."
"I nearly… told my cousin I was gay but I am a coward in the way the right thing isn't always the one you should do. Especially if you do not want to be sent to a re-education camp."

**

HOB OF OLD

Freya read it in one of the row of battered paperbacks, a mix of self-help and inspirational tracts, which Rosa kept on the window shelf in the loo: that a long-term relationship is like a house, its rooms, decoration and orientation so familiar that they define our worldview to the extent that, once living there awhile, we can't imagine ever inhabiting other spaces. No wonder Freya and Jamie's own home improvements had been so traumatic and so exciting, when toilets swapped places with beds and windows appeared in walls never before seen through. The new kitchen they'd put in a few years ago with its modern equipment and wipe-clean surfaces might be better than the worn lino and grease-encrusted hob of the old, but what happened to the ghosts of all those dinner parties past? What of the family breakfasts when she gazed unseeingly into corners and through doorways now vanished, legs of lamb and Christmas turkeys pulled from the oven now junked, the layers of experience which coated those spaces which then so completely ceased to exist? Now she had wiped clean the new surfaces of their life together too.

That night, under her duvet in Rosa's front room, Freya lay awake imagining her way around every room of 10 Rayner Gardens. By dawn she was satisfied that a virtual version of the place was embedded in her mind. Those memories were so much more important than the bricks and mortar. Priceless really. Though not worth actual money. So why shouldn't they flog the thing itself?

From THE LITTLE BOOK OF NEARLY

Write your secret Nearly in chalk on the wall.
Wash the chalk off with water.
Keep the water in a jar.

On a sunny day
write your Nearly on the wall
with water in big letters.
Watch it disappear.

Now
sell the water.

OLD LETTERS

After finding that box of old flyers and letters and throwing it at the wall of the box room, Jamie intended to sweep up and burn its contents, but chickened out of course, and instead spent hours on his knees shuffling through this mulch of bitter nostalgia, sorting through the debris of their life together, trying to decide what to bin, then failing to bin anything. Now ephemera was spreading out across the surfaces of his lonely house – like this torn A4 poster which he'd found in a pink cardboard folder on which Freya had written LETTERS: PRIVATE in felt tip. This was scribbled out and added in biro was: STUFF 1980s. BAND. PLAY. MEN ETC. In the folder was a flyer promoting the Men's Sexuality Group, hand-lettered by Martin, decorated by the cartoon figures he used to doodle on everything. And here was that poster: printed off-set litho on bright red paper. It featured a blurred monochrome photo of a child on a toy scooter with a cartoon thought bubble. Caption: "PLAY POWER" hand-lettered in thick felt tip, advertising a benefit at the adventure playground he'd worked in, the Proper Job he took to prepare for parenthood as Freya's belly began to swell and the band set off on tour with new singer and guitarist secured.

He remembered photographing that boy on his pedal scooter, who was togged up in coat and gloves, scrupulously pushing his vehicle along a series of steps, running the wheel as close to the edge as possible, but not once going over the brink. It was Freya who had pointed out the kid to Jamie, commenting how much time children spent not actually joining in with the games, not doing anything much but clearly in a state of mental play in their heads. It was something he'd written into his strategies and talks ever since, the importance of giving children space – the breathing space they need in which to dream.

Frey arrived at the playground that day in her best gear causing a flurry of gasps and curses from the users. "Lezzy. Weirdo." Her hair was cropped ferociously at the sides, her fringe dyed electric blue that day, exactly the colour she'd reverted to recently. Jamie was embarrassed but proud as he slipped his arm around her waist and the playground erupted in wolf-whistles.

"Chunk dropped me off," she said, wriggling free of him.

"I thought you'd fallen out with him. Patriarchal arsehole you said he was."

"Yeah well, arsehole with motorbike. Mind if I hang out with you lot here?" Soon she was playing football with the boys, laughing at their banter and, when one lad shouted, "Pass it to me, ya stupid woman!", with a blood-curdling yell she booted the ball into his crotch and ran at him like a wild thing.

From THE LITTLE BOOK OF NEARLY

Whisper your Nearly story into a paper bag.
Seal it.
When ready,
give it to a friend to open and listen to.

CUSHIONS

The Men's Group met in the front room of the home of a fellow member and founder of the Anarchist Building Co-operative, whose girlfriend had recently left him to move in with Penny the Plumber – what was his name? Bad acne and long hair, heavy glasses, moved to Leeds after. They sat on cushions on the floor in a circle around Jamie who put an imaginary Freya on the hotseat in the middle of the space and talked to her. He said how terrified he'd been to see her in the playground attacking that boy. But she'd stopped, lifted the kid high up in the air and tickled the petrified youth. The rest of the gang piled in, and a hilarious play fight ensued. After that they bloody loved her, chased her round the place like puppies. Jamie told his Men's Group the anecdote and they nodded approvingly.

"I think you're so amazing, so brave and uncompromising, Freya," he said to the cushion in the centre of the circle. "But it really pisses me off – yes, and makes me really sad – that you won't acknowledge publicly that you love me. If you love me. I want you to acknowledge you love me." The Builder sat on his grey corduroy knees and scratched his beard, urged Jamie to repeat the final words over and over, talking to the cushion which now represented Freya, so that the full significance of the words could steep in his psyche, like leaves of mint in hot water. The circle of men watched the incantation. Martin had been there that night, Chunk too come to think of it, watching intently.

When Jamie swapped places and sat on the pillow occupied by his absent girlfriend, he was startled to find he could articulate her feelings very clearly.

"I do love you. And I want to be free. My body belongs to me, not you." The builder and the other brothers smiled with satisfaction at this conclusion. At a previous Gestalt session the builder had burst a cushion thumping it too hard to let out the trauma of his break-up with Penny, sobbing and raging, flayed by rejection. Whatever happened to him? Still plastering the bathrooms of the radical? Unlikely.

Switching cushions again, Jamie moaned about her blunt refusal to express any kind of romantic feelings for him. They were friends who fucked sometimes. No handholding, no staring warmly into each others' eyes. He could understand where that urgent suspicion of all things male came from. But still.

"Any feedback anyone?" asked the builder guy. Chunk seemed very upset.

"Maybe you should move onto the hot seat?" asked the builder. Trevor, that was his name. Irritating, self-righteous character come to think of it.

Chunk moved into the centre of the circle, sitting on the cushion that had previously been the surrogate Freya. He recounted a dream of his from the night before. "I was in a weird version of The Rainbow Garden which was like an aviary and a big crow-like bird kept flying at my head, pecking at me, over and over."

"Do you want to put the crow in the hot seat, tell us what it said to you?" Trevor asked. He had a thick beard that he scratched all the time, and little round glasses. God he was annoying. But not a bad leader of the group really, and in Gestalt Therapy nobody explained what your dreams meant, the idea was that everything you dreamt was part of you.

Chunk closed his eyes, moved his head, spoke, "I'm a crow and I'm evil and strong and out to hurt you. I'll peck you and jab you till you do what I want."

Chunk shuffled to the other cushion to confront his dream crow. "I'm good and strong too and I know I can swat you away but I don't want to hurt you. I want you to leave me be, let me do what I want." Trevor asked him to repeat that line, over and over. And in so doing, the theory went, the inner conflict which the dream referred to could be resolved without ever needing to be articulated.

"I'm good and strong. I don't want to hurt anyone. But I will do what I want. I have the right to do what I want."

"Super," said Trevor. Chunk said he felt clearer, freer. And this was miraculous, that they each had it in them to express and flesh out these variations of themselves, to find a voice for all their demons, the stars and supporting cast of their deepest dreams. Martin went to make a pot of tea then and the group relaxed, lolled around discussing fatherhood. They decided in a perfect world responsibility for children would be shared equally, not only between mother and father but everyone else in the commune they'd be living in.

Back in his cold, 21st-century kitchen, Jamie jiggled his knee to shake off pins and needles, swallowed a mouthful of cold coffee. All that time spent being so personally political, so anti-sodding-sexist, so non sodding hierarchical, so child bleeding friendly. OK so Freya had been messed up by the patriarchy but what about him? Really! Had she ever put an imaginary him on a pillow and

tried to see its point of view? Had she buggery! Now he
spotted a faded square photo he'd found and then dropped
on the floor, of the housemates on a demo, Freya punk sulky
in tight jeans, braces and bovva boots, Chunk in uncool
denims, smiling face blurred, Jamie so skinny in those days
with his floppy hair and roll-up. Can't tell now what the
march was for or against – there were so many then.

Later that night at The Rainbow Garden,
housemates Freya, Chunk, Martin and Jamie smoking and
drinking in the front room like people did back then,
laughing about the chants and placards on the march, a
Joan Armatrading record playing. As the room sang around
them and a conversation about non-monogamy and
possession dwindled to stoned silence, they moved gradually
closer, looking deeply into one another's eyes, gaze
switching from friend to friend. They held hands next in a
circle, then rubbed each other's shoulders and backs,
zinging and tingling, hands through each other's hair,
exploring each other's bodies. Martin seemed tense,
shoulders tight; him and Helen had been arguing lots.
Martin stood up and staggered woozily off to bed. Soon after
Chunk put his hands to his neck and pulled off his tee-shirt.
The other two did likewise. Freya reached behind her back
to unfasten her bra. And massage continued by the light of
the gas fire and assorted candles, with murmurings of love
all round. Spaced night high with possibility, rushes of
desire and jealousy and other feelings harder to describe
somewhere between. Unlocking and opening a door these
three. Their eyes meet, bodies touch, hands and mouths
explore. But then Freya was standing, stretching, bare-
breasted, extricating herself, picking up her fallen tee-shirt,
saying sorry guys, she had work in the morning. Gave each
a parting hug and kiss. But the warmth kept spreading
between Chunk and Jamie and they carried on stroking,
smiling, unzipping and undressing completely, exploring the

textures of each other's stubbly cheeks and warm mouths, and then moved onto the bed. And awoke to a new world.

Or rather, woke with headaches and sore lips from stubbly kisses in a swamp of embarrassment. They couldn't look each other in the eyes as Jamie slid out of bed, slipped away quickly to wolf down muesli and rush off to work, wobbly, glowing, pondering the implications. He remembered feeling proud that they'd actually done it, a self satisfied sensual overload, but guiltily relieved that he still seemed to fancy women more. Now he knew what it felt like to stroke a bristly chin, to put a fleshy column of cock in his mouth, to feel the firm muscled warmth of a naked male pressed against the length of him, to pump and pull his friend to squirting orgasm. A doorway of erotic possibility had opened. He was relieved too that he didn't feel himself flung through that door and locked out of the hetero-room. Not really gay. Not gay enough to be teased or sneered at or beaten up in alleyways round the back of pubs. But a little bit. Not as gay as his own daughter who only last year had felt driven to declare herself utterly so.

Chunk and Jamie kept their distance after that night. Not long after, Chunk announced he was leaving the country.

"A guy I met Inter-railing in France lives in California and asked me to play in his band." How cool did that sound. They had a farewell drink down The Premises. Was it the Human League or Heaven 17 playing that night? The collective of his friends lined up in a row to hug him at the end of the evening. And life went on, until Freya's body, which belonged undeniably to her, but undeniably gave Jamie intense pleasure when he popped in to visit it, began swelling up with someone else's body within. This idea fascinated and freaked them both, opened the door into a new phase of adulthood, closed the door on shared living and loving.

He felt guilty now, a fraud. Why couldn't he celebrate her rebelliousness back then? Which bit of him had wanted her in Laura Ashley frocks, gazing placidly into his eyes and knitting bootees for the new arrival? Fast forward to the 21st century, which bit of him resented his Mrs having built her business as his career hit the buffers?

Jamie made a mug of instant coffee and returned to his den, spilling a trail of the milky brown liquid up the stair carpet and into his room where he sat himself groaningly down beside the heap of memorabilia. They'd produced an Anti-Sexist newsletter round about then, and he'd had the words of a song printed in it. Where was it?

In the same file was a cluster of old magazines, covers creased and faded, smelling of off-set litho printing ink, the oily scent of the revolution: Oz, Resurgence, Achilles Heel. Jamie opened a copy of Spare Rib. A letter dropped out. Freya's loopy handwriting. So much of it was familiar – the texture of the paper, dried out and browned with age, the purple ballpoint ink. Oh yes, information then wasn't a huge, indelible ball of digital dust in a cloud somewhere but made up of scraps of various materials you stored or lost, or came across unexpectedly years later.

And here was one such: irreplaceable, one moment captured. He pulled out the folded sheet of paper, lined, with a red margin, holes punched in the side, written in purple biro with the address drawn with a Rotring pen in 3D effect capitals, like a comic book title, coloured in crayons, and a trace of a scent – or was it simply a recollection? – of the ammonia smell of her dyed hair. The tone of it was familiar: ardent feelings laced with complication. *"I think I might love you but it's so complicated… don't know what to feel… why must feeling so much love cause so much hurt?"* Nothing was easy then, all feelings challenged, all relationships questioned.

It was a draft, unsent, full of crossings out, the letter stopped, unsigned, at the end of the page. He turned over the sheet of paper to read from the beginning. And then he saw. The letter was written to Chunk, not him.

PING ME

This time Freya met Tyler Jackson in the top floor café of
Waterstones, Piccadilly – she'd suggested the venue – for a
brief meeting arranged, cancelled and then rearranged by
his personal assistant who accompanied him now and
guarded his time as if each half hour was a precious stone to
be polished and set precisely in the crown of his magnificent
diary. At the allotted hour, Freya emerged from the lift,
mobile once again pressed to head, pretending an important
call. The P.A. was too engrossed in her texting to notice, but
Tyler rose from his seat for the briefest of air kiss, then
sank back.

"Freya: Poppy." Poppy smiled politely and broke off
tapping on her mobile to reach out and shake her hand. She
was an attractive young woman with the face of a different
woman painted on top: lips, eyelashes, eyebrows, tan,
blonde hair dye, all carefully applied. Freya sat opposite,
apologised for her lateness and continued to riff about a
high-powered project she was on the verge of clinching.
Poppy's phone whistled and she took the call, whispering
fiercely. Tyler interjected that he too was in a rush today
and perhaps they could get on with the meeting? He made
clear that from his company's point of view this Taqribaan
jaunt was important, not a jolly for Freya and her new beau.
She laughed at that description of Carraday, but Tyler
remained serious, his tone cold and dry.

"I'm glad this amuses you, but actually it's pretty
damn vital to my business."

"Really? They're going to be interested in us two?
In Nearlyology?"

"They're gagging for novelty, the press lap up the
weird and quirky, something they can write punning
headlines about. It doesn't actually need to mean anything.
You fit that bill – and can charm them too no doubt. Freya, I
am keen to continue supporting the Nearly Project. But
these donations have been hard to justify to the board. We

150

had a bit more of a struggle than I'd anticipated getting this one through, frankly. However I've asked Poppy to take advice about setting you up as a registered charity. My people can sort the paperwork, find trustees, give you the services of an accountant."

"No problem at all," said Poppy in a tone that suggested it was going to be a huge problem.

"I'm bowled over. That's too kind. But I'm not sure…"

"That means we can classify our payment as a charitable donation. Can't we, Poppy? Don't worry, we'll do it all pro bono. From our point of view it allows us certain flexibility with our options re. tax management, my accountants say."

"Is this some kind of tax – thing?" she said, swerving away from using the word dodge. Poppy took out an iPad and began hammering on it far too ferociously to actually be writing anything.

"No. Absolutely not. Not really. Perhaps nearly. Which should please you." He smiled briefly and she did too.

Freya used her usual technique when faced with big decisions of saying she needed to defer to her imaginary board, assured him this seemed like a wonderful opportunity for which she was very grateful but which she would of course have to discuss with Mister Carraday and other team members. Poppy looked up, nodded sagely; her phone rang again and she growled at the screen and switched it off.

"Sure. Your guru needs to be reassured I appreciate that. No need to agree today. However," he leaned over the table and placed his hand on her wrist, weighting it down firmly as he looked straight into her eyes. "Freya, I'd like your assurance today that you yourself will do what you can to make this happen."

Her muttered assent meant the deal was done. Was she really prepared to fail to win round Carraday? Tyler glanced at the screen of his phone, then slid it into his pocket like a cowboy holstering a six-shooter. "We must dash. Ping me tomorrow, yes?"

"I am so pleased to meet you, Mrs Seward. Thank you for this opportunity," said Poppy with alarming sincerity and kissed Freya on both cheeks. Then the young woman's phone rang again and she was muttering into its flat surface as they made their way to the exit.

Freya sat alone with her decision and started on the work of convincing herself that this was the only way forward, a unique opportunity, really a very remarkable coup. The expression *perhaps nearly* hovered nervously around her as she finished her coffee, but she left it hanging there and set off up Regent Street in search of something smart and light that wouldn't crease too easily.

GRINDING

The Doughnut of Doom Jamie named it, the Polo Mint of Mortality.

"Please try to keep still, sir."

The nurse laid him down on a shelf under a layer of paper, left the room and pressed the button to send his most sensitive body part into that hole to be appraised following an injection into the glans administered by a student nurse under instruction to "point it to six o'clock then... in". Left in a cubicle to tumesce in his back-to-front gown, then brought in to lie on a flat bed while a thing like a giant white plastic toilet seat made grinding noises as it advanced ominously towards his groin. Jamie's genitals were sent through the ring of the CAT scan, headphones piping David Bowie's 'Let's Dance' over the deep growl of the machine. Afterwards he was sent home with the instruction to generate orgasm via intercourse – not on the cards in his case – or masturbation in order to aid the de-tumescence, achieved only by unleashing fierce, painful images in his head of young Freya, naked, pressed against the wall by Chunk, his old band's rampant drummer.

One week later Jamie was summoned to collect the results of the scan, during which time he'd replayed the two scenes over and over with every permutation: the doctor's prognosis, the drummer's rutting, out-takes from a weird porno medical horror movie. At the groovy new cancer centre he approached the desk where they found no sign of his appointment on the computer in front of them despite his name being flashed up in GIGANTIC CAPITAL LETTERS on screens all around the building, clearly visible through the glass walls. Jamie was sent to yet another desk and then to a blandly reassuring who said there was "absolutely nothing to worry about. Hopefully." But in the corridors Jamie saw plenty of those who had plenty to dread: the tell-tale wigs and headscarves, the ones who hadn't received the all clears. Jamie thanked his lucky stars and prayed they'd remain lucky for as long as possible before someone would tell him, "Sorry sir, this time it's for real."

"Now I see here you were offered a trial on the Hinchcliffe Society programme but declined."

"That? Well, no I didn't get round to it."

"I can rectify this right now if you wish." A box was ticked on screen and he was given another appointment for the next week concerning therapy that might be beneficial. A reminder pinged up on his phone before he'd left the building.

By then Jamie's imagination had fixed on a version of events which felt as clear to him as genuine memory. The cancer scare he'd dismissed, but the story of Freya's affair with Chunk grew more and more vivid. After coming across the letter from Freya to Chunk, the slight doubt over whether Pippa was actually his child peeped into his mind like the first green shoots of a creeper emerging in a garden soon to be overrun, and his marriage was now a demolition site with certainties crashing and new views revealed as walls fell and cold wind blew through the rubble of once intimate spaces. Now as he sat in the waiting room toying with his smartphone, Jamie was incandescent with self-righteousness.

"I've been waiting for more than an hour!" he railed at the receptionist. "This is insane."

"You tell 'em, man!" muttered his neighbour in the queue, a stooped black guy with baggy jowls and rheumy eyes. Jamie groaned as he sat down beside him. A young woman doctor walked past them, honey coloured skin and a relaxed, flowing stride. The two men watched her admiringly, heads turning like spectators at a tennis match as she sashayed by.

"Now she's a beauty." The man purred under his breath. "Mi-lawd, it's miserable sometimes, getting old." He let out a soulful sigh. "She don't even notice me, man, and if by some miracle of God she did and start coming onto me, I couldn't do nothing about it. The bird's not stirring on the nest." Jamie smiled in embarrassed, floppy-cocked brotherhood, but then buried himself in an old copy of Vogue which he'd picked up from a stack at the reception desk to avoid being drawn into sexist banter. Half an hour later the expert appeared, besuited and tanned, trundling an overnight suitcase on wheels behind him. Eventually Jamie was called through.

On the desk was a row of plastic contraptions and a beige-coloured computer monitor, behind the desk a man with orange flesh and perfect teeth.

"Good morning, sir. Do sit down. Apologies for the delay." Smile. Glance at clock. Smile. "I represent the Hinchcliffe Society which makes a device the honourable Doctor believes could be beneficial for men with your condition."

"Do you know how long I've been sitting out there?!"

The rep's smile slipped. "I am sorry, sir. My train was delayed."

Jamie's outrage wilted as fast as a lost erection.

"Oh, that's all right."

"Well then."

The expert's complexion glowed with synthetic healthiness, like a GM crop of fresh apples. He reassured Jamie again that there was no sign of cancer, then read aloud a statement about the trial being undertaken on the basis that the hospital took no legal responsibility for any problems however unlikely arising.

"My consultant told me there were three possible outcomes, ranging from recovery to dire awfulness. I've been waiting to find out which group I'm in."

"Statistics damn statistics, eh! Doctor Gunawardena is very keen on these. But it's our belief that sexuality doesn't work quite like that, not in real life. Put a brain through an MRI scanner and the neuroscientists discover that sex – like pretty much everything else – is converging with the rest of how we feel about things. We're bundles of sensations and thoughts. Now it says in the Doctor's notes here that you were… 'excessively expressive' at your last appointment."

"Really?"

"So we'd like to ask you to write about *your* sensations and thoughts on our new forum: 'EDspace'. This is a key element of the Society's Penile Reclamation Plan, but still at the beta stage and the Society is keen to facilitate user engagement in trials."

"Who's Ed?"

"It stands for Erectile Dysfunction."

"Catchy title."

"In exchange we provide a booklet of physical and mental exercises and mind-experiments, a chart containing dietary advice – fish oil and green tea are highly recommended – all this for free, plus one of these state of the art VEDs: a Vacuum Erection Device." He pointed to the tubular plastic gizmo on the desk. "So, we may not really have identities or sexualities or memories, but in an uncertain world, having the means of production to generate a usable erection may still be of help to the contemporary male."

"Sounds handy. Do they know what causes this condition?"

"Not really. When first diagnosed by Sir Eric Hinchcliffe in the 17th century it was of course considered a disease of the weak-willed and sexually degenerate. Evil thoughts and self-abuse were blamed, prayer, leeches and abstinence the cure. Recent research links the condition to an accident or physical trauma, intense sexual activity or simply... well, decrepitude basically."

"Nice."

"Our current Director has developed a gentler and more multi-disciplinary approach to its rectification."

The plastic tube was presented with all its additional cylinders, rings and gel. The man measured Jamie's penis with a ruler, and a pipe cleaner for the circumference. He entered the figures on the keyboard. "It's very common for the circumference of the flaccid penis to be more than its length," the expert explained reassuringly as he noted down the girth and extent. "Now here's how it works." And he produced a plastic coated A4 card showing Jamie how to grease the end with goo, clamp it over his cock and pump it impressively erect, then deflate it, then reflate it, preferably ten times over a period of twenty minutes, this process being designed both to increase the level of erections and to rectify to some extent the bend which had appeared in his deformed, half-hard member.

Next he had to drop his trousers and push his penis through a hole in a see-through plastic globe much like the one that Pippa's pet hamster once used to career around the lounge in. His shortened, kinked penis was photographed from different angles, hopefully as the first half of a hugely impressive before and after shot. A series of questions followed, with scores for answers from one to five tried to hone in on the precise nature of his problems.

"But none of these questions mention sexual pleasure. They don't ask whether 'intercourse' is actually enjoyable any more – they assume it's a feat that has to be performed. As if the only reason why men have sex is to prove that they can."

"As your notes say: 'Excessively expressive'. Which is why we want you to log on and share with us whatever thoughts you have of this kind. And encourage any friends you might have to log on too. The Forum is," he read from the screen, "intended to provide an opportunity for men with a variety of issues to re-write their erectile narrative. Apparently."

BUZZ AND ZAZZ

Mumma Carraday sit on the sofa, curtains drawn,
lights of the fancy flat screen telly jazzing in her
thick glasses. Those smiling tellymenandwomen engaging
with her morningnoonandnight in endless bloody
cheeriness. Make you want to put a brick through the
screen and wring the neck of little white-haired bundle on
the squeaky black leather armchair which she got
conned into buying by a smarmy cold caller.
She loving it, mind, a sprinkling of money magic, this
monstrosity in the midst of herknickknacks and jeejaws.
"Luxury!" she saying, close her eyes and smile
like a cream-filled moggy. In the kitchen he flick switch,
pull mugs from dishwasher, drop tea bags in, empty the
contents of the plastic box of cutlery into the correct drawer
as the kettle boil, slotting the latest round of dirty plates
in the racks of the machine, unwrapping and inserting the
all-in-one powerball. Cyclical activity, round and round,
the cosmic wheel of rinse and rebirth,
the all-in-one powerball of the universe.
"Cup of tea, mum?"
"Ooh – lovely, Greg."

157

"What you watching?"

"Oh..."

No idea. That the truth of it. Ma floating in zones without
name mostly, and why shouldn't she. He sick of his own
endless questions – how how she? what what did she..?
when when? Torture to her when she not locate an answer,
names lost down the back of the cushions of the chair she
spending her last days in.

"Some bollocks. Patronising twaddle they feed us geriatrics.
This man herewith the tan and the pristine teeth:
makes me think of whatsit... you know...
diddlysquat... reheated frozen shepherd's pie."

"Ha! What do you want for lunch, Mamma?"

"Not this geezer. Cheese Sandwich will do me. "

But she not switching it off.

"All right."

Ma Carraday, Socialist crusader once, now losing it.
But then she never quite finding it again after
Daddy leaving, when life become what the social workers
call somewhatchaotic, sending him out like a yowie
to the emotional outback.

The air thick with Nearlyness then, black clouds of its
buzzing and zazzing. Carraday crouching by the water's
edge, hands over his ears, longing for silence.

He like a lyre bird, bright and ornate as a
psychedelic record cover, fast as the whirring
Magic Boomerang he watched on telly as a kid
which stop time when the boy throw it, like he wanting
time to stop now.

The boomerang Dadda sending was light and cheap
decorated with many spots of colour. When he throwing it
up into the air the thing react like any other stick,
no sign of its returning neatly to his hand, let alone freezing
time so he can play tricks and catch villains.

But bunyip pet Boomer's a lyre bird now, fanning its tail

opening its beak and snapping at the Nearly Dust over and
over, like scissors snapping through the bug black air, a
cloud, a murmuration,a swirling vortex of uncertainty,
a twister curling and spinning, down into the throat of
this bird, belly growing fuller with the mass of juicy specks.

Old Carraday watching his Mumma watching the telly
people adjust their faces from jollity to concern
as they turn on the sofa to face grieving widow of
decapitated journalist before it's time for sport and the
weather. Jolting out of reverie by his mum saying,
"I spoke to my sister. Told her I was coming."
"You what, ma?"
"Nellie. In Bournemouth. Told her you needed
whatchamacallit. Respite. And that tosser of a husband
of hers can get his finger out and come and collect me.
Nice car he's got. Under seat heating. Lovely."
"Wow – really?" He need to phone Nellie, check this call
really happened. Sometimes Mumma was pin sharp,
other times doolally. But this sounded real.
"Warms the bum up lovely. And from their bathroom
they've got a view of that great big beach. Remember, Greg?
Bournemouth? That collie what buried your sandal
when we went that World Cup summer?"
"If you're sure you'll be OK."
"Nice place. Shame they're so bloody dull. And Tories.
Do me good though. You too."
Next time he look at her she sleeping again. He turn down
the goggle box and leave her to snooze.

ROCK GIANT

Jamie left the hospital, stood at the bus stop with the pump
and its lubricants and extra plastic bits in a Tesco plastic
carrier bag. He recollected the story of an old lady who'd
had her bag snatched by two youths. She was very upset

159

because it contained the body of her dead cat which she was carrying to the vet for burial. His phone buzzed in his pocket.

"Hi, is Janey there?"

"No – this is... my phone."

"This is Ashok, the publican at The Oak. We've got our open mic night starting a new season. Someone called Janey left this number? She phoned and left her details, saying she might like to do some songs?"

"Oh that was me: Jamie. Yes. Yes. No, not Janey at all. Sure." A booking. Well, sort of. A foot on the ladder. He'd forgotten scribbling his details on a sheet of paper one night in the pub. Who knows who might hear him? Could lead to more gigs. Tours. Festivals. Record deal. Record deal? What were they called now? Did bands still get recording contracts? Or instead build a cult following on sites like Soundcloud, Bandcamp? He glanced down into the Tesco bag and the imagined bandwagon of his life as a late starting rock giant was stopped in its tracks.

Later he made himself a cup of camomile tea, cut an avocado in half, scooped out the stone and ate the flesh with a blob of lite mayonnaise, lay on his bed, pulled down his trousers and underpants, applied the goo and started to pump. Through the plastic tube he saw his flaccid prick stir and arise, then gradually and impressively expand. The effect wasn't unpleasant, though the base hurt a bit. He felt himself tingling in places he'd not tingled in for some time. He tried to apply some sexual imaginings to the mix, half-heartedly ran through his tatty mental library of erotic images, frantic youthful couplings, occasions of sexual lusciousness with Freya, that later-life easiness of doing to each other what they knew worked. Ejecting her from his thoughts, he pictured pin-ups of his teens, Bond Girls he realised were today well over seventy and possibly dead, back then younger than his daughter now. Fantasies faltered, trickled away as he dozed off. And jolted awake with a full-blown memory.

Him and Freya in his single bed in a shared house decades ago, Ian Dury on the hi-fi and them in the naughty naked nude, sash window open, walls covered in political posters, postcards from art exhibitions and European travels. Freya had said that the world was their oyster. And he looked down at her of course unshaven bush, her legs open to him and to the warm, spring air. This wasn't a hippy trippy free love memory – these were the days of articles in Spare Rib on self-examinations, speculums and pessaries, sexual exploration by and for women, and every desire could and should be acted on, spoken about and rigorously explored. They lay in bed talking about past lovers, his guts squirming with jealousy and desire as she reminisced about old boyfriends, but when the situation reversed he could feel her tense and flush at his revelations, her politics so fierce and her flesh still so peachy. And then they were laughing and tickling and in and on each other, fucking again, trying to fuck a new world into being. And maybe made a new being too. A shoal of sperm flickering through the warm dark towards a single egg which only one of them would pierce, enter and melt into. Was that the moment when Pippa was made? Was it or not? How could he know?

Jamie detached the device, yanked up his trousers, cleaned his hands on a towel and picked up his guitar to see if music might help to fix his aching parts. This Hinchcliffe 'condition' had suddenly put him in a place beyond normality and he was eager to re-enter the clothed, healthy world. Jamie put on a bright shirt, a black pork pie hat to cover his baldness, tuned up his instrument and ambled down to the pub, once a dark brown smelly boozer now re-sprayed in the gastro pub's inevitable grey green emulsion and infused with the aroma of onion marmalade, garlic, Cumberland sausage, crushed new potatoes grown by some local ex-banker artisan on his allotment. Behind the bar, the publican was polishing glasses.

"Hi Ashok, I'm Jamie."

"Yes?"

"You called me earlier, about playing."

"Oh. Yeah. OK. Upstairs."

A bluegrass band sang on a tiny raised stage, young people in their early twenties, so fresh-faced and keen it was almost unbearable to watch them. Standing at the back of the room, he found himself wiping tears from his cheeks as they sang: a guitarist with a new grown beard, a blonde girl singing, smiling hard, mouthing the words of the lines she didn't sing, then pouring forth a stream of melodious vocals. Much sooner than expected it was his turn to be summoned to the microphone. Jamie pushed through the tables to the front, stepped onto the stage, the compere adjusted microphones and levels while Jamie sorted through the printed sheets of his words which he'd brought with him, placed these on the music stand, nerves robbing him of the ability to strum, remember and sing all at the same time. OK, everything ready.

The compere announced, "A big hand for... Jimmy." And he was off. Halfway through the first song, Jamie dared look up from the music-stand, saw eyes upon him and felt his voice grow stronger. Only then he flashed back to the humiliations of the afternoon and fluffed a chord. Nobody seemed to notice. When he finished there was a rustling of applause.

Jamie climbed off stage and made his way to the bar to order his long-awaited free pint, smiling in expectation of strange looks and maybe some compliments. After all, hadn't he sung his bleeding heart right out? But no – not a flicker. And he couldn't complain; after all, the next act had taken to the stage and played their songs without Jamie even registering what they sounded like, so immersed was he in his own awesomeness.

Was anyone really listening? Who gave a toss? The girl singer from the previous band gave him a thumbs-up as they stepped away from the stage and for one absurd

162

moment he brimmed with pleasure at her attention. She of course saw only someone looking like a friend of her dad's. Get real Jamie. Please please get real. Another drink might help. To enter some marvellous new phase of resolved integrity. A wave of jealous sorrow crashed against the wall of him and flooded in. Ohhhhh where was Freya who he knew now he loved forever and forever. He wanted her so much to talk to and cherish, even the bits that drove him nuts. But images of her and Chunk poured over him, on which floated horrible doubts about Pippa's conception. At a table now he spotted those nice students he'd met with Martin that time watching the footie. Hello hello. Remember me? They smiled but looked alarmed, didn't invite him to join them, so he sat down anyway. Awash with self-pity as he drank down another scotch and half listened to some other crooner. A bit pissed to be honest but wanting to get clear get far enough away to come clean. This certainty that he hadn't had time to get his head around the whole shitting situation and if only he could assend accend aascend Sabrina – is that your name? It is? Wow you left quite an impression. Her friends moving in to block her from him when they were talking that's all, like walking to the top of a hill, and look down on it all, put the whole thing in context the whole effing thing of how his love – and rage – for her, and love of his daughter and... O my g o d -- these lovely young people he could talk freely to maybe get it. so pissed now it dosnt make a... You know what not a bloody DAMN what anyone... What was he saying? That anyone. That any bloody body would ... o there was street now and cold on his face blur of shop people traffic him having this urge to urinate here now maybe against this wall no one seeing probably and if they do then WHOGIVESA!! Nothebloodyboss anymore like for all those years bosss daddy lonely in the middle being reeeeezonable and sensible and unfree having his creativity hammered flat his sense of self like that kids book Flat Stanley paper thinnn mister middling friggingmanagr line toeing no more no noooooo

163

SINGing at the topofhis voice. Song by the lung. Gibberish words but all seem to flowww. Just come to him, rhyme chasing rhyme. Love and glove. Languages Sandwiches? Better. Where did that

What exacvtly? He couldnt muchremember how he found himself homenow. Big Dave the student guy held him up and asked for his address. His too big for him clattering about freya free house with its shadows and belongings and ... Negative space. You know?? Come in guys come in all welcome. No? Sure? OK. YOu have a bloody clue what he's feeling, so sad angry hungry And still chuffed if flustered by tat fight withthe blasted nearly man. THoufh he felt guilty for hurting the oldweirdo. Whsose managed to get freya besotted, really, deeply nbesoted. Good to kick out tho to give him what for

Which is painful. When you see her talking without any o f the love..... The love ..... o god.... The lovelovelovelovelove

Is all you need da da da da da ah

O shit

Fallimg updtairs toothbrush? No maybe morning for nowa piss an d a splash pof cold water to freshen up ooo o o o o o
I
Need

To

Sleeeeeeeeeeeeeeeeeeeeeeeeeeeeeeeeeeeeeeeeeeeeeeeeeeep

0000000

Waking up 1 half hours later bold as brass from a dream filled with crystal clear clarity about the whole business yes in the dream he was you know on his way he was live on

164

stage he was spotlight beaming down and him not naked
but wondering why nothing came out of his mouth...
dumbstruck but nobody seemed to care the crowd were
walking off he was Singing his heart out and and and AND
AAAA NNNN DDDDDDDDDDDDDDDDDDDDDddddd d
d d d d

d

      d

d

          .

O!!

forgotten now soditsleep

z

z

mm

z z z

ARAB MOON

Everything moved quickly after that conversation with
Tyler. An email arrived from the Jackson Trust offering
support in kind to the charity, a brand-new state of the art
mobile phone was delivered by courier one morning,
presaging a stream of calls from an organiser in Taqribaan
to fix flights and rooms, then a link sent to the event
website with details of their panel session and workshops.
Another courier arrived with a big delivery of lapel badges,
pens and folders, plastered with the company name, which
Freya diligently assembled into the packs to take with her
to hand out to delegates. The agreement was that Freya
would run workshops in *Nearlyology and Social Media*,
Carraday would attend and sit on the stand distributing
leaflets and badges. He was now used to playing this role at
the Nearly Store. Carraday wouldn't appear on any
platforms, but instead 'act in an advisory role', in other
words shut up and look wise: the Guru of Nearly. Freya
would sit on one panel to talk about *Imagining
Nearlyfutures – the abundance of selves in the digital age.*
Her words would be simultaneously translated, as would
the contributions of Emirati panel members to whom the
English guests could listen on their headphones. The two of

them were to receive small fees for their attendance as well as all expenses. On their return a further payment would be made to Seward Associates, which would go a long way towards wiping out Freya's debts. Oh, heavenly joy.

"We're very keen to meet you in person Mrs Seward and of course to hear the wise words of your eminent colleague we've heard so much of!!" wrote Mustapha, senior administrator, in one of many exclamatory emails exchanged in the run up.

Cars collected each of them early one morning and carried them through the bleary dawn to Heathrow. Freya was no stranger to this kind of travel, but Carraday arrived in the airport departure hall that morning, carting his usual small, brown leather suitcase, looking sleepless and terrified, like an overgrown schoolboy on his first field trip, and asked to borrow Freya's 'portable telephone' so he could call his mother who was staying with her sister in Bournemouth. He seemed relieved and a bit disappointed when his aunt insisted she was happy as Larry, sunning herself out on the balcony, and there was nothing to worry about.

Hours later, they arrived at Dubai Airport, a kaleidoscope of mirrors and lights, were welcomed by a smiling guide and swept by taxi to their hotel on the Taqribaan Corniche where they had been booked into adjoining rooms on the ninth floor. When they convened in the lounge having unpacked, Carraday was still wearing his customary white shirt and black suit, curiously appropriate in this land filled with people in robes of black and white. Despite his weirdnesses, Freya marvelled at how reassuring it was to have Carraday with her on this trip. He actually did look the part: eminent, dapper, gruff, until he switched on that winning smile and their new Arab minders basked in its glow.

AMPLIFIED WAILING

Friday in Taqribaan, the Sabbath. The air was hot and dry, baking but not unpleasant. A boy in baggy shorts and flipflops played in the fountains, filling his baseball cap with water from jets arcing out of the concrete, then, in the absence of a sister or enemy to pour it over, tipped it over his own head, giggling madly. Mother, chic in black burqa and gold designer handbag, her eyebrows, partially visible, immaculately painted, looked on, gently amused. Dad, big bellied and proud of it, dressed in big shorts and MAKE BABY NOT WAR tee-shirt in gold on black, iPhone pressed to ear, was more concerned by all that wetness and messiness, but too absorbed in his call to assert his authority. Was the tee-shirt's slogan an expression of his heartfelt politics, or something in English emblazoned on the garment he'd happened upon in the Dubai Mall? Father waved at his wife absentmindedly and turned back to his phone conversation. Freya watched from a café table at the Casbah, cafés and shops slotted between white stone arches, with a ferris wheel like a mini London Eye and stunning view of the Khaled lagoon, the Space City of Dubai in the distance. Only Starbucks and a couple of other coffee chains were open today. On the air she heard the amplified wailing of the call to prayer from the domed white grandeur of the nearby mosque. And as she watched the Mosque, caught site of Zane from Webberations, walking out of Starbucks.

"Well, fuck me sideways!"

Freya was sitting opposite Carraday and between their shocked guide Mustapha, huge and benign in his white dishdasha, and Britta, a speaker from a Berlin start-up with bright red lipstick and a fiersomely toothy smile.

"Excuse me, Doctor Seward?" asked Britta.

"Pardon me. I think I saw someone I know." She stood up, preparing to chase after him, but it was too far and too hot and Freya couldn't be sure it was Zane. So she sat down again.

"Entschuldigung but I'd watch it with the expletives here," said Britta in a stage whisper.

"OK you're right. Sorry." I must be mistaken. This is a strange place, thought Freya. Strange how often in these situations some unexpected person crops up. An old school friend or work colleague appears randomly in the midst of a holiday. Strange too how ordinary anywhere is when you're actually in it, places from news reports and movies revealed to have air and cars and pavement and Coca Cola signs just like home, though far, far hotter and filled with new smells, scripts and sounds. Strange too that she was sitting here opposite Gregory Carraday. This man made a convincing guru, sitting ramrod straight, attractively eminent, staring ahead. Britta was attempting to network, but Carraday's silence flustered her. She tried to make conversation. "Berlin is indeed a cosmopolitan city and yet at the same time quite small and provincial really." Words dried in Britta's throat and she looked up at him nervously, in awe at the great Nearlyologist's inner resolve. Or inner whatever it was.

"I think I've had a Nearlyincidence," Freya said. Mustapha looked alarmed, but laughed his booming laugh.

"Nearlyincidence? What is this?" asked Britta.

"When someone we know comes within a whisker of crossing our path but doesn't quite."

"I see."

"Except in this case perhaps it wasn't really him at all. What do you call that, Mister Carraday?"

"Um..." The others looked at Carraday awaiting the knowledge. Carraday shrugged. "Not bumping into anybody?"

POWERBALL

Saturday. A few of them from the Expo took a car over from Taqribaan, where all alcohol was banned, to find licensed premises in Dubai. They paid through the nose for real alcohol which they drank as they sat on the terrace of the bar, watching the fountain display, gigantic jets of water lit up in multicolours, rising and falling to pumped music, "including Shik Shak Shok, the Arab world's top-selling dance number", the guide book said. Booming explosions, fireworks wrought of water, the most precious substance here, seemed a fitting symbol for the technological mastery of nature. "The beam of light shining upward from the fountain can be seen from over 20 miles away, and will be visible from space making it the brightest spot in the Middle East, and quite possibly in the entire world," Freya read aloud from the guidebook. Carraday opened his eyes wide, said, "The All-In-One Powerball of the Universe." And closed them again.

The marketing officer from Anotherfuture.com, a sardonic Liverpudlian, sitting beside Freya said, "It's like sitting in an orgasm." Which made Carraday frown and Freya laugh like a drain, reminding her how Jamie could make her snort with laughter in situations like this, his whispered asides setting her off into fits of giggles which she struggled to contain. At the next table, Arab women in fully veiled burqas posed while their husbands took photos. At home did they have albums of their anonymous shrouded selves beside world destinations, the Liverpudlian wondered aloud? "Here I am at the Eiffel Tower; here's one of the two of us at the Taj Mahal." Here in the Dubai Mall, brightest spot in quite possibly the entire world, global corporates resplendent, the black and white robed Arabs, the rich western tourists dressed for clubbing, mingled and browsed and proudly paid way over the odds for their branded goods. The group from the Expo ambled about the mall for a bit, then squeezed into a cab to speed back across the bridge to Taqribaan, cracking jokes about the Burj Khalifa skyscraper, shaped like a hypodermic needle, so tall that the outrageously expensive penthouse flats at the top were said to be almost permanently shrouded in cloud, which served the rich bastards right, according to Margaret the Expo administrator, drinker of many Guinnesses, who lived in Dubai and so knew.

When Freya woke up the following morning from a dream of grey London corridors, the ninth floor view from her room reminded her even more of the space cities of Sixties sci-fi. And yes, if we ever colonise Mars, she realised, this is what it will look like: shopping malls under a huge glass dome, airtight skyscrapers looking out over the astounding desertedness of the planet. Is this heaven or hell? Not her cup of tea for sure. Spending so much time on Planet Carraday was a strain also. If she was honest, he didn't give out much, and what he did share was peculiar. On the other hand, she felt free to wander off without him to explore the other stands, to stop off and network with participants, to sit for short periods in the baking heat. She was free to think and do what she liked, yet was always glad to return to Carraday's familiar smile and the man's quiet and benign affection.

In the cavernous hangar of the Taqribaan Expo people dressed as gigantic tablet computers and mobile telephones danced the samba through the aisles of stands, following a clown in a Noddy car and two women dancers in pink lycra on stilts, like Paralympic flamingoes. In Aisle 45B Tyler Associates had sponsored a stand where Carraday would sit next to a screen on which played a looped PowerPoint display about Nearlyology and the Virtual World, beside a classroom set aside for Freya's social media workshops. Each day, thirty teenage girls sat at tables gazing at her, needy, their stern teachers waiting to see what educational benefits would unfold. Freya said hello, today we're exploring Facebook and suchlike. Then her interpreter, Nada, spoke at length. The audience still look bored and baffled.

"Oh kay..." Freya pressed a key on her computer and the first slide of her presentation appeared fuzzily on the screen behind her. She began to describe the immense potential of social media marketing to the new start-up business, then paused to find the interpreter in the midst of a whispered phone call in Arabic.

"So sorry, miss, I must go. The Minister wishes to meet one of our esteemed special guests." And Nada was gone, leaving Freya to convey her message through sign language and short sentences.

"You know Twitter?" Yes, much nodding and smiling. "Um... useful too." More smiling. Someone even taking notes. "Facebook also. Can. Be Used. To Promote Your Products." And after forty minutes of this a hand goes up.

"Yes?"

"But aren't you concerned about the role of social media in creating bubbles of opinion in which zealots can feel their opinions legitimised and normalised? Also the whole issue of cyber bullying of children and adults too?"

After the sessions, Freya and her burqa-clad assistant dished out the stiff, glossy paper bags supplied by her funder, emblazoned with the company logo. Inside were the usual goodies: folder, biro, notepad, sticker, brochure, leaflets and a little lapel pin of the logo: a sparkly J for Jackson. Participants queued up keenly, though some she didn't actually recognise from the session, but politely they communicated as much friendliness as they could via their dark eyes and flashes of carefully made-up eyebrows. The intensity of their interest was alarming. She couldn't gauge who understood what, nor why anyone here would be remotely interested in what she and Carraday thought.

"Misses Seward your workshops here have been a spectacular success," said Mustapha, the next morning in the hotel reception, so tall and handsome in his brilliant white robe and checked headdress, arms folded like a muscular genie.

"Why thank you – you've had good reports?"

"Not yet, but I am confident they have been extremely informative."

"Thanks."

"So today you make your speech and then on Wednesday afternoon depart. We hope you will return to Taqribaan. And you too Mister Carraday, of course." Mustapha beamed at his friend eliciting one of Carraday's rare, brief smiles in return. "It's an honour, sir, to have you visit."

'Oh yes, well I'd be very keen to come back. Extremely keen," said Freya, never one to say no to future possibilities.

"OK. This is good. And your bags of luck are most well received I think."

"They do seem popular don't they."

"May I take one also for my wife and son please Mrs Seward?"

"But of course." Their enjoyable chat was disturbed by a sigh at her shoulder. Carraday, despite Mustapha's adulation, was looking more and more like a fish as far out of its water as it was possible to get without drowning in air: this wrinkled, wiry man fidgeting in the Emirate heat.

Sitting beside Carraday in the car, Freya riffled through her carefully prepared notes and decided they were all gibberish. Carraday sat poker-straight as he always did, staring into the middle distance. Whenever she did public speaking this last-minute panic would engulf her.

"I don't know why you get so worried, Frey. Your talks never go wrong," Jamie used to say. But the next one might.

SIMULTANEOUS TRANSLATION

Around Carraday fizzing the nearlyness, demons of
possible failure hissing at his ears so that he bat at them
with his wrinkly hands. Mouth feeling sore, constricted.

Worm of doubt curling like a collar round his neck and
squeeeeeeeeeezing.
Who are these people? What this all for?
A world so strange it like one grand hallucination.
Wailing from speakers along the corniche the call to prayer,
men in white robes carrying their prayer mats. But stranger
still to Carraday the land of the conference with its urgency
and sense of purposes which nobody yet manage to define.
What are they doing? The minders and administrators
so polite and kind but always with an eye on higher bosses,
leading them here, there, delivering them to this door,
this meal, this car.
And soon after he sit in the audience watching MrsSeward
being led on stage in conference room four to a row of desks
covered with a cloth, jugs of water, microphones,
folded cardboard name signs. The badge he have pinned
to him saying Prof. Carabby, Ministry of Nearly UK.
A surly gent give his headphones to put over his ears and a
box of technical trickery to slip into his jacket pocket.
Soon, think Carraday, someone telling us what's going on.
A smooth presenter fellow, neat goatee beard, linen suit,
a bounce in his step which tell you he a Somebody,
pretending to be ordinary. And when he start to speak,
the headphones click and buzz and a disembodied
voice explain what he saying, simultaneous translations
in a flat, hurried tone. Conveying nothing. Words flow forth
but not signify. Bathing in jargon
and generalisations. Native speakers laugh at jokes
which no one bother to Englishise.

CRACKLE

The speaker who was billed to speak before Freya stood up,
clicked on his presentation. Not a lot happened. Frantic
backstage staff rushed to the podium to fiddle while the
paunchy speaker made remarks. Freya looked out into the

audience – and to her amazement saw Zane. At the back of the hall, that dark-suited man disappearing through the exit. Surely this time it was. Now the first Powerpoint slide appeared on screen and the talk began: infographics of organisational structures, lengthy quotes from books which he read aloud very slowly. The moderator looked at his watch and sighed, tried to catch the speaker's eye. No joy. The interpreter's flat voice babbling on from headphones, "umtheassociatoftheemirateseducationfundfortheseumtypes ofdevelopmentareunderthejurisdictionof...theappropriateoffi ce... in our... workwithawiderangeofcommunitiesthroughoutthetheregionm uch... progressisbeingmade..." Freya felt her eyelids drooping even as the adrenaline coursed through her and the diaretic side-effects of her caffeine intake were felt in her bowels. And then the crackle of applause.

Freya stood, walked up to the podium looking out at the hall of faces. No time to lose, she rattled through the opening passage of her talk, thanking the kind hosts, apologising for her lack of the language and in-depth knowledge of the regional situation. She noticed that the audience were looking not at her, but at the handsome young moderator who must be a celebrity here, judging by his aura of self-satisfaction. Glamorous Moderator smiled wanly, tapped his watch. "Well thank you Mrs Seaford for your wise words. But sadly we're running behind and lunch is being served. Thank you to all our speakers for..." His voice was drowned out by seats flapping back into upright position, as delegates poured out towards the exit and the tables of food. Relief and outrage coursed through her veins.

"Thank you thank you." At the buffet lunch, Freya was congratulated by Mustapha on a first-class presentation. He introduced her to someone important in the Ministry, but deference to foreign guests lost out to urgent gossip about the first speaker whose talk had included some thinly veiled criticism of Government policy which were causing ructions. A journalist rushed over to interview Freya for a television channel. He too had deep dark eyes and a set of large and perfect teeth. But even as he questioned her and she spoke live to camera, Freya saw her interviewer glancing away at the Glamorous Moderator. Doctor Freya Seward was and wasn't where the action was. Here egos were teased out into the open and then, once coaxed into view, given a good kicking. Next she looked around for Carraday who was tucked away behind a palm plant with a plate of wilted lettuce. By the time they sat in the car on its way back to the hotel, both felt wrung out.

Freya looked across at the car next to them and into the eyes of another replica Zane. She looked away quickly. "Mister Carraday, I hope you're not too unhappy here."

"Not too unhappy, Miss Seward? Yes, that describing very well how I feel."

INTERCOURSE

Jamie tapped in the URL for the ED Space Forum while he was also listening to the BBC news and watching a YouTube clip of an old Madness video he'd seen at the gym where he'd gone to plod for ten minutes on a running machine and sigh in the sauna. Now on his laptop he was confronted by garish blurred photos of curved, twisted penises, followed by a cold, dense databank of medical information, and – tip tap tip – through to the forum itself. And he found himself reading posts laced with such depression and distress that he had to put his computer on sleep mode a moment while he went to open a bottle of wine.

Back at his desk, glass of Merlot to hand, he prised open the lid of his laptop like he was opening the gates of hell. Hinchcliffe's was described here as a full-blown medical condition; there were conferences about it, arguments over funding research into it, differing opinions on effective treatments for it, frank accounts of injections, bends, traction devices, surgical interventions, pumps – and pain. Hinchcliffe World. There was a lot of talk of length and girth and the tormented isolation of men scared of failing to be normal, a questionnaire posted by an American institute offered a choice of boxes to tick next to descriptions of its various symptoms.

He sat in a pool of light at his laptop. He yanked down his pants, applied lubricant and attached the pump to himself. He pumped and deflated, pumped and deflated. But at the end of the evening, after he'd detached his red, swollen member from the tube with a sound like *thwunk*, had exchanged posts for some time with a Danish man who was furiously bitter about the lack of interest in his condition, he hit the sleep button again, closed the lid, washed and went to bed, failed to sleep as well as his computer did, lay awake pondering this disease which wasn't really a disease at all, one which apparently caused serious depression in over 40% of the diagnosed, which could lead to relationship breakdown, isolation, loss of self-esteem. And realised that he already knew these things to be true.

Jamie would

> get over it. He was in his mid-fifties for god's sake, separated from his wife – what right did he have to expect a sex life at that age? Except there was that nice Italian woman who worked in the Café Del Mondo sometimes.

> meet that nice woman in the Café Del Mondo who always stamped his loyalty card twice and remembered his name. He would never dare ask her out, didn't even have the confidence to look her in the eyes.

> meet that nice woman in the Café Del Mondo. "By the way, what's your name?" he'd ask when he went up to fetch his latte. "You know mine." They'd fall into conversation.

> meet that nice woman. Tell her that his wife's left him, that he now suspects his daughter may not be his daughter.

> meet that nice woman, skip over the getting to know each other, the machinations and trysts. One way or another she's now in his room. They're on the bed together...

> meet that nice woman in the Café Del Mondo. And everything at this stage goes blank. A terrible sinking feeling. Whiteness and silence. He wouldn't be there. Her wanting him in the first place – ridiculous.

> meet that nice woman in the Café Del Mondo. She'd serve flat white never thinking twice about him.

> meet that nice woman in the Café Del Mondo. Since when did a sexual fantasy have to be realistic? Hadn't he imagined encounters with supermodels and neighbours and women sitting opposite him on buses over the years without any trouble?

> meet that nice woman. Tell her that his wife's left him, that he now suspects his daughter may not be his daughter.

> meet that nice woman in the Café Del Mondo. And now it felt different. Felt like those guys who go to prostitutes and pay them to sit with them while they cry.

> meet that nice woman in the Café Del Mondo. They're in his bedroom and as they walk in he'd feel his belly contract, glance in the mirror to see hair oozing out of his follicles, snaking down his neck and brow, dark brown and soft. His new friend also seemed to be rearranging herself, wrinkles smoothing away, fat on her hips making its way up to her cleavage. They slip between the sheets morphing into amalgams of all their favourite sex symbols. They embrace, their mouths connect, she reaches down.

> meet that nice woman. And a terrible moment would occur when his body wouldn't do what it ought to. And a long, cold walk home in the night. And a decision to

178

maybe go to Starbucks, even though they don't pay their taxes, next time he wanted a flat white.

> meet that nice woman. And they'd talk. She'd tell him about her abusive ex-lover who flew into rages and beat her. She'd suggest that they undress and snuggle up in bed and talk.

> meet that nice woman. Tell her that his wife's left him, that he thinks his daughter may not be his daughter.

> meet that nice woman. But it would need to be online. Some site where he could set out his stall carefully, present all his benefits, slip in odd code words for overweight like cuddly and... whatever the other code words are. And he could also describe his condition, explaining also that he was sensual, able to please, whatever the code words were for being up for non-penetrative experiment.

> meet that nice woman and with a huge sense of relief he'd realise there was no possibility of anything sexual ever happening between them at all. Now, at long last, so long after it should have been, he was capable of enjoying the company of an attractive woman without that entering into it. And now he could look around the Café and see beyond it outside the window a wonderful world of joyously intercourse-free encounters.

> not meet that nice woman.

> meet the nice woman. Take his coffee, sit down and continue reading his very interesting book about the Playfulness of the City. He'd look up to admire the bright spring morning on the high street.

> meet the nice lady [woman?] and she would smile and put her arms around him and they'd hug each other tight, he'd close his eyes and breathe her in and open wide again to find her transformed into Freya herself and all being well being well and all manner of thing being well.

> meet that nice woman. Tell her that his wife's left him, that he is certain his daughter is not his daughter.

COOL GLASS DOORS

She was being watched, Freya Redcoat was certain of it.
These white robed minders with their thick beards and eyes
dark as anti-matter hovered in the lobby, on the stairwells,
around the edges of the restaurant. They watched all the
delegates – they were employed as minders after all – but
her treatment was different. When she caught that guy's
eye he turned away and whispered to his accomplice. Years
ago she'd have angrily written it off as the objectifying gaze;
now, with much relief and a hint of sorrow, she knew that it
wasn't. What were they muttering to each other about? Who
were these guys talking to on the mobiles which they held
clamped to their heads at all times? Or was this her white
Western paranoia? Could she read what was happening
around here? And there were these Zane lookalikes which
hovered in her peripheral vision. Men in suits – well, there
were always plenty of those at events like this. She'd
checked the lists of exhibitors and found no mention of
Webberations, though the hall was filled with stands of
similar online providers and advisors. Freya was so
engrossed she bumped into the man ahead in the breakfast
queue.

"Oops. So sorry!"

"Excuse me." The short, neat, middle-eastern man
turned to face her and smiled politely. His eyes weren't
quite aligned – one must have been made of glass – and, like
a TV presenter looking for the live camera, she couldn't
discern which one to speak to.

"The Nearly Lady. On the Jackson stand, yes?
From UK?"

"England. Yes, the United Kingdom. So called.
Disunited most like."

His blank expression showed no interest in her
nation. Neither eye lit up. "I see. Allow me to introduce
myself: Mister Hakim, Maktub Hakim. I recommend the
scrambled eggs."

"Freya Seward. Hello Maktub. You live here?"

"For now. I am from Istanbul and hope to return there. You live in London I think." He said flatly. "I went once on business, yes, and once with my family. Buckingham Palace. Harry Potter." His tone implied he hadn't liked it much. "Your first time at the Expo?"

"Yes."

"Yes." And before she had time to say anything nice about the city, he moved away from her to check out the row of silver hooded dishes containing grandiose mounds of baked beans, falafels and chicken kebabs.

Freya and The Istanbulian with the dodgy eye collected their coffee, juice and rolls, stood together in the sparkling marbled splendour of the hotel restaurant holding their trays and glancing around for somewhere to sit. He nodded in the direction of a table in the corner. Once settled Freya shook out her napkin and placed it over her knees, lifted her fork, smiled as her new friend spoke in Arabic to the others at the table, men in suits who roared with laughter at whatever he'd said.

"Bon appétit." He didn't speak again as they ate. As she chewed on a mouthful of warm fluffy egg, her neighbour put knife and fork down on his plate, stood up and walked out of the room. The man sitting to her left on the table looked horrified, began speaking urgently to the man on his left. Freya stared through the hotel's tinted windows into the ferocious blue sky beyond and began planning for the day ahead. She looked round and Maktub was back in place sitting opposite, his hand on a small box wrapped in purple tissue paper. He leaned over and spoke quietly.

"Nearly Lady. I wonder if you might do me a favour."

"Of course."

"A gift for Mister Jackson. Perhaps you could take it him." He slid the box across the table. One of the other breakfasters glanced at it, looked away, ate on.

"Yes, that's fine. I mean, what is it?"

"A tiny gift in gratitude for a favour he has been doing for us. Best not to be placed in hand luggage but no problem in your suitcase. It would very much be best not to break the seal but – be assured it is all perfectly... 'above the board'?"

"It's 'above board'. There's no 'the'. Yes. Well, I'm not sure..."

"Ah, my mistake, apologies."

"Well we Brits are terrible at learning other languages."

"This is true. Very much so." He sounded cross rather than amused. She was used to being feted at these affairs, even in ex-Colonies her quaint accent would be cooed over, respectful references made to the Queen and The Beatles, Leicester Square and, god save us, Maggie Thatcher. But the affection was wearing off these days. Mister Hakim picked up the box again and pressed it into her hands.

"Please. It's only paper. Simply a rather beautiful notebook from the Blue Soukh which he expressed admiration for on a previous visit. He thought his wife would like it. Tell him from Mister Maktub Hakim, yes?"

"Well – thank you on his behalf." Freya took the box, picked up her mobile and opened her notes app, tapped in his name which he spelt out to her letter by letter. The man from Istanbul stood up again, bowed slightly, dropped his napkin onto the detritus of his breakfast tray and walked away.

FLUSH

Freya didn't unwrap the box but, back in her hotel room, she shook it. Could be a notebook. But it was done up very beautifully with tissue paper and ribbon, secured with sealing wax. She couldn't undo the parcel to take a quick peek. Probably bank notes thought Freya Redcoat, super sleuth. At the expo her expenses had been paid to her in cash without a receipt, from a safe opened up by a senior administrator, with a key he kept on a fob along with a bunch of car keys and house keys. Anyway, best to keep the package sealed and tell the truth of how she came by it if asked at Customs. Although she'd have to fib at Check In, when they questioned if she'd been asked to carry anything on board. Now Freya sat on the end of the bed and opened her laptop, clicked on the overpriced hotel wi-fi access button and tried to get a grip. She slid deep into the info flow as into a warm, relaxing bath, growing calmer as she picked up on this morning's memes, campaigns and virals, gathered news of politics, obituaries, funny pets through the chatty posts of associates. But still that guy's face and suspicious gift jolted her back out of her web wash. She thought with a pang of Dan in Brighton, as if he was a familiar, long-term friend. Then laughed aloud and bitterly at the absurdity of that.

In the bathroom, holding the laptop with one hand, Freya yanked down her trousers with the other, and sat on the toilet, peeing as she googled Zane's name yet again. Still no success. Was she a screen addict? Probably. Her analogue friends liked to tell her so. Jamie used to make sarcastic remarks about how much time she spent staring into Apple's dark mirror, clicking on laptop keys, tapping on the phone, but her defence was robust. She wasn't gawping at a dead screen; through its lens she was watching and wandering in a rich cultural landscape. OK there were the silly cats and snaps of bread risen and meals about to be consumed, but every community thrives on the exchange of trivia. On the same device she could read a novel, catch up on missed radio and TV, follow unfolding news, sign and share a petition, write a business letter or loving note to Pippa, undertake research for work. But true, much of her time was spent in this state of noodling, starting one task before sidestepping into another, perhaps more fruitful, perhaps not.

Now she sought reassurance, that in the midst of this strange place and time she could connect with her online gang. She browsed her feed as she fired off another note to Zane demanding a refund. But a minute later she was guiltily reading some drivel clickbait about Brad Pitt being spotted at a wedding reception and agreeing to pose with the bride. That led her to watch a three-minute YouTube clip of Thelma & Louise, to read about a new social media tool and comment on a thread in a Women in Technology forum on natural metaphors for the internet.

MISTER LAPTOP

"I so hate the moral panic about it all," she'd said to Rosalind one morning back at the flat after reading out an article on children's online behaviours. "Society goes soppy with nostalgia about the joys of village life but freaks out about new ways to gossip and mingle."

Rosa stood behind her reading the screen and massaged Freya' shoulders while she read what her friend was writing. "Bullshit, Frey!"

"Oh god, not you too!"

"It mashes up your head that stuff. It's changing who we are. We're filling in boxes, not really writing. Patting ourselves on the back over and over."

"That's crap, Rosa."

"Bull. Shit." Rosalind said she hated the web but used it all the time, bombarding her friends with links to petitions, photos of global suffering, conspiracy theories about corporate greed. She was also frank about her use of porn.

"Me and Mister Laptop are going to get us some orgasms," she'd say before carrying her tablet off to bed with a glass of water. Freya brushed her teeth trying not to overhear the moans, real or virtual, emanating from Rosalind's room. Freya put on headphones in bed and propped her hi-tech tablet up against her knees to do what she'd done in bed most nights for years: fall asleep watching Newsnight.

But now Freya was using Mister Laptop to calm herself down in a Taqribaan hotel room, shitting out fear-induced diarrhoea while getting her emails done. Time to close the lid and wipe and flush and wash and put on make-up, descend to the mirrored, chandeliered lobby via lift and a stairway from the finale of a Fred Astaire movie, to find her minder at the desk who, looking even more sinister than usual, handed her a conference-branded linen bag containing the day's consignment of lucky bags. Freya pushed through the cool glass doors and out into a wall of heat to walk to the car and be taken through the streets to the conference hall.

TRICKY WALKABOUT

MrsSeward go again workshopping
with her flip charts and lucky bags,
Carraday do walkabout in the calm streets of Taqribaan.
He clutch close a Nearly piece from words he got him
at the fair where he sit for hours with FreyaSeward's flyers
and rotating powerpoint slides about Nearlyness In The
Digital Age while he next to a sign asking for Nearly stories
which pretty much everyone ignore except a few who come
straight on over knowing what they need to write.
Including this one. An Arab woman he realise hovering
around the stand, small figure in full veil, he pretty sure it
being the same lady keeping walking past, stopping to read
the Nearlies he pin on cards to the display boards.
He go for a toilet break and after, as he turn into their aisle,
see her bending down over his chair, but she spots him and
scuttling off as he approach. He find this note after,
crumpled, hand written, stuffed in the top pocket of his
jacket he leave on the back of his chair.

185

"I nearly died when a bomb hit my home in my land where the earth is on fire. But travelled here where I nearly feel safe. So long as I keep my head down and don't challenge the authorities. But I so want to challenge them. Thank you."

NEEDS BURYING

Back in his hotel room he lie on the floor, head under the
desk, and with his felt-tips make a drawing of her,
eyes downcast, an aura of fire around her and he wrap it up
in the complimentary flannel from his
huge, marble bathroom.
At dinner time when Mrs Seward go back for more from the
buffet, he quickly slip into his pocket
some roast chunks of barbecued meat from his plate,
fold in a tissue and steal in a trice, these dark hunks of flesh
wrap into flannel then truss up tight with a broken lace
he pick up from a bin in the lobby. And now it need burying.
Once dark he go down in the lift, past young woman
playing grand piano under the huge chandelier.
Bridge Over Troubled Water with cascades of notes
like Dubai fountainwater, pianist's swan-like arms bare in
shiny evening frock, in the midst of all that glam she still
looking boredasshit.
Carraday he slide past and out into the heat of the night,
cross the road through lanes of honking taxis and start to
walk along the corniche, ornamental planting wet from a
lattice of hosing. He arrive at the spot where prayers blare
from speakers embedded in the ground.
Tricky walkabout here where so many hover.
But he need to bury this spell in the earth to keep that
woman from harm. Carraday on his haunches,
scrape at the ground to make a hole.
Taking some digging. A courting couple approach and
Carraday stand back quickly.

186

The duo smile at him curious, the man glance behind as
they walk away and mutter something to his
cuddling girlfriend. He hearing how women can be flogged
for sexual behaviours in public here.
These two lovers not so scared.
As they walk off,
Carraday reach into pocket and pull out the soggy brown
parcel, push its bloody mush into the ground.
Let hate seep out and die.
Can't get out of his head images
of explosive belts, exploding clothes exploding heads.
Then he hear shout behind him, Carraday turn to see
figures in white robes approaching, man voices loudening,
one with hand raised. Fear grip hard.
In a strange land terror and chaos open up sudden around
and he running quick quick, heartbeat whamming
his chest. Head he for the road seeing these
dark men crouch where he been digging and imagine them
re-digging, yanking out his weird meat thing. Imagining
their fear and rage at this strangeness, their hunger to
hunt him. Ducking through traffic and down a sidestreet of
dusty shops under gaudy plastic signs, windows stuffed with
boxes, sullen Arab keepers in the doorways,
Carraday leg it to the back entrance of the hotel, check out
if anyone eyeing him, then sneak back
into marble cool, past travel agency office, to mirrored lift
and up up up to safety.

From THE LITTLE BOOK OF NEARLY

Make a mobile phone out of cardboard.
Carry it with you everywhere.
When it rings
answer it.
Who nearly called?

WRITE AND BURN

Stepping out of the lift find a maid outside his room,
her cart parked across the door, stacked with sheets
and toy sachets of shower gel, body rub,
shampoo and conditioner. She murmur her apology,
pull the cart to one side to let him through and
he safe again. Only now realizing Carraday his hat gone.
Where did it fall? A crowd discovering it,
torture it to telling them his whereabouts?
From the window he try to see but he too far up to look
straight down. Pressing his foreheard to the cool glass.
Carraday make work for the spaces between
and is familiar with the terror of near discovery.
Hotel life be special hard for Carraday what with
he wiffying home daily to ma to be sure she OK
and then he need extra vigilance to keep death
only nearly for she.
He do counting in the night he do pacing and push ups.
He hide his making after all clean and normal for the
cleaner to not find it, for Miss Seward to not know how he
wants her. He can't write and burn as there's a
smoke alarm in the ceiling, so instead he turn up the TV
and speak in the midst of the racket he make,
mutter and shout his prayer-type things.
His bullshitmagicnonsense
no more stupid than everyonebloodyelse's.

JAWS

In the sitting room of Rayner Gardens, in the room which
had become his control centre, art studio, office, pigsty,
Jamie was writing a song. He'd been at it all day. He
hummed and strummed, stopped to note that he ought to be
doing other things, like house cleaning and looking
hopelessly for paid work, then continued, fixated. He

scribbled words, sought out chord sequences, recorded on his laptop, added falsetto backing vocals, tapped on boxes for a percussion track. Lyrics arrived on his tongue without filter: truths and fantasies, puns and metaphors, weird words that somehow fitted. Threads of a new tune were spun around the bones of borrowed chords until a new pattern emerged; played over and over, the song became some kind of memorable, fell into dull familiarity, then sometimes Jamie hit on a riff, a flourish, a rubbing together of sound and meaning which made the whole fly awhile.

The doorbell rang and it was Martin he found outside the door, collar upturned against the cold. "Hello Elvis." He walked in as if he owned the place, past Jamie to the kitchen, plonked himself on a dining chair.

"Listen to this." Jamie fetched laptop and little speakers, hurriedly set them up on the kitchen table and pressed the keypad. His reproduced voice burst into song accompanied by chunky, rhythmic chords, squeaky harmony and thudding percussion. Jamie heard its flaws but still couldn't stop himself thinking, not half bad. Martin listened, impassive.

"What do you think?"

"Of it so far? Rubbish."

"OK." It was. They glared into each other's eyes. A beat. And smiled.

"Only joking."

Jamie prepared to accept a compliment, but still it didn't come. Martin opened the fridge, presumably looking for something to snack on, then closed it. He went to the French windows onto the back garden. As an ex-housemate Martin knew the knack for unlocking and opening the doors with a thud of the hip. "The garden's turning into a bit of a wilderness, mate. Don't you have a mower?"

"What do you really think?"

"Really think? Really?" Martin prodded the earth in a flowerpot on the windowsill where a tired, yellowing

189

geranium was clinging onto life. At the sink he filled a jug with water then poured some into the pot.

"Hello – are you there?" A silence as the two old friends looked at each other. Third time lucky: "What did you really, really think – of my brilliant song," Jamie asked. Martin looked blank. "Of the song I played you."

"S'all right. Tune. Words. Good. Yeah."

"And? Be honest."

"Well, it's all a bit… embarrassing isn't it, mate. Old guy making pop. Sorry."

"Well that's honest."

"Like me trying to talk to you about what I'm wanting and not wanting – sexually – at my age. All a bit..."

"What?"

"When we went to the pub that time, there was something you were about to tell me."

"Oh, I can't remember."

"Really? Afterwards I felt bad – thought maybe it had been important.'"

"Oh – about my health? A kind of… erectile problem type thing I've got. Plaque in the cock that makes it kind of twisted."

"Gross."

"Not terribly nice. No." He explained more about the symptoms.

"Not easy to talk about. And I didn't let you. Apologies, mate."

"No, not easy."

"Like your wife says: A bit you know."

"You've seen Freya?"

"Before she went off on her jaunt."

"What jaunt?"

"Oh, she didn't tell you. She's abroad on business. Pippa came too which was nice, for dinner round our house. Connie's designing her new website." Jamie felt a tug in his gut. "It's going electric blue. Looks rather smart."

Martin had always been good at bursting his friend's bubble. What did Jamie think he was playing at, really, making music? This was all some hideously trite late life crisis. Accept the slide into dotage, become a character part in younger lives.

"The two of them were talking about the little put-downs they get as older women, the subtle messages in the media about what's uncool, not the done thing at their age. I thought: bloody right." That sounded like his wife, and yes Freya was right. This wasn't mid-life, this was the beginning of the end. He was being cut lose from adulthood and sent into limbo. What the hell, better be embarrassing than dull. Old age at least offered freedom from caring what anyone else thought. No one else to amuse but themselves. Then again he could hear Freya reminding him the world was still run by old men. It was traversed by wrinkled dinosaurs of rock on never ending tour. Freya also said that their generation fought for the rights of those whom society deemed "a bit – you know". Wasn't that exactly how women, gays, transexuals had been mocked and belittled? Wasn't the history of liberation struggles a history of The Bit – You Know?

"Anyway, I thought I'd do something about it for a change. Like you said. Like Frey was saying. Take a stand. Revive the spirit of those Anti-Sexist Men's Groups of yore." Martin took a card from his pocket, wrote something on it, slipped this into the breast pocket of Jamie's shirt. "Better go. It's feeding time soon. Let me know what you think, mate. You might want to contribute."

Later that evening, Jamie opened the jaws of hell again, stared into the screen, typed in the url printed on the card Martin had given him. It opened up a title page: 'Nearlysex.com'.

Posts were illustrated with images and animations, half comic, half erotic. One of them was a cartoon, based on the blowjob clip Jamie had seen on Martin's laptop that day at The Oak. Each time the lips moved up and down, words appeared, written on the shaft: Same / Old / Same / Old. Around the woman's head speech bubbles kept appearing, moans of orgasmic ecstasy turning to groans of boredom. Mmmm...Ahhhh...Ummm...Hmmm... The 'About' page read:

There's plenty been said by men about having great sex. But now I want to talk about sex when it doesn't happen or happens but not like it used to. Are you enjoying the pleasures of a relationship not based on orgasms? Or is the absence of sex always evidence that something's wrong? Can older bodies feel as sexy as younger ones? Are you trying to revive your sex drive with massage, sex toys or porn? What works? Might cuddling and conversation be better? Do you feel liberated or decimated by the prospect of losing your libido? I'm going to be as honest as I can be here and hope that might encourage readers to be honest too. Please do tell.

That was what was wrong with the Hinchcliffe site: it was like a discussion of food without reference to taste. He thought of those TV cooking shows he used to watch with Freya, ogling over quenelles and foams and reductions they couldn't smell or savour. Those earnest ED Space questionnaires didn't ask how sex felt, or how it didn't feel any more, didn't ask about desire and fantasy, didn't mention porn, that big bad box of sweet, shameful sex chocolates, never more than a click away. Oh yes, it was time to tell.

DIFFERENT KIND

No sound through the plate glass only the neverending
hissinghumming of hotel air conditioning.
The big sky and water, dinky cars on the road below,
and on the verge a cluster of toy people jostling,
holding banners, Arabic words in red on white sheets.

And he seeing down there, on a stick like a pin,
a small dark disc could maybe be his hat?
But around the demonstration the city rumble on as ever.
Veiled women walking slowly along the Corniche,
robes flapping like the black bin-liner he once seeing
by the reservoir being spied on through binoculars
by enthusiastic bird watchers.
Walking through the world covered up and looking out.
It's what he kind of aims at, his suit anonymous, his speech
proper and polite, manner plain enough to keep people
at bay, and inside his clothes, his secret signs,
painted with dots and squiggles in felt tip and powder paint.
Making him itch and leave in his trail a light
multicoloured dust, but not enough to be troubled by.

In the Nearlyverse the black bird of secrecy flap her
plastic wings and sail aloft, spotting from on high the
thinks bubbles of the populace which float above each head
like plump little clouds, seething with private desires
only this creepy crow deciphers.
Carraday take the lift down to the restaurant for the next
round of buffet. At the next floor a guy blustering into the
car, suave in smart, dark suit, trundling his
smart leather suitcase and matching hand luggage.
This fella dabs his forehead with a white handkerchief.
"Hey Mister – you speak English, yes? And drink, yes?
Of course you do. Let me give you this. Seems a shame to
waste it and I have a flight to catch.
Sudden change of plan."
He pull out of the case a brown paper bag and
pushing it into Carraday's arms:
a half full bottle of scotch whiskey.
"Hey, take it. Courtesy of Webberations Plc.
I'll be back in normality soon, thank God.
Out of this dry hellhole. Can't wait for a big, cold beer."
"Oh – really? Well…" The man step out of the lift and the
doors sliding shut.

"Thank you," Say Carraday to his flustered metal reflection.
Like being handed a ticking bomb. What to do with this?
Hit the button and go straight back up to his room.
Where he pace about, catching sight of himself
in all these mirrors: mad fella clutching hooch.
Shame to waste it though he not
drunk spirits since way back. But MrsSeward maybe.
He wrap the bottle in one of the tiny white towels folded on
a shelf above the bath, embroidered with the hotel's name
and logo. Finding her room he knock on the door.

EMOTICON

Freya yawned luxuriously as she brushed her teeth and
prepared for an early night before the journey home the
following afternoon. She was scented and glowing from a
piping hot shower, pleasantly weary tonight having failed to
sleep much so far in the anonymous plush of her four-star
room, brain sifting through the events of the day, featuring
so many encounters and strange flavours. The workshops
didn't relate to Nearlyology in any meaningful way, but
Carraday's Nearly Story Collection Point had indeed proved
a good gimmick at the Expo, catching the interest of a few of
the flock of passing visitors. Her workshop was simply a
basic introduction to social media, which seemed to satisfy
participants, and she always mentioned how digital tools
allowed us all to create our own nearly selves in cyberspace,
so it was all sort of part of the project. And sounded quite
cool. But the sessions were knackering; frankly she was
looking forward to getting back now. Freya reached into her
wash bag for floss, fingers rummaging amongst bottles of
conditioner, a tub of anti-ageing cream, found a fold of foil
down behind the flannel, felt its edges hoping it was an
Aspirin, her head fugged up and throbbing with the stresses
of the long, hot day.

She froze, mouthed into the mirror: "Oh! My! God!" And pictured Rosalind saying when Freya was off for her recuperative weekend in the country with old friend from work, "I've popped you a little prezzy in your wash things to pep up the proceedings."

"I don't do drugs any more, you know that, Rosa."

"Not yet you don't, but you know, things change. Anyway, now you can if and when you want to, lovey. Like your Carraday might say, keep them so you can always be nearly doing them." Thanks to Rosalind she had unknowingly smuggled a tab of LSD into the United Arab Emirates. If they'd had sniffer dogs at customs she'd have been handcuffed and deported, or be in prison by now, awaiting a public flogging probably. Her guts twisted with fear as Freya pulled out the foil and ripped it open. Yes, there was the tab: a square of paper with a smiley face on, an edible emoticon. She put it on the tip of her finger and reached for her reading glasses to look at it properly.

There was a loud hammering on the door. Freya yelped in panic. She pushed her finger into her throat and gulped. What made her do that? Some crazy instinct to waste not want not?

"Coming," she cried out, put her mouth under the tap, coughing and gargling in an attempt to regurgitate the tiny square of swallowed paper, but no luck. Heart pounding, legs wobbling under her, wrapping herself in the hotel's white dressing gown and belting it tightly, she went to the door. And opening it enough to peep out, found Mister Carraday, hunched over a white cloth which he clutched tight to his chest under his suit jacket. In her state of shock Freya was more relieved to see him than angry at his disastrously timed arrival.

"Sorry to trouble you Mrs Seward but...""

"It's you."

"Not meaning to disturb you."

"Are you on your own?"

"Of course. You all right, Mrs Seward? You seem –
kind of strange."

HOOCH

MrsSeward look completely gobsmacked when she open the
door, but deep relief when she seeing it's him.
He explaining about the fella in the lift. Thinking she'd
laugh and welcome him in, but MrsSeward stand rooted,
staring blank. She look up and down the corridor
then beckon him in. "Well – we're going home tomorrow."
Ask him to pour out the hooch in two plastic tumblers
he find in the bathroom, wrapped up in cellophane.
A splash of water from a plastic bottle provided gratis.

NYINGGGG

So relaxed and cleansed such a short time ago, now knotted
with fear about what she'd ingested with an inadvertent
gulp, Freya closed the door on Carraday fixing drinks in the
bathroom while she quickly slipped off the wrap, grabbed a
blue silk dress off the only hanger in the wardrobe, pulled
the soft fabric over her head and wriggled into it, looked
herself hard in the mirror on the back of the door, ran her
hands through her wet hair, slapped her cheeks and urged
her reflection to get a grip. No effects yet, of course. Hang on
tight. As the door opened and Carraday emerged from the
bathroom with two tumblers of whiskey, she reached her
hand out to switch on the light, but then didn't.

"Look at that night," she said, went to the huge
glass wall of her room and its view of the highway, the palm
trees, the deep dark of the water, the lights of Dubai in the
distance. "Amazing, don't you think?"

"Indeed," he said. He stood beside her with the
tumblers, handed her one, his tree-like quality so reassuring

196

here as her heart's pounding slowed and she awaited the rush of whatever it was she'd taken. Together they silently admired this antiseptic viewpoint on a strange land, Carraday's piercing eyes beaming out like lighthouses. "Cheers," she said, tapping his beaker with hers. Her legs felt like jelly. She picked up the two heavy cushions which each morning the maid would arrange carefully on her bed only for Freya to drop them onto the floor. "Let's sit." She dropped them onto the floor now and sat herself down. Carraday carefully folded himself, like a complicated deckchair, till he leant against the bed, arms wrapped uneasily round spindly knees. Freya took another swig of whisky.

"God, that's good. Never expected it to be difficult to abstain from alcohol."

"I'm not drinking whisky in years, MrsSeward."

"Really?"

"Bad for my brain and body. Used to be relying on it to excess, other substances too. But this once."

"You're sure? It would be a shame not to celebrate our being here."

"I agree." And they drank again. Oh, the deep grip of it. And in this place of prohibition, enticingly wicked too.

"You were a drinker once?"

"Oh yes, Mrs Seward. Oh yes. Perhaps better not to go into it."

"OK. But let's go into something." She poured them both another. "Tell me... did you ever do drugs? Acid for instance, LSD."

"Did I ever?" He laughed his dark laugh. "It's probably why I'm like I am."

"Like you are?"

"You know."

"I drink a few more units per week than I think I'm supposed to, but I do find that I can stop it when I want to, so I'm not too concerned."

"My father heavily heavily drinker."

"You mean he had a drink problem?"

"He was a drink problem. A big, big drink problem. Let's not going into that either."

"Well tonight, Mister Carraday, I have a drug problem." And Freya took a deep breath and explained how her so-called friend Rosalind had left a tab of LSD in her washbag which she had accidentally swallowed when Carraday surprised her by knocking on the door. She thought he might laugh at her, but he seemed shocked and seriously concerned, looked deep into her eyes.

"How you feeling this right now, Mrs Seward?"

"OK. Normal still. I think. Well, maybe a bit... ooh... nyingggg."

"OK, ah – please don't panic. Let me being your guide."

"Excuse me?"

"Let me act as your shaman. I can be doing that." He was excited.

"You're most... kind," said Freya.

"Good. First: you might require some food, while there's still time." It was true. Freya was ravenous. They went down to the restaurant again for yet more buffet food, sat at a table by the dark windows wolfing down kebabs. By the time they headed back to her room she was flying. The space between the lift and her room appeared bafflingly vast, the patterned carpet a map of wriggling roads and rivers she might never manage to traverse. Thank heavens for Carraday guiding her through.

FORUM SOMEWHAT

"So you've had some success with the Vacuum Erection Device we gave you?" The orange-skinned man from the Society was reading Jamie's latest notes on the computer.

"Some. It doesn't hurt so much and the bending isn't quite so pronounced. The pump's not unpleasant

198

actually – except when one time my testicles got sucked into the tube." Jamie was dressed in a suit today as well, for the first time in ages, and he liked the feeling.

"Ouch! Now, I see we did stipulate that in exchange for the VED you might contribute to our forum?"

"I have a few times – and look at it regularly, found lots of useful information there – and I'm sure it's important that we who have this condition share with fellow sufferers or whatever. But basically I'd like to propose that you include a permanent link to a blog I have some involvement with. To broaden the focus of the forum somewhat."

"Pardon?"

"To cover wider issues around sexuality, masculinity – and health and ageing. A colleague of mine has been developing something I thought might interest the Hinchcliffe Society. I brought along my iPad so I could show you the site." He flipped the cover open, clicked the switch and handed the tablet to the guy.

"'Nearlysex'?"

"I wondered if the Society might be interested in working with us actually." The expert tapped and pinched the screen, raised his eyebrows and kept them raised, coughed, tapped again.

"It's quite… graphic. I'm afraid our budgets are all allocated."

"I was thinking more about a collaboration, actually, between our site and your 'Ed Space'. We could maybe frame it within a wider – and more positive – debate. The thing is, I have strong links to a charitable trust that we could jointly apply to for a start-up grant. And considerable experience of raising funds from trusts due to my experience in a senior role at the Council."

"That is rather different."

"Have you heard of the Tyler Jackson Foundation? It's only small, but their funding criteria emphasise innovation in the health care and what they call well-being sector and I do have… a good contact there."

From THE LITTLE BOOK OF NEARLY

Nearly Pleasure each other
with treats, a warm hug,
a hot shout, a lingering kiss,
a hint of kink, a fingering,
a giggle of guilt,
a randy remembering.

UNFATHOMABLE SUCHNESS

Freya couldn't get that Redcoat voice out of her head. When
words came to her she imagined the letters pouring from
her mouth and floating in the air. She described the view to
herself and the room was filling up with the description:
nouns, verbs, adjectives arising and jumbling. She tried to
think very simply in order to keep the words short and
manageable, but no, her mind was loquacious, garrulous,
verbose, blathering, multiloquent, deblabberous. To stop
herself making more words she made pictures instead, lots
of variations on herself, like cartoon characters. She played
with her singer self, her radical dancer, her flirt, her
politician and her adventurer, her supermum and singleton,
her brainiac and bummer, she stared at the ceiling and
watched it beginning to squirm with what she realised must
be the nearly dust. She was child, teenager, neverwoman,
everywoman. She turned to look at Carraday and found he
was glowing like the sun and she thought, "Oh god, I am
becoming absurdly stoned."

    And still they sat in the darkening hotel room and
he talked, his voice slurring as he carried on drinking, her
mind warping around his words. It seemed he was talking
about his drunken (sloshed, plastered, intoxicated,
inebriated...) father. And it crept up on her, and then it
pounced, the full narcotic rush, and it was all starbursts and
weird and segments of obsession with this corner of the

bedspread, this unfathomable suchness of the back of her hand. And his presence glowed brighter and hotter. The spreading awareness of each other's presences actually, their bodies' closeness, blood pumping to places it usually doesn't, and the brain blotting out all the usual, making a hiding place between them, redcoat and the magician, hunkered down in the dark like teens at a house party. She looked at him looking at her, eyes locking, that astounding smile sending out showers of sparks, and in silence she reached out to him, their hands not quite touching but massaging the space between them, hands and bodies closer and closer for what seemed like an eternity. Until the eternity was over.

And then they were touching. His face close, stubbly chin, lips like a sexy tortoise, tasting unexpectedly fresh, but he pulled away, whispered nervously. "MrsSeward?"

"Mister Carraday?"

"This is not right. I am your Shaman. I need do the good job correctly."

"Yes."

"So I mustn't take advantage."

"No?"

"No."

"I'm a consenting adult. Enthusiastic even. Albeit a stoned one. But I can handle that." He didn't seem convinced, and neither was Freya completely, trying to keep hold of the corners of her unpegged normality while she thought this thing through. She desired her Nearlyologist for sure now, something she'd never/hardly ever, contemplated before, though his physical presence had become a good thing for her, a sanctuary. And in this time and place it seemed natural. Strangest of times and oddest of place, mind. But safe she thought he was, and she was freeeeeeeeeeee.

"No, really, it isn't right, Mrs Seward." He was trying to stand up, rocking forward onto his knees.

"I told you, I can handle this."

And then they were on each other again, making her glow and hum and yearn, except for disconcerting moments of reverting to worse than normal and a feeling of having a body made of cold spam.

But then the glow returned stronger than ever and she unfastened the top button on his worn white shirt and gasped. "Your chest!" He tried to cover himself, like a shy girl covering her cleavage, but she saw: his skinny body, covered with tattoos, crossed with patterns, some faint traces, others fresher. No, not tattoos – blue lines like scars, dobs and whorls of encrusted paint. "Oh my god. Let me see." She unwrapped him from his shirt and felt like she was revealing a mummified archaeological find. This chest with its white hairs, powdered with that coloured dust he always left in his trail. So this was what it was: dried flakes of poster paints he daubed his body with. Carraday looked like he'd crawled through psychedelic barbed wire. He had his eyes closed. And when she looked at the scratches again realised it's only ink – under the dry, cracked paint he was covered in biro marks, a dense etching all over his body. Which she found something like erotic in her new stoned universe. And later in the dark she unbuttoned herself and pressed herself to him in such a way as to cover the bagginess.

ROOT ITSELF

She touching the map of him,
the journey he scratching across the outback of his skin
overandover. The drawings he make to keep
the big pain out. She stroking them. He feel his versions
surrounding him and entering him, the snake in his loins
asking to root itself into her, but Shaman voice saying no
no way. They kissing and through their mouths pour all the
unspoken. Been a long time.

Brush of hair and press of flesh, desirous eyes so right
right up close. Her whispering OmigodsorryIneedtowee.
This voluptuous siren going off to the bathroom and
walk slightly stiff in the hips same as when she only an
elder shopper plodding into the Café del Mondo.

NEW KIND

It was later still and they were on the bed now, bridging two
twin beds actually, bit saggy in the middle, but she fully
high now, pupils large, brow sweaty. Carraday high too on
her spirit seeing her hands tracing the marks across his
body. And then she slipping out of the last of her clothes.
This was a new kind of free, nothing to prove, no
expectations, no map except the symbols etched on the
surprisingly suppleness of the old man's skin. This was a
man who'd done drugs enough in his time, as had she
actually back in the day, but nothing had ever felt quite like
this before. Free from her marriage, her country, her sane
mind, with a man too abnormal to suffer from any normal
inhibition or guilt. And now the acid was happening like she
remembered it used to. And one moment he was the most
beautiful angel man she'd ever clapped eyes on, her body
more succulent than it had ever been in youth. And now she
was a blobby pink jelly and he was bare-chested, barefoot
and stick thin. Blancmange and a bag of bones. She became
aware of the bulge in his trousers, an exclamation mark
sticking up out of him in a surprised sort of way. And she
considered this surely the cockiest cock she'd ever come
across the cock cockcock like clock by the bedside became
and far more more interesting, so filled with its clockness it
was, and the two words sort of rhymed which was also
fascinating and ordained and she could lie here beside his
trousers full of exclaiming appendage wondering how it
would feel rooting about in her and she could think

anything   go   anywhere   tictoctictoc   the clockclockclockclockclockclock.

Surrounded by a drizzle of white sparks. A fizzing hiss. Like a gripping dream as all memory evaporates except the remnant of a hunch. This snow of possibilities which could turn to hot ash and burn them up. Needs controlling which is what he does with his spells and cutting-up shit. Pacify. When you walk past houses in the early hours and feel them ache with the energy stored there – all those happenings to come. Here Carraday and Freyaseward arise in their nearly form, sculpting the speckled air, making pillars of it, spirals, whorls of it, thrones of it for the palace of their nearlydom. Autumn leaves of almost to kick and hurl. O the gibberish. O the lunacy. She was holding back laughter. Old people contemplating love was ridiculous, far too old to spirit away the everyday, these two couldn't slide into sexuality, like luscious fish sleek into a stream, they were too bloody clumpingly real. So deeply embarrassing. And she could feel every drop of desire dry up. Ah but hum but O but the buzz of it. Close her eyes and she's anybodyanywhere. But he so feverishly keen, the horny old howsyerfather. Who'd have thought? O dear.

"Mister Carraday, I'm sorry."

"Yes, MrsSeward?"

"I don't want us to actually... I'm sorry." Now the atmosphere shifts with a whoosh.

"No no, this is right and fine. Whatever you wishing. Absolutely."

"But it's lovely like this, being bare beside you."

"Whatever you wishing."

"Whatever *we're* wishing.... Doodle me. Please."

Now it was later much later and she was naked on her front on the bed and he was straddling her, bare except for his suit trousers which itched her thighs a little as he bent down and drew on her as she'd asked him to with the free

204

ballpoint pen they'd found in the drawer. And sometimes it was rather nice being drawn on and sometimes tickled like mad and sometimes it hurt like she wanted more hurting in a bite me spank me kinky kind of way and sometimes ouch it hurt in a will you please stop that immediately way. Which he did and said sorry. Is that all right? And now it tickled like mad again and she giggled and jiggled. Which burst the bubble of the ritual utterly. And now all was cold, this strange old man on top of her, in this insane place, probably men outside the door in white robes, holding Kalashnikovs or scimitars. She was scared now, shaking slightly, and Carraday noticed and said, "Are you chilly, MrsSeward?" climbed off her and then pulled the duvet down to cover them.

Now she stood in front of the mirror and her body too was covered inky lines, a map of a nearlyplace, a tree of all the ones she might have been, emanations of those she could have been expressed in symbols she might decipher if she tried very hard.

Now some tide turned and whoosh again she was missing Jamie and his body and their old house, and her homeland, and everything Englishly familiar. Carraday was weird like that creepy guy at a campsite when she was thirteen, the stubbly, stocky farmer who called her into his office to give her a box of eggs from his chickens to take to her mum, then stood close to her for far, far too long, her clutching the box of white eggs, him breathing hard, smelling of mould and diesel, lost in some furtive depths she couldn't fathom, then she slipped free and said thank you and was gone, the moment quivering in a shameful corner of her sexual memory ever after.

Neither spoke a word and both breathed many sighs of relief when they realised there was no need to. They lay together in the dark until at some point each of them slept a little, then awoke to lie awake again, her paralysed with complexity and almost high on guilt. Carraday got up in the night to go wee. His scrawny body, willy dangling,

205

head not as bald as she'd assumed it was under that bloody hat he seemed to have chucked out at last. Then he slipped back into bed again and held her tight and stroked her hair, her back. The vibrations of attraction. She felt cherished like she hadn't felt for years, the opposite of how she might have been, the baggy older woman in the bed of young Dan. She felt safe as she slipped away into sleep.

Awoke when the bedroom door clicked shut and he stood above her fully clothed again, smelling of the baked street. "I taken the liberty of putting a Do Not Disturb sign outside. Fetched you some breakfast." He'd bought boxes of orange juice, a bunch of bananas he'd washed in case, a box of figs which seemed somehow appropriate. Eat Me.

"What a good Mister Shaman."

"Thank you MrsSeward."

She woke up again and found him staring at her with those deep dark green eyes of his. Looking at her like she was some kind of treasure.

"I want to show you, Mrs Seward." He was on his knees opening a suitcase he'd fetched from his room next door, inside was his collection. He pulled out the hefty old laptop, opened up screen after screen of his peculiar creations, talismans made of plastic toys fused with sticks of wood, covered in patterns scribbled in biro; a lamb bone attached to a broken doll's head and a body of mushed-up paper... "Manifestations insist themselves out of me, and I trying to make one photographic image of each one before it goes. Then the original I consume in fire, or make disappear by various means. I never meant to keep the pictures. Better to let them go completely. But lately, since you been a presence, I feel that I ought to. You – encourage me."

"Mister Carraday – Gregory. I mean these are... remarkable." They kind of were. And the story was good too, what a great narrative: The Outsider Artist making work for nobody to see. He was more animated than she'd ever seen him, spiky limbs flying about, words tumbling forth.

"I made spells on my Mumma's behalf, to try to make him to stop. I wrote bad words on me. Never let him see, burned them up before he had a chance. And charms for Mumma. If she knew she'd think I was barking mad. But it's Boomer who telling me, helps me dig the holes."

Freya catches sight of herself in the mirror, a moment of realisation: this is happening, has irreversibly happened. In bed with this... man proving himself before her very eyes to be an absolute weirdo. That's a terrible thing to think. This person with issues. This wild-eyed bag of bones. Carraday proudly displaying a stream of bright colour photos of the strangest amalgamations: pen lids and bits of mobiles and string tied round and round then wax dripped on then dabbed with bits of paint and lumps of papier-mâché. Which she can see now in a white-walled gallery, on a plinth, untitled, mixed media, a red spot showing it's been sold for pretty pennies and she's showing a client round under a very stylish black and white photo of the Artist Himself and at the front desk a neat stack of the catalogues of this important maker of Art Brut.

"I love them, Mister Carraday. You shouldn't throw them away."

"I photo each like this before, but I make them to bury them, MrsSeward. That the whole point."

"Maybe from now on though you could keep the object and throw away the bad energy?"

He shook his head.

"Worth trying, perhaps? You could make an incantation, make the dust of the Nearly but keep the amulet? To ward off bad stuff."

"You believe I should continue making them though? You don't think they're a complete...?"

"Not at all!"

"You believe they ward off the most negative aspects of our Nearly thoughts?"

"Well, perhaps." He closed the heavy, battered laptop, swaddled it carefully in the scarf, padded over to his open suitcase, placed it carefully in and snapped the lock closed, slid back into bed shyly. "I'll carry on as ever I think if you don't mind." Looking like he wished he hadn't showed her now.

"Tomorrow – oh god! – back to the UK. Mustapha's ordered us each a cab. Shall we make our own way to the airport? Don't be late though – and don't forget your passport," she said in a rush of efficiency, but then reached out her hand, stroked his wild hair into place. "You're an amazing man." He smiled proudly.

The next time she woke up, he was gone. She rolled over and slept again until 11.30. In the shower she washed and scrubbed herself until all ink traces were gone, then packed up. There was no sign of Carraday in the foyer or the restaurant, no answer when she called his room from reception. The wooziness of the drug was gone mostly except for occasional surges. Sitting in the back seat of the car taking her to the airport, she tried not to worry about him, refusing conscious thought about the night before. She went nervously through customs and security, then queued to buy a paper cup of coffee. Carraday was at the gate. Freya noted in a glimpse that he looked flushed and dusty. He avoided Freya's eyes and she didn't go to great lengths to catch his glance either, in the cold light of air conditioned, UAE day.

On the flight home to Heathrow she watched movie after movie, catching up on old favourites and recent releases, but kept falling asleep and dreamt Daniel Craig and Jamie were fighting a savage Paddington Bear. Carraday sat rigid, staring at the seat-back in front of him, slept, jerked awake, looked ahead of him again. Freya slipped off her headphones and stroked his shoulder.

"All right?" No answer. Under the thick, woollen suit jacket, his arm was hard as lead.

"Tell me, what did you make of your foray into the real world, Mister Carraday?"

"Not convinced of the reality of that place. Not from where we were."

208

"Excuse me?"

"That not being the real world at all."

She felt a bit hurt. Hadn't she brought about this opportunity for Carraday to experience this brave new place? Hadn't she opened her arms and more to him and still he felt as distant.

"But didn't you think it was amazing to hear the call to prayer? To see Islam in action. Shed a whole new light on it all for me. Made it real, bizarre but normal too. A place I 'know' now."

"I think that's very strange if I'm honest." Then he laughed. "But then, Mrs Seward, I am very strange."

"But you're not, you're original, intelligent, brave."

"Me? Very strange. Believe me." He closed his eyes. It seemed this topic was not up for discussion.

NICE HANDS

When Freya first met Jamie all those years ago, she nearly fell in love with him for his bearlike sex appeal and dry sense of humour and nice hands. Instead, she loved him for helping her pick her first electric guitar, showing her how to shape a few chords, saying he loved the agitprop lyrics that she scrawled in her notebook, and which he helped turn into angry pop songs. Then when she started thinking this big blonde bear of a guy might be the one for her, he'd do that thing with his eyes, his face all hangdog, staring at her as if he'd burst with sorrow if she didn't give him a hug. That pissed her off, because he was cramping her right to be who the hell she wanted to be. But she also couldn't resist hugging him back, which of course meant soon afterwards they were in bed, which was pleasurable. But her heart resisted all that yearning and neediness. Yes, she was a bit screwed up then and reverted to screwing around and why not at that age? She spent a lot of time being hit on by zonked male musicians, being the sexy lead singer, a role which was flattering and scarily exhilarating when it wasn't a drag, all that fending off of men, the leering and pestering. And when she stopped fending off and let things happen, these acts were seldom as hot as anticipated, involving aches and stains and stickiness and boredom and walking home too late at night – although once or twice, well...yes, pleasurable. Then lonely.

But she loved being single and a band member, no ties to stop her working late on riffs and solos, struggling for hours to get that hefty electric guitar to stop whining and make a pleasing noise for her. Designing the posters and the clothes she wore, dyeing and patching and painting herself as a punk rock goddess, phoning up venues and bullying the others to get there on time – all that was rewarding. On a good night she basked in live performance, though it petrified and drained her, the nerves beforehand, the eyes drilling into her body, all the gyrating and snarling she needed to do as she struggled to play the right notes. And she loved that she could spend all day reading a Margaret Atwood novel and this counted as research for material for a song she was supposed to be working on. Freya was resistant to commitment for politically sound and perhaps other reasons.

On the day Freya discovered that what she'd thought might be a weird allergic reaction or a dose of flu was actually first signs of a pregnancy, she arrived at Jamie's place intending to confess all, to tell him she was going to have an abortion, and expecting the news to result in a big fight and the end of their relationship. He answered the door to her with his guitar round his neck.

"Hiya. Do you know the chords to Stand Down Margaret?" He threw the stub of a still smoking roll-up over her head into the street.

"C, G, D, B minor...? I don't know. Anyway I'm not in your poxy band any more." He stepped aside and as she passed, Freya reached up and over his guitar to kiss him on the lips, which pleased him.

"Why? Is the band going to cover it? "

"Might." He called through to Martin, "Try B minor."

"Nah, sounds all wrong," called the bass player from the bowels of the house.

"Shit idea. And he's way out of tune," said Freya.

"Might not. Might use the chords with a different melody."

"OK. Even more shit idea. Hey, we need to talk."

"Yeah? You pregnant or what?" He was joking of course.

"Yeah. I am." Silence. "Like I said, we need to talk." And now he was standing open-mouthed. Like, literally. She'd never seen that before. Freya was building up to bursting into tears, but Jamie got there first. As Martin walked through from the back of the house strumming, Jamie howled with joy and flung his big arms around her. Poor Martin looked about to faint.

'Wow. That's like. Wow. Shit. Wow," he gabbled. Jamie was singing, "I'm going to be a dad! I'm going to be a father!"

"Woaw!" said Martin, shocked. His friend was running around now, dancing from side to side like he was in a very clumpy production of West Side Story. Martin began playing the two chords over and over. "Dance, Daddy, Dance!" he sang, "Dance, Daddy, Dance!" Martin sang as tears streamed down Jamie's big face. And Freya didn't have the nerve to produce her mauve A4 hardback poetry notebook which she'd been using to write down the address and details of the abortion clinic. Later "Dance Daddy Dance" briefly became one of their most popular songs, an upbeat dance number that could be spun out for up to fifteen minutes with plenty of solos if people were dancing enough and they'd run out of new material: *out of nowhere someone come / the tip tap tip of ten new toes / beat the soft drum / beat beat / our baby come.*

Freya hummed the tune as she rested her head against the window of the taxi. She didn't think about the past very often, unlike her ex, who moped about in his memory daily like it was a huge park very near where he lived in which he could roam around freely, discovering different pathways through it and interesting places to stop and drink coffee along the way. For Freya, life was more like a novel she wouldn't dream of reading twice, or a movie – currently turning into a bit of a thriller she was shocked to find, and so she wanted to know what was going to happen next, not what else might have happened differently before. To be honest she found it hard to think of her own experience in terms of nearly other things, even though she saw the potential marketability of nearlyness in relation to all kinds of digital issues. When strong feelings did assail her, like lust or whatever it was she felt for the bloke at that conference whose name – Dan – she had almost forgotten, the impact was powerful and disconcerting enough to lead to results, like the derailment of her marriage, or her decision all those years ago, hours after her pregnancy test, as Jamie lifted her in a bear hug and soaked her X-Ray Spex tee-shirt with tears of joy.

At the time Freya decided that her initial thoughts were some kind of defence mechanism, that she'd always wanted a baby and that man. Only now, in the early hours on the train home from the airport, jet-lagged and addled after Taqribaan, she reconsidered this and wondered to what extent the shape of her whole adult life had hinged on that mistimed announcement. A guilty secret she'd been too cowardly, or maybe too uncertain, to reveal. Did she have a child and a husband because she was too embarrassed to explain what she'd really meant that day? How nearly childless, single? And now so almost alone. Then again, had she spent the night with Carraday in Taqribaan because she desired him, or had she felt pressured, despite all her protestations at the time about enthusiastic consent? She'd been high on acid after all. Perhaps it was the drugs talking, a spaced-out aberration, or even an accident driven once again by a sense of embarrassment, a need to make something happen in that moment? O god. Luckily no copulation happened. But why did the actual actually matter so much? Carraday was right: so many things nearly happened or didn't quite, but didn't he see that what did unequivocally occur was so different, so fixed and definitive? O god.

"Hi Hon. Did you sock it to the towelheads and the men in suits?" asked Rosalind as soon as Freya appeared at her front door, weary in a flight-crushed posh outfit this early morning, trundling that business-like black suitcase behind her.

"You can't say things like that, Ros."

"But I just did."

"I mean you mustn't."

Freya intended to let rip at her about racist cultural stereotypes for starters, and then the trauma of the planted tab of acid. But Rosalind had bought smoked salmon and eggs for a welcome-home breakfast so Freya bottled out of explaining what the trip, chemical and geographical, had led to. Instead she told funny stories about orgasmic fountains, then washed and went to her room hoping to sleep. Dropping her case on the floor, she unzipped and disembowelled its contents of clothes, wash bag, papers, maps, pulled out the neatly wrapped present to Tyler from Mister Hakim. Tearing off the wrapping, she opened the box. And found it actually did contain one hundred hundred-dollar bills. Too exhausted to think about anything else that day, she pulled shut the living room curtains, dropped the box onto the floor, curled up in the familiar, musty embrace of her very own duvet and fell deeply asleep.

TRUST AND TRANSGRESSION

The next time he logged onto Martin's Nearlysex blog, Jamie found more comments had rolled in. He'd been promoting it heavily on the ED Space forum which seemed to help. A little world map on screen showed small droplets of activity from all round the English-speaking world: men were beginning to tell things – about their hard-ons and limpnesses and aches and pains and weird desires or lack of them, of their guilts and kinks and secrecies. Blank-eyed, he trawled through these deep seas of damaged masculinity. Shipwrecks of relationships, shoals of loneliness – and then sometimes men described what kept their love alive; they were bright little submersibles passing through the dark, they were bubbles containing lucky couples breathing the air of trust and/or transgression.

Some talked of having transcended sex – they'd given up on bonking but found a closer bond with their partners instead, some had found bondage and other love games, united in tightest embrace of late life kink. Some saw sex as a distant memory from the first flush of love, soon pushed out by work and kids and loss of interest. Some had split up and found themselves alone, miserable in bedsits, hectic with online dates, blissed out from evening classes in tantrics, tango or massage; others stuck it out, tied up in knots of silence and lived in unspoken, mutual despair; some had surrounded themselves with sex toys and trappings, some had simply cuddled up, and to their shock found new seams of the sensual in late night, lights out fucks and fingerings. Here he found ugly abuse too, and disquieting messages from the desperate. All human life. But was he looking at a lake of liberation or a huge new well of loneliness and suppression? It was all too much, all too confusing. He pictured Martin, Captain at the helm of his secret blogship, broadcasting words of wisdom to his brothers. How could he tell which of these might be closet abusers, bullshitters or borderline suicides? Sinking in cyber suffering. He imagined Martin summoning all these souls to a rally in a hall somewhere to share and engage in some massive emotional exorcism.

"Does Connie know about the site?" Jamie wedged the phone under his chin as he spoke to his friend whose voice murmured to him, sitting in the dark scrolling through the glowing gifs of heaving flesh.

"Sure. Connie helped design it. She was a bit shocked when I told her what I had in mind. But by then she'd been to see the Nearlyologist herself."

"And?"

"I don't know if I should..."

"Up to you."

"Connie told Mister Carraday things she'd never told me – like that she nearly ran away from our wedding. She told me that immediately before the ceremony a voice whispered to her, 'You don't deserve this. Flee!' And she had a vision of running in her wedding dress down the aisle and out into a field of snow. Except it wasn't snowing and she wasn't wearing a white wedding dress."

"I don't get it. She dreamt this? Or a friend of hers encouraged her to run?"

"A voice told her. She is very clear about this. A voice in her head persuading her, she shouldn't be happy with me, she doesn't deserve to have Stanley. She told Mister Carraday that last summer she was standing on the top of a cliff in Cornwall with our son in his arms, and heard a voice telling her to jump. And she says she very nearly did."

"But surely, not really. Connie would never..."

"Well – that's what I think. But she's convinced she 'nearly' did. And this voice in her head keeps telling her: that Stan doesn't love her, that she mustn't let herself love me, because she's a piece of filth for breaking up her first family."

"Carraday's planting ideas in her head."

"She says not, that he hardly spoke actually, that he sat and looked at her while she talked about all these negative feelings she's been bottling up. And then it was easier to tell me."

215

"All thanks to Mister Bullshit Carraday."

"Do you know what, mate, it feels good that she's telling me this."

"Oh for crying out loud. The bloke's a phony, a fruitcake, a human time bomb."

"She doesn't want a sexual relationship for now. I'm getting used to it actually. Feels kind of like a new departure. Thanks to Mister Carraday."

"Good old Mister Bollocking Bloody Carraday."

"You OK?"

"Congratulations on the website by the way. Hope you don't mind but I've been talking to some people about your site."

"Great. I want to spread the word."

"Actually I have a proposition for you, about some funding. I think you'll like it. I got an email from The Hinchcliffe Society. I thought they'd run a mile but it sounds like they might be interested in working with you. The only downside is my having to go cap in hand to my smarmy half-brother."

RELATIONSHIT

Since returning from Taqribaan, all Freya's demons had taken up residence in one small cardboard box under her temporary bed in Rosalind's lounge. Freya battled against debilitating feelings of guilt, drowning out those negative thoughts by consulting her Top Tips for Women Managers, her Things To Do lists and motivational podcasts which she played on her phone in the dead of night when sleep failed to come. Still the doubts would rise like mist on her horizon some days and she buried her head in the duvet and wept.

Rosalind must have been wondering why her friend was distracted and irritable with her on the pleasant afternoon they'd set aside for catching up a week after Freya's return. Amazing how winter sun can make the dreariest places seem delightful and ripe with potential. It was the sort of day when it's a pleasure to zip up your coat and see steam rise from your lips as you breathe, at least that's what Ros said she felt, linking her arm with Freya's and chatting about her plans for an exhibition of Foot Prints.

"They'll sell like hot cakes, Frey, and make my fortune. Or at least pay for a flight back to Australia and some frigging sunshine."

Here the sunlight faded to steely grey, streetlights began to glow then shine, the chill grew chillier. The two women sat on a bench in the park and talked until it was evening and the air turned harsh and sad. Then they strolled back into the shopping centre and into The Oak, which was quieter than usual in the bar as the publican had turned off the usual selection of Dylan, Winehouse and Coldplay in honour of the live acoustic music emanating from a room upstairs. Folky people, shaggy and geeky, with guitar cases and hand drums, kept arriving at the bar, ordering drinks then heading up to the events room.

Having made a vow to avoid 'relationship shit', Rosalind talked at length instead about an idea she had for a new performance piece involving steaming piles of Relation Shit. Which was good because Freya didn't want to have to tell Rosalind about her night with Carraday – nor about that box of money lying in wait for her in the dark under the sofa bed, emanating dreadful possibility.

"How come he wanted you there, Frey? Must have cost him a bomb to send you out to that conference thing." Rosa sipped her vodka and tonic, leaving traces of purple lipstick on the rim of the glass. She was wearing what looked like a second-hand wedding dress and pink and green stripy tights under a blue duffel coat.

Now Freya took a glug of warm white wine and prepared to answer questions. "Well, I helped promote his company, showed he has a social conscience, that he's switched on about digital possibilities. I think I was good value."

"And he didn't expect to shag you."

"Tyler wasn't there – I told you, and of course he didn't, Rosa. Is it so hard for you to believe that I might actually be good for his business?"

"Oh yeah, you're too old for anything else of course? Sure. Except you are actually still quite hot in your wrinkly way. So how is it now you're back?"

"It's good. I'm working very closely with Tyler."

Rosalind raised an eyebrow.

"Stop it!" said Freya, laughing. She explained to her sceptical friend that since the Taqribaan trip Tyler Jackson had gone into overdrive helping her to fundraise for the Nearly Project, taking her off in taxis for meetings with CEOs of start-ups and corporates.

But it was a bit strange. Increasingly he treated her like an employee. Although Freya was introduced as running a "marvellous community project to which we're giving a helping hand", the conversation moved swiftly onto other topics and she was left gazing out of the window at whatever stunning view of the river or park or London cityscape the boss had made sure his office overlooked. So far none of these high-flyers had been women. Tyler and the CEO talked business together while she sat there like a lemon. When the men ran out of steam Tyler would raise the possibility of sponsorship for her Nearly Project, Freya would trot out the same spiel each time about her plans, but the response was minimal. Her role was, she felt, to make smart remarks about social networking and social responsibility, but mostly to shut up and smile. The thing is, she quite enjoyed it, in a horrible way. There was a skill to facilitating good networking between Tyler and these various movers and shakers, associating him with the right mix of benevolence and pragmatism. Quite what the meetings were supposed to achieve eluded her.

"I mean, what was the point of that?" she asked Tyler directly, in the taxi back to the office, after one lavish lunch which he'd bought for a chief executive of Something International. "The sea bream was delicious and he seemed friendly in a fishy sort of way, but why spend all that money?" At the restaurant she'd taken a peek at the bill before Tyler slapped down his gold credit card on top it, and she'd been appalled. The fish wasn't *that* bloody tasty.

"Relationship building, my dear." He brushed crumbs off his stripy tie and cradled his stomach cheerfully. "He had some invaluable insights I thought." Relationshit. She wanted to ask if any of these companies were actually going to sponsor her project, but she couldn't. Freya hadn't actually told Tyler about the money in the box, not yet. Mister Jackson hadn't mentioned Mister Hakim nor given a clue that he was expecting a gift from his Taqribaan contacts. Freya had pushed the box under her sofabed at Rosalind's and left it there, trying not to think about all those notes inside. Anyway Freya could still tell him she'd thought it was a box of chocolates or something, which she'd forgotten all about. But the days went by and after a week or so Freya realised she couldn't hand the gift to Tyler now without looking dodgy. He'd look in the box, look at her strangely and she'd fall apart. So she still hadn't said anything. As Rosalind chattered, Freya stared at her vacantly and realised she was in the process of committing a crime.

"You feeling OK, Frey?"

"Fine."

Rosalind was looking behind Freya, eyes wide.

"What's up, Ros?"

"Don't look round but..."

"Tyler?" Freya didn't dare to turn her head. She could picture him at the door of the pub now, his charming smile turned evil, his henchmen flanking him, hands in their pockets, walking towards the two women. The game was up. She'd feel hands grip her shoulder, pulling her from her seat and bundling her out into the dark evening, then pressing her head-first into the back seat of a black car, Freya crushed between these two thugs in the muffled interior, the pulse and swish of the windscreen wipers as they drove through the dark, rainy streets, raindrops glowing golden under passing headlights. Then she'd be bundled roughly out again, down a side street and in through the heavy metal doors of an empty warehouse. She'd be struggling properly by now but these guys grip her tight then slam her down into a beat-up office chair, Freya screaming loudly until a big, heavy hand clamps itself over her mouth. Panic as gaffer tape is wrapped around her wrists, an oily handkerchief stuffed down her throat, some kind of sack pushed over her head through which can be heard the ripping sound of more tape being unrolled, then wrapped around her skull. She sits, petrified, in the pitch black, awaiting questioning. Then a dry metallic click, the cold barrel pressed against her temple.

"No – it's Jamie."

"Jamie? Where?"

"He's gone upstairs. I think he's going to sing."

TWO THREE FOUR

On a slightly raised stage, watched by a few clusters of people nursing pints and wine glasses, stood Jamie, in a pork pie hat and a sky-blue Hawaiian shirt patterned with palm trees and dancing girls. He'd bought that shirt in a charity shop in Brighton, but Freya hadn't seen him wear it since. He was holding a little guitar. As the two women entered, a song ended, there was a ripple of applause.

Jamie coughed, smiled, said, "Thanks. One more." And he started to play again, *a one two a one two three four*, remarkably confidently. At the front of the audience was a plump, busty woman with curly hair, dyed purple, who clapped hardest of all at the end of the song. One line of the lyric: *"you think you've lost the plot but… you're nearly there*." They couldn't really make out many of the words through the buzz of the heavy black speakers, the noise of pub tills, punters chattering across the over-amplified jangling of what she now saw was his old ukulele. But it sounded… well, like real music again, not like the punk frenzy of The Longstockings, more like a musician playing at a folk night. A bit of a shock, really. And then Jamie looked over and saw them too. He smiled and carried on singing with only a slight glitch in the rhythm. Another ripple of applause and he said, "thankyouverymuchmyname'sjamiethankyouandgoodnight" and then went to sit next to the plump woman, put his arm briefly on her shoulder, said a few words in her ear, nodding in their direction, picked up his pint and waddled over to their table.

"Well, hello! Didn't expect to see you here."

Still reeling from shock, Freya turned away, then felt bad, wanted to say something nice about his act, couldn't think of anything that sounded quite right, felt angry that she felt guilty, and so kept quiet while Rosalind did the chatting.

"Who's your friend, you secret superstar you?"

"Oh," Jamie blinked, waved an arm vaguely. "She's a regular at these gigs. She's from Rimini." As if that explained everything.

"You don't speak Italian."

"We get by."

"Cool. By the way Jay, I saw that mate of yours – Clunky? – the other day, over from the USofA. He asked after you. Seemed keen to make contact again," Rosalind said, eyeing up this new Italian woman rather too blatantly.

"Really?' Jamie frowned. "Was Chunk staying with you, Frey?"

"No – I've been away – you know that. United Arab Emirates. I didn't even know he was around. You didn't mention that, Ros."

"Slipped my mind. I bumped into him in the frozen foods aisle at Sainsbury's. Didn't expect him to recognise me. I only met him that one time with Martin."

"You are memorable if nothing else." Jamie glanced at her outfit.

"He'd bought fish fingers and baked beans and kept going on about how that was all he ate in the old days of your band. On a big nostalgia fest. But it sounds like he's doing all right for himself in the Big Apple. Grown himself one of those sleazy grey pigtails though."

"I'd like to see him," Freya said quickly.

Jamie turned to look at her, said, "You two were close back then, weren't you."

"We all were, weren't we. Members of the band, of the extended Rainbow Garden communal family. I liked that last song by the way."

"You two especially." Jamie glaring now.

"What do you mean?"

"You know."

Freya turned away, saw Rosalind's frown, wondering what are these two up to now? The exes were kicking off this strange spat about a friend from long ago. Dipping back in time, they were accessing the memory files which they'd assembled and maintained together for so long, recalling experiences which they'd very nearly shared, but both saw from their own point of view. Sullen rage flared up around old jealousies and mistrusts neither could even articulate. Now they'd broken apart, the demons of the past were freed to spring out from the fissures in their love. And they sprang with a vengeance, their old friend caught in the crossfire.

"Chunk was a great support to me back then – when you were acting the moody rock god."

"And to me, when you were acting the randy punk diva."

"OK, that'll do," called Rosa, standing up between them. "Home time, guys. Wish I'd never mentioned your precious drummer boy."

"Anyway. Good to see you both." Jamie tried to saunter nonchalantly back over to the table of his new Italian friend.

AIR WAS THICK

One eyed snake say Sewardwoman possess him make him
hiss. In the garden he feel her influence
baffling and freaking him.
O he know this is shit this voice hearing baloolah
but it aint half hard to shake off.
"You're changed, son. Have you got a lady friend?"
Eyeing him suspicious from her armchair.
"No ma. Not I."
"All right, Gregory, whatever you say."
He feel the nearlyness of MrsFreyaSeward,
the scent on his skin, the whisper of her voice in his ears
at night when dreams don't come.
He surrounded by the possibilities of her now.
In the Garden he burying all kinds of amulets
to protect him: a coffee cup she drink from, her biro,
chewed and rich with her spit juices. It not lust, though.
Infact lack of desire for her spooking him even more.
This devil woman surround him in imaginings.
All those nearly cards he gather and hide seem to be talking
to him now, all those possibilities tempting tempting.
Make something happen, they say, get off the fence. The air
thick as thick and no lyre bird arising to devour the dust.
Carraday itchy, his paint scratching body sore.

They were probably wondering about that woman he had been chatting to at The Oak. Like he said to Martin trying hard not to blush or sound a bit smug, he had met that nice lady at a previous Open Mic Night. Jamie was up on the tiny stage with his ukulele and music stand. The room was packed and extraordinarily loud; nobody was trying very hard to hear the music.

"OK a big hand for a good friend of ours... it's... Danny? No. Timmy? Jammy." A screech of feedback, a smattering of claps as he clattered to the microphone, fiddled with stands and leads, muttered "One two one two," then began to play and sing. It filled him with huge relief that next to nobody was listening. Soon it was over and he sat with his pint, as oblivious to the next shy strummer as they had been to him. Then a woman's voice cut through the babble, said, "Scusi. I am liking your first song. Bellissimo." He looked up to find a small, tubby young woman sitting in the seat opposite, corkscrew hair, apologetic smile. She looked vaguely familiar.

"I like very much."

"Excuse me?"

"Your music."

"Oh. Really?"

"Really – very much."

"I'm Jamie."

"Hello Jamie. And I am Paola, Your Greatest Fan." She stood, reached out her hand and shook his, squeezed back into the chair.

"Pleased to meet you. Have we met...?"

"At the Café del Mondo. I work with Beatrice – I'm the Other Waitress." She pulled a face then smiled again.

"Of course – I know you. Yes – hi." This one was always very friendly when she served him his flat white, maybe not as memorable as her slim, sultry workmate.

"The second song? Derivato Dylan– but also quite nice." Paola insisted on buying Jamie a bottle of beer and they shared a table to watch the other acts. Shouted bursts of conversation between numbers revealed that she had recently moved to London looking for work. Unemployment was high in her hometown and she found the place stultifying and provincial, although Jamie thought life in an Italian seaside town sounded fantastic. She used to go to bars at home where live music was played, sang backing vocals in a band for a while. "You know Ragamuffin? No? Like punk meets tango – meets Italian boys with big egos."

And the Open Mic was a cheap night out for her, a good way to meet English people and avoid the clutches of her extended family who kept badgering her to attend events at the Italian Church or Italian Bookshop in London where personable but uncomfortable Italian men would be nudged in her direction. Jamie was surprised when Paola let slip so quickly that she was single. When the next song ended and he offered to buy her another drink (which she declined), she chattered about the break-up of her last relationship with an ease that made it clear to Jamie that he was too old for him to register as any kind of sexual possibility. So that was fine.

Over the next few weeks his new Italian friend came along to most of the open mic sessions in various pubs in the vicinity at which Jamie would pop up and sing his songs. Mostly nobody noticed him. Sometimes the slightest dip in the volume of chat seemed to signify some level of interest. It was reassuring to realise as a punter that you could shout loudly to your neighbour throughout a musician's performance and still clock whether you liked their music or not. And it was also possible to be annoyed by performers who became irritated with the audience's lack of response. Having Paola in the audience to gauge response was useful as well as pleasant. She was certainly not an uncritical superfan; she took notes on his mistakes as she sipped her half of lager and floated amongst the punters checking how audible he was and what feedback she could overhear. Paola would hum along to songs she knew, and Jamie persuaded her to sing harmonies with him on a couple of numbers. Another night she started chatting to a guitarist called Billy who had long brown hair tied in a ponytail, played beautiful, intricate introductions to Van Morrison songs, then howled their lyrics tunelessly. Paola told him how great he was and asked him if he'd accompany her and Jamie. Of course he agreed. The three of them were beginning to feel a bit like... well, a proper band, sort of.

"It's so kind of you to support me like this, Paola. Really."

"My cousins in Tunbridge Wells keep telling me, come visit with us. I say to this, bollocks. I am in the land of Jam Beatles Ian Dury. I want to meet English people. Can't afford proper gigs in the city. So. I am your Super Fan."

"Well that's very nice. And part of my supergroup now!"

"Don't flatterer yourself. Super nothing. Words are OK but your voice is quite rubbish actually. But you are antique yes? That's OK. Tunes: OK."

This was ridiculous but it was fun, to be a man of his age and girth and baldness, standing up in front of strangers and singing his heart out. He stood still a moment and savoured it, looking out at a sea – well, a small pond, a pool, perhaps more of a puddle – of faces looking up at him, except for the ones concentrating on each other. That plummy blonde twerp was braying to his bored girlfriend about his new bloody iPhone for godsake. A young man with twirly moustache and thick beard like a woodsman stood right at the front and stared ahead oblivious, like he could equally have been in an empty field as a packed pub. Jamie checked the tuning of his ukulele with the gadget clipped to the neck which flashed green when the note was right, and arranged the sheets of paper on the music stand. He knew it was unprofessional to read the lyrics, but found it impossible to remember even his own words these days, or else he was too scared of forgetting them to risk it.

He strummed the introduction, then opened his mouth and began to sing. And he was music, was minstrel, was balladeer, was singer-songwriter doing his eternal thing. OK, he knew his voice was not great and the strumming was crude – like Costello, like Cohen, like Dylan, like a multitude of talentless people too. But these days he could try hard to do well and also not give too much of a damn, whereas in his twenties it all mattered massively, so that he had to act cool and pretend that it didn't.

At home he strummed and hummed away till words came, then scribbled something down and hummed and strummed again. The line was sometimes driven forward by an idea, sometimes one rhyme led to a cascade of others, the words hooking themselves naturally into a tune. One phrase might be heartfelt, the next was nonsense that happened to fit the rhythm. He wasn't expecting to make earth-shattering poetry, but perhaps fill up a few minutes of time with something that made you tap your feet with words that might stick in your head on the walk home. For the first time in many years, words seemed to tumble from him and he was allowing himself to enjoy that.

And was this heaven or hell to find himself back at Paola's place after closing time, to be watching her rolling a joint like he was back in nineteen seventy something? She didn't have a Pink Floyd LP cover on her knees; it was a laptop case which caught the crumbs of tobacco as she snapped a cigarette in half and tipped out its contents into the Rizla paper, folded up the joint and licked the gum. He knew he couldn't smoke any of the emerging spliff, though he hadn't admitted that yet. One puff of a ciggie left him gasping these days. But the smell of it was nostalgic, and the amazing openness of evenings like this, talking about music and the differences between their countries and all

227

that typical stuff, when he didn't have to get back to anyone, didn't have anyone to get back to.

"Broken English. That's how you say, yes, Jamie? This language so much of us in the world is speaking."

"Broken English, yes, that's an expression. Though what everyone really speaks is American, I suppose. I love the way you speak English though, Paola."

"Because it's funny. Make you laughing? Patroniser shit person."

"No no – it's sort of poetic, original. Broken English in Broken Britain. That's what the politicians keep saying we are."

"I don't like this 'it's all broken rubbish everything is screwed up' talking. Nothing is perfect and getting it better is complicated. Like learning a language is, right? I try I get it correct. Eventually."

"Eventually. Very good."

"For now, Broken English: trying to get by with a few words and pointings. Nobody quite sure if we understanding correct."

"And. Speaking. Very. Slowly. Just. In. Case."

"The English do this very much. Speak loud and expect us foreigners to understand."

"It's. Very. Late. I. Should. Go. Home. Comprenderoni?" She laughed and he rose from the sofa with a groan.

"You don't wanting this smoke? OK OK."

Walking home alone under the sodium glow of the streetlights, he hummed a new tune. Back at the house he tidied up a bit, washed up, caught the end of an old movie on telly about a giant killer spider, went to bed. Jamie thought, I am who I am. No one else to please. Have I ever felt like this before? I make my decisions, no one to boss or be bossed by. Waking up in the night he clicked on his mobile to find some soothing Radio 4 podcast to bore him back to sleep again. And later woke up, clicked on the Facebook icon to be confronted by a post announcing the sudden death from cancer of that nice finance guy who'd waved to him from his old office. Benedict was his name. Here were photos of the man as a boy, as a football player, as husband and father, messages of respect and sorrow. Jamie added his own. Tragic for the family. But was that it? Think "so sad", and then roll over and go back to sleep? No narrative shape, a random end out of the blue, a book finished half-way through. If Freya was here beside him he'd snuggle up to her, chat about Benedict a while, then discuss what they each had planned for the next day, then kiss and say goodnight and roll over and sleep. All the deep knowing of each other comes down to that. Love and understanding. In the morning he climbed out of his bed, dressed, snatched keys and wallet, opened the door, locked it behind him, stepped out into the road.

AND

arrived seconds later on the other side of the road perfectly safely.

He put his hand in his coat pocket, pulled out his mobile, found the contact details for Tyler's office, and hit the call button.

A KILLING

Mumma daffier than ever. She sit looking like a demented
chicken, confused, emptied, like how he feel quite often.
But in the night she sob and moan and fall herself
out of bed and he can't hardly lift her.
Ma Carraday is well crook and crooked too. Looking
confused always, affronted, like someone cheeked her
but she can't tell who.

Carraday in the middle of a dark wood try to get his head
around all this. He's been doing his thing filling nearly jars
with water to help her get well, grinding up old
prescriptions and sprinkling the powders in like Beechams,
with a needle jabbing tiny pricks in his fingers to make
droplets of blood to tint the water with, then go to a bench
in the park where Mumma once loving sitting, and he open
the jar when nobody looking and whisper into it,
then stand and write his mother's name in the grass.
But he knows he's kidding himself really.
Mum's dying and her son's a headcase.
Sometimes he take the serpent line to this TylerJackson
jerk's business in the Big City to sit by FreyaSeward at a
desk doing not a lot though they treat him like a someone,
Mrs Seward on the mobile always working her
business thing, setting up sessions, her looking flustered.
MisterTylerFlamingJackson been burbling on and on at her.
Beyond burbling; he pestering, niggling, flannelling,
all kinds of not very nice thinging recently.
"Mrs Seward?"
"Yes, Mister Carraday?" She say, that voice warm
mocking gentle.
"You OK?" Her smile crumble, teary quiver.
"Not really. Thanks for asking."
"Don't worry," Carraday say, wanting to go stroke her hair,
wishing her curled into him and sobbing onto his jacket.
And then he think of his arm round his woman proud strong
heroic. Thinking he can sort out this mess of that bully and
MrsFreyaSewards' sorrybrokeness. And this time he know
sudden how. His poor Mumma sick of living, she say so
sometimes in the night, when he lift her up off the floor and
clean the shit off her and wipe her good.
And this flat of hers bought years back with Dad he know
now worth a killing. Seeing it in Nearlyverse the story of
the Property Spirit how in his dreamtime
the House Man he full of gold, his lungs, his belly, his cock
all golden, and the Needy one creep up in the night and grab

230

him wrap his hand across his mouth as House he thrash
and wriggle some and twist and then go sudden limp
and the Nearly Man ripping open his stomach and pull out
the gold which he take back to his woman to help
pay off the debts.
That what he do.

CULT FOLLOWING

"I finally spoke to my brother Tyler. I got past his fearsome assistant, Poppy. My brother sounded weird though – I wonder if he's going bankrupt or something. He didn't sound happy. Anyway Martin, he said we could send him a proposal."

"It's a start, mate. But tell me more about Paola."

"She says as a new immigrant it's reassuring to know a proper Englishman. We go for walks in the park. We talk about... all sorts of stuff." The young Italian barista and the ageing Nearly Musician were spending a lot of time hanging out together. Paola spoke a great deal about her troubled relationship with her mother and how angry she was about the politics of her native land. At least that was what he thought she talked about. To be honest Jamie found her speech very hard to follow – the accent was strong, her English poor and his hearing poorer. But he was delighted to give his full attention, to look into her eyes as she smiled sparklingly, frowned dramatically, gesticulated Italianly. He conversed to her at length about his songwriting and found this very inspiring. She seemed to devour his words. "Yes, oh yes," she said breathlessly, like an acolyte at the feet of Jean-Paul Sartre. They could comprehend enough to realise they were, broadly speaking, in agreement about culture and politics. Like one of those deconstructed classics that featured on TV chef programmes, their relationship contained good ingredients combined in strange ways.

And his music had attracted a cult following in Italy, Paola assured him. She'd set up a Facebook page for his songs which every day received dozens more 'likes' from friends of friends of friends of friends of Paola's. The comments on the page were all in Italian; when he asked her to translate them, most turned out to be about locating good fresh parmesan and the high rents for flat shares. But when Jamie uploaded a new song to Soundcloud, Paola posted a link on the page and dozens swiftly clicked on it. When later Jamie checked the statistics to ascertain how many had listened to the whole song, no-one much had. Still, it was flattering to have such an active site. Martin was certainly impressed. He beamed strangely at Paola when the three of them met in The Oak, and spoke to her in Italian, in which he was alarmingly fluent.

"Una sola lingua non e mai abbastanza."

"Assolutamente."

"Yes," said Jamie. Absobloodylutely."

THE PLOT BUT

Another atrium of glass and steel, another icy receptionist looking up from her screen to point them to a sofa under an anonymous abstract canvas, another water cooler, copies of the FT and Vogue to flip through, and another glass elevator whooshed up to the Umpteenth floor, Tyler, Freya and Carraday were led down a thick carpeted corridor to an office where an assistant ushered them in to sit before another contact of Tyler's behind his – yes, still always his – huge teak and leather desk.

"I've brought along my associate, Doctor Freya Seward, and the eminent Nearlyologist, Professor Carraday. I do hope that's all right."

Of course it was, and the three of them sat together across the desk from today's Captain of Industry, Carraday silent in meditation as the others conversed. Freya did her spiel about The Nearly Project and the great work it would do with the underprivileged. The businessman smiled and said how inspirational, and then he ignored her and Carraday, but chatted at length with Tyler about colleagues in common, businesses she'd never heard of, and Tyler's links in the United Arab Emirates, at which point in proceedings Freya was called on to talk about her workshops there. All three men nodded sagely and the meeting concluded with a burst of conversation in which Tyler expertly referred back to issues they'd touched on previously and Carraday smiled and said something random and possibly wise that no one quite understood.

"The rhythms of the Nearlyverse vibrating."

"Indeed, Professor." Tyler told his potential client he knew the perfect people to help his client and would promise to ping over contact details by close of play.

"Terrific. Do let's keep in touch and all the very best with your marvellous venture." Handshakes and air kisses, then they retraced their steps down through the building, escaped outside and off to prepare for the next appointment. Carraday absented himself to do walking meditation in the streets around. The other two found a nearby branch of a coffee chain with free wi-fi. There they grabbed a sandwich and coffee and caught up on emails, sitting next to each other, hammering away at their keyboards.

It was becoming clearer to Freya how all this worked. In the taxi Tyler let slip that he was on a retainer and/or paid commission from a number of companies, most of them providing solutions to things: financial services, I.T. or human resources. He made his living by brokering introductions between these UK companies and companies in the United Arab Emirates. When some years back he'd been 'kicked upstairs' into a powerless Directorship with the company he'd founded, at first it was no problem getting his foot in the door with business people he knew. But as time

233

went by, those contacts retired or moved on, or realised Tyler was no longer the mover and shaker he had once been.

"Fresh corporate meat was needed," Tyler said, clawing the air with his fingers and growling. And so Tyler's team would find a good cause, research into contacts in the business world, celebrities and politicians too who might be interested in supporting a charity focused on that issue, and then, having hooked or almost hooked one big name, used this as bait to set up meetings with others. This could be valuable for the charities and projects, and some of his work was funded by the good causes, based presumably on results. But in other cases, the good cause was clearly sought out to help attract specific clients.

"Blue suits you by the way," said Tyler unexpectedly after the next meeting as they emerged from rotating doors into the street. "Matches your eyes, my dear." He was referring to Freya's new blouse. She'd bought it the week before when its rich floral pattern and neckline caught her eye in the window of a store she'd never normally venture into. It did suit her, and felt luxurious to wear. She'd paid for the garment with some of those dollar bills from the box she'd been dipping into recently, using different banks to exchange them for sterling and each time convincing herself she could pay it all back one day.

"I have to email Taqribaan urgently," said Tyler, eyes focused on his phone, scrolling through messages. They hurried through the throng of Central London. Pulling a fat black wallet out his jacket pocket, Tyler handed her a twenty-pound note and left her to queue for their usual order while he secured a corner table near a plug socket and logged on.

From her place in the queue Freya looked around the room at its hushed customers with slim silver laptops, headphones over their ears. Tyler was settled with his iPad, busily writing to his contact in the UAE. Could this be Mister Hakim? Freya's stomach churned. She paid, placed his drink before him on the table and sat down opposite. Tyler muttered thanks, took a sip, then stood up and made the universal sign of 'will you watch my things please while I go to the toilet?': a questioning look and circular swirling of a finger over his possessions. A curiously trusting ritual this, Freya always thought. When working in public spaces, complete strangers at neighbouring tables would signify in this way that they were about to exit the room for five minutes, trusting her with protection of their valuable laptops, their bags, stuffed with credit cards and cash. She had been tempted recently to grab the goods and run.

What Freya did today wasn't that. Once he'd taken the stairs leading to the Gents, she slid herself across to Tyler's chair and clicked the screen out of sleep mode. Here was Tyler's screensaver of his wife Di-di in a bikini on a Caribbean beach, the document Tyler was working on covering her chest; there was nothing for, by or about the Istanbulian in his in-box. What a relief. The email was to Mustapha though, referred to some "useful connections made at the Exp" etcetera etcetera. There was an enquiry about the name of the head of procurement at a travel agency. And then she read: "Glad FS was a hit. Badges very well received I gather!"

Then she noticed another email – from her own husband to his loathed half-brother, called simply 'Proposal'. What on earth? She clicked sleep mode and moved back into her seat. As she did, Tyler emerged up the stairs from the Gents – sooner than she'd expected. When he looked in her direction she was almost back in place, half standing, reaching out to take a sip of her skinny latte. Did he look strangely at his computer as he sat down, as if finding something about it had changed?

FLURRY

An A4 flyer in the window of the pub had his name printed on it. The spelling was only a bit wrong. Inside, Ashok the Publican called out to him from the bar with a matey smile. "Your band are here, James."

"Jamie – I'm bloody called Jamie."

"Sorry, Jimmy. There's a room upstairs you can use to stow your gear till you're on. We're expecting quite a crowd. It's amazing – I heard on the grapevine that with you being so old, word's gone round that you used to be a big star in the Seventies, whose gone mental or been in rehab or nick or summat and is making a comeback. Good for you, eh. What can I get you to drink?" Jamie took the stairs two at a time humming the opening song of their set and pushed open the door with his foot.

"Hello guys!"

Jamie heard a flurry of activity like a mouse trapped in a laundry basket. Looking up he saw Paola and Billy the guitarist standing apart, hastily arranging their clothing. He felt himself morph in a moment from megastar to member of the living dead.

HORRIBLE

Back at Tyler's headquarters Freya refreshed her lipstick and dropped down to chat to Gareth in his tiny cell of an office at the back of the accounts department where, she noticed, his two assistants worked on their Facebook pages as if engaged in deep economic analyses. She knocked on the door and squeezed past brown boxes of invoices and annual reports to stand beside him.

"Gareth, sorry to trouble you but do you by any chance have the budget for the materials we took to the expo? I'm planning an information pack about the project and need to compare print prices." The accountant went to his filing cabinet and dug out a file. Call him a Luddite if you like but he was a firm believer in keeping paper copies, he explained, though his young assistants teased him about the wasted trees.

He looked through the paperwork, frowned and said, "It's all in a bit of a mess, dear. Let me do you an Excel spreadsheet of the key figures and email it over." They chatted for a while about the weather and grandchildren – his daughter had recently given birth to a second child and he was itching to show off some pictures of the new arrival on his phone. Gareth was probably in his mid-sixties, and still a chain-smoker, "last one on the planet", he joked bitterly, face permanently flushed, teeth stained and breathing rusty. As she knew he would, Gareth soon referred jokily to his horrible addiction and took a packet of Marlboro out of the jacket on the back of his chair, palmed a cigarette and lighter, headed for the lift.

Snatching the file from his desk, Freya shuffled through the cluster of invoices, print-outs of pie charts, typed budgets with scribbled comments and additions. How on earth to make any sense of this? What was she looking for anyway? After all, it was Freya who had done the thieving. But she'd only dared to take the box because she assumed the present it contained was in thanks for something illicit.

Time passes and the longer that the anticipated bad thing doesn't happen, the easier it is to convince oneself it never will. The world seems so cheerfully as it is – why should it ever change? Like on a sunny day, it's hard to believe we'll ever need a warm coat. But then a tiny cloud drifts across the sun and immediately we shiver and curse our feckless optimism. Freya jolted in her chair. Gareth was looking at her through the tiny, wired glass window in the office door.

EMAIL HER

Hi Jamie, Sorry to miss you when I was over in the UK. I hope all is well with you — and Freya too maybe. Martin kindly sent me an MP3 of The Longstockings and I've been playing it ever since. Bringing back a whole era and I've been doing some thinking. Would you let me fly you out here to talk? Be great to see you. My P.A. can get flights on the firm, so you have only to email her to sort out best dates. Your old friend, Chas (Chunk) x

Sent from my iPhone

OVERZEALOUS

"What the hell are you doing?" The sweet smell of fresh tobacco smoke enveloped her. Flushing, she waved her hand across her face to cool herself.

"Gareth! You gave me a fright. I was... trying to make sense of this. Sorry. Way above my pay grade. Sorry." She closed the file, stood up, pushed past him to the door. "No head for figures. Sorry." And left the room. The receipt she'd seen for the little silver lapel badges stated that each one was made of silver, top quality. She'd been handing out free packs to punters worth in excess of one thousand pounds each. And Gareth knew she knew that – or at least thought that she might do.

She felt herself jumping into the void of the crisis. Like back when she was freelancing for the Council on implementing their tourism development strategy and the Doctor Who story broke and she stepped out of the building to find two reporters from the tabloids waiting on the pavement. She stood at the bus stop next to a guy reading the local paper, its headline, 'COUNCIL'S PR WOMAN IN TIME LORD LIE STORM'. There are days when shit hits fans, houses of cards come tumbling down. There's no time to think at all. She was on the phone for hours to the Leader of the Council, then the Head of Service, then a clutch of her best media contacts, trying to explain the mistake. She'd only said in passing to a journalist that the star had agreed to attend the launch of their youth strategy, when in fact she'd emailed his agent who hadn't quite replied yet. Freya had thought it was such a wonderful idea that the actor's office was bound to say yes. But the journalist was out to have some fun teasing the Council for its shortcomings, so phoned the BBC who passed them on to the agent. The agent had no idea what he was talking about and when she did find Freya's email, took pleasure in mocking the nerve of this jumped-up PR person who had fibbed to appear important. The journalist wrote a witty if scathing opinion piece for the local paper and then, oh so pleased with himself, thought it might amuse some colleagues whom he was out to impress on the Sun and the Mail, so emailed it off to them – job done. It wasn't a serious story, nothing more than a jokey *'And Finally…'* filler, with a headline to make it sound like a scandal about serious criminality; the article itself acknowledged this was no more than an embarrassing slip by an overzealous minion. Luckily the story wasn't featured on *Have I Got News For You*, but it did go a bit viral on Facebook, reposted by the Council's opposition group. For weeks her whole body was numb with embarrassment. Too tense to sleep, she lay awake playing through what she should have said and done, over and over. She sat at her desk again, unable to move. Then without letting herself think about what she was intending to say or why, she called Jamie.

"Hi." He sounded so far away.

"Can I come and see you?"

"Why?"

"We need to talk."

"We need to talk," he mimicked her spitefully, then felt guilty. "What about?"

"What about? I want to see you, that's all. To talk. Explain. I don't know. I'm sorry. We've messed things up. Let's talk, please."

"When?"

"Tomorrow?"

"I'll be away. I'm taking a trip."

"Really. Where?" There was a pause.

"None of your business."

Freya stood stock-still, thinking nothing, feeling nothing. She called Carraday next who, after many rings, answered the clunky old mobile which he only ever used to phone his mum. He spoke slowly as he walked, enunciating carefully through the racket of street sounds.

"Hello? Gregory Carraday speaking."

"It's Freya."

"I'm on my way home right now, Mrs Seward. Have Mumma to see to, sorry. But please – be having no worries. Everything going to be right right as raining."

STILL LIFE WITH CHRYSLER BUILDING

Travelling through time and space, on a plane to New York and the 1980s, scenes from that time in Jamie's life played over and over. He was back in a dank cellar, walls covered in old mattresses and egg boxes, a drum kit in the corner, keyboard, mics and guitars connected by tangled black leads. He was hearing the words and chords, which he'd scribbled drunkenly on a piece of paper torn from a notebook the night before, gradually coming to life as Freya sang, Chunk tried out a few drum patterns and settled on one that gelled with the rhythm, Martin fumbled towards a bass line. Music was happening here, harmonies arrived at, riffs repeated. And he was pouncing on the drummer to beat the living shit out of him.

Jamie played with the touchscreen TV in the seat-back. He changed the perspective of the map of the flight, he swooped his finger around the plane logo and the line of its flight behind. Then pressed the minus key over and over – – – – – – – – – – – – – – – – and saw the continents shrink then the globe appear then spun it till all he could see was the dark side speckled with tiny lights, then shrank it further until the globe was a bauble in the cold immensity.

"That's cool," said the young man sat next to him, taking off the headphones he'd worn for the first half of the flight. "How do you find that?" Jamie pressed his neighbour's screen to take him back through menus to the Flight Chart application. Then they fell into conversation.

"I was terribly lucky. A job came my way in Chicago – in social media?" Was that an actual question? Jamie struggled to hear over the engine's hum. Apparently not. "I met an amazing American girl – gave me a lift back from a conference in Brighton, and we fell madly in love. All moved a bit quickly actually. We're getting married – first child on the way. I know – how lucky am I!"

"How what?"

"Very very."

In a few months this guy will be immersed in nappies and night feeds. He looked so young. Jamie settled into advice-giving mode and his new friend soaked up the tips and anecdotes.

"And these days it's you and your wife on your own?"

"She's in your kind of field actually – I think. I'm a bit vague about what she does actually. But no, we're not together any more. It's a very empty nest."

"I'm sorry."

"Well, good luck with the new life." Conversation dwindling, he was about to put his headphones back on, then thought to introduce himself. "I'm Jamie by the way."

"Hi Jamie, I'm Dan, Dan Sampson. Pleased to meet you."

"You too." They smiled warmly at each other then re-entered the zone of in-flight entertainment. Jamie tried to doze but found himself looking at the back of the neck of a young Latino woman a few rows ahead across the aisle, winding her flag of black hair into a loose braid, letting it tumble, then rewinding it. Some years ago this would have made him ache with yearning. Now he had to concentrate to keep focused on her as opposed to the elderly couple behind who seemed to be watching movie clips of their grandchildren on an iPad. It looked like they were filming themselves waving at the screen, maybe taking a selfie. And there he was: distracted. It annoyed him that he couldn't focus on the sexually attractive even as he wondered at the appalling amount of life he'd wasted desiring the unattainable.

On the little screen his planet was revealed as a dot on a spec in a blur of cold hard foreverness. Night flight thoughts. On the small screen of the kid across the aisle Iron Man whizzed towards his foe, all set to wreck a few more multi-billion-dollar chunks of gadgetry and save the day.

As they prepared for landing, he looked down through the plastic window past the wing and the darkness to the trove of golden streetlights below, rivers of headlamps flowing through intricate latticework of streets, reservoirs, flyovers, sports pitches. Such extraordinary ingenuity was involved in keeping so many lit, fed and moving around on this big round lump of rock. The plane began its slow descent. All these people anticipating a bite to eat, a warm hug, re-entry to a cold home in need of heating, reanimating with lamps and recorded music, turned from a cold, empty space into cosy sanctuary. Out there somewhere in the dark were the transit camps in chilly deserts, the truckloads of desperate illegals heading over hard bumpy roads towards checkpoints and border guards. How many people at this moment were ambling home from the pub or a nip to the corner shop or a secret tryst or another round of the same old same old, stopping outside a house to glance in through the window at those arrived, at peace, at home? How many people on our globe at any one time are nearly home?

Jamie had come all this way from his home to have his say, to unburden, to speak the words he'd been avoiding. Confessions and accusations had been replaying in his thoughts for weeks, over and over. As the plane touched down he wondered if he dared.

At immigration the guy at the desk pointed at the glass pad. "Fingers." Jamie pressed his hand to the cold dark screen. "Thumb... Other hand... Thumb." Passport control guy looked at his passport photo then at his face. "Take off your hat and glasses. OK. Wow." The big guy looked him up and down once more. "A lot's sure changed since that picture got taken." Handed it back. "Sir, have a great visit." "Thank you." "Ya welcome." And he did feel welcomed by this rude New York warmth; it reached through his British reserve like a hand grabbing his lapel. Stuff was happening here: conversations, fights, clinches, exchanges. At baggage reclaim he saw the young man from the plane hauling a huge blue suitcase off the conveyor belt and gave him a wave. In Arrivals, Jamie found his way to a yellow cab past a cluster of rival drivers offering deals, gave the address and, as Martin told him to, asked that they go over the Williamsburg Bridge because the view was meant to be good. The driver shrugged.

"Up to you buddy."

SO WRONG

Installed at the Institute of Directors beside huge windows overlooking Waterloo Place, her drinking black coffee amidst this Georgian splendour, him on a small malt whiskey, unusual for him so early in the day, and a glass of water to wash down his Parma ham, salami, pecorino and rocket on French artisanal sourdough baguette, Tyler Jackson was talking at Freya Seward. Around them were the drones and guffaws of other huddled businesspeople, laptop keys clicking like locusts. She heard snippets of conversations about web presences and social media strategies from all around.

The Institute was becoming a regular destination for them. While they ate their smart snack lunch, Tyler took it as read that she would listen attentively to him going off on one about the rivals who'd done him down over the years, the Whitehall bureaucracy that was squeezing the lifeblood from the business world, the interventions from Brussels – "Don't get me started!" – that had apparently done so much damage to everything and everybody everywhere.

Round about then Freya lost track of his stories and began imagining which choice Australian insult Rosalind would use to describe him. Tyler was telling her another story about his new role in consultancy. "Probably the most useful thing I've done is raise some serious dosh for a children's charity in Azerbaijan. Helped to set up a foundation. I visited some of their projects, witnessed oh, such terrible conditions, and I'm pleased to say saw some huge improvements also, thanks to the funds I raised. We were treated like gods there. Of course I was working for a company which the press accused of exploiting child labour. Which, to be fair, was true, my dear. In my experience, when hard-nosed business meets the need for a feelgood factor, things can happen fast. I remember when I first met the Managing Director…" Some expression involving a dog's anus perhaps.

London shone like a glossy postcard outside the window, sky too blue to be true, today that pillarbox was pillarbox red. It was a day to be on a school trip to the National Gallery, or to be demonstrating, marching down the Strand shouting "Out! Out! Out!" Certainly not a day to be sitting here in luxurious boredom pretending to give a damn. But the box of bank notes from Taqribaan which she kept under the bed in Rosalind's front room was already more than half empty. Whether or not he knew about the

244

gift that she'd never delivered to him, Tyler seemed remarkably confident that Freya was in his debt and thus duty-bound to listen to his tedious anecdotes. People rattle on about the wonders of storytelling, but stories can be so, so, so dull sometimes, every little detail spun out into an elaborate, tedious vignette. "It was back in nineteen ninety three – no, maybe four. No – three. Spring as I remember it. We had travelled across the border in a jeep driven by an extraordinary little fellow. He'd lost his eye in a skirmish with smugglers..." The two of them were locked together, and this was intolerable. "Perhaps you met him in Taqribaan?" mused Tyler, leaning forward to brush baguette crumbs from his tie. He raised his eyes and glared at her with sudden malevolence. It was a gut instinct that pushed her onto the attack.

"Mister Hakim? Yes. But Tyler, talking of Taqribaan, those packs you sent over for me to give away at the workshops..."

"Packs? For the Expo? What about them?"

"I know how much the little silver badges cost." For a moment Tyler froze.

"Really? And?"

"Well. I don't think that's appropriate for a charity, to fund bribes." Tyler appeared non-plussed. "They were billed to the charity."

"Indeed. Which will gain from the benevolence they will hopefully help to generate."

"They're too bloody expensive."

"Expensive?" He smiled. Leaning back in chair he tucked his tie back inside his jacket. "Yes. Very much like the women whose chests we hope they will shortly adorn."

"I had no idea."

"You should see your face, Freya dear. Like a smacked arse. Did you think you'd uncovered some sinister crime? I know my dear brother thinks I'm a capitalist villain, but I expected better of you. The expenditure is completely above board."

"Really?"

"Utterly."

"Have you spoken to Jamie about this?"

"No – why on earth would I? Freya, I don't think you appreciate how much time and money goes into the nurturing of valuable contacts at this level. We're not talking local Council websites now, my dear. These people are so immensely rich that one can make a very good living out of schmoozing and flattering them, whether or not it actually leads to any specific outcome."

"So, all these meetings and lunches – may lead to absolutely nothing? Like those screenwriters who make big money writing movies nobody ever makes."

"I would prefer to describe it as a form of insurance: we humble citizens shell out monthly in case our house burns down or gets burgled. My esteemed clients need to be connected at the highest level, just in case. It's my job to reassure them that they are." And he was good at it, although how reassured they should be feeling she wasn't too sure.

"I think it's bribery, Tyler."

"Do you." He smiled, then stopped smiling. "And on that topic, Freya dear, I gather Mister Hakim gave you something to give to me." And there it was, said. But while Freya opened and closed her mouth, hopelessly seeking a legitimate response but failing to, Tyler simply carried on talking.

Freya stared straight ahead as Tyler launched into his next tale of another brush with the super-rich, this time in Brazil. She looked at the black railings outside the window opposite and pictured Tyler's head spiked on the top of one, neck bloody, mouth still speaking. Oh, the power of imagination!

In the street, a gaggle of school kids passed, heading, she expected, for the National Gallery, gabbling like geese herded by their anxious teachers. She imagined them as the vanguard of an occupying force. She envisaged the hush broken by their hubbub, a quiver of alarm as a flurry of strangers entered, then a loudhailer squawking and a voice shouting out that the building is being occupied. Freya Redcoat marched at the fore – not the messed-up, sold-out Mrs Seward of this miserable day, but the vermillion-clad, magnificent, imaginary one, marching at the head of a crowd of radicals pouring in through the shiny black gloss doors, the be-suited managers fleeing petrified as the communards swarm in. These rooms beginning already to ring with proper argument, music, animated conversation, people deciding together what was right and then making it happen, what was wrong and kicking up a fuss about it, banners hanging from the windows, communiqués being written. She imagined all this happening on old typewriters like Rosa's hefty Remington; this would be a revolution of silkscreen posters and off-set litho-printed statements rather than blogs, sites and twitter feeds. This would be Greenham Common meets the Diggers meets Hornsey College of Art meets Occupy. Midnight gigs on the rooftops, the re-formed Longstockings, like the Beatles atop their Apple offices, playing loud and free, their radical punk anthem *Stand Up, Sit In, Shout Out, Fuck Off*. To occupy: such a satisfactory notion, moving into a place to which we have a moral right of access, seizing control, spending days and nights there, living together, remaking the rules, deciding on the spot what to make happen next. This would be the forging of the Nearlyversity, the people taking over the bastions of power and refusing to shift, setting up discussion groups, seminars, publishing and debating new ideas. We don't need authority to tell us what an education is, we can make an approximate one of our own. We don't need a weatherman. Only a gust of a wind of change to blow all this shit away, and blow her out from this stickiest of situations.

"Excuse me, Tyler. I need some air," Freya said, picked up her laptop, slotted it into her shoulder bag and walked to the exit, weaving through the maze of desks. Half an hour later Tyler Jackson looked up from his iPad and realised she'd gone.

WOW

The taxi deposited Jamie in Greenwich Village and left him standing on the corner of – wow – Bleecker Street, surrounded by bags on the 'sidewalk', searching through his pockets for the slip of paper with Chunk's address on. Chunk Webster lived behind a battered door beside a graffiti-covered wall. Jamie pushed the bell which buzzed glumly. Nothing happened for some time, until the door slowly opened onto a vast expanse of floorboards, white walls, carefully lit corners and canvases, ceiling traversed by pipes and vents. It was opened by a large old man with familiar eyes. For a few fleeting moments the image of young Chunk was superimposed upon this revised version. Then the two identities melded into one. Thirty years evaporated with a sigh, and his friend was transformed forever. No doubt Chunk was also seeing his youthful friend morph before his eyes from young man to strange old guy. How cruel. And yet the thrill of seeing each other again was charged with the proximity of their past.

"Hey wow – well – wow."

"Hi Chunk. Yes, it's me. You're looking good!"

"Wow. And you...!"

"Older, bigger, balder."

"Well – Jesus, man, you're not so bad."

Chunk was fatter but hunkier than he'd been as a skinny youth, kind of distinguished too with long grey/white hair tied back, a weird squiggle of grey beard on his chin. He was Alpha Male Extra Large in an oversized grey linen jacket which complemented his colouring and disguised his bulk.

"Come on in."

How many times had Jamie imagined this scene in which he swung a punch at Chunk, knocked him to the floor and leapt on top to grab his neck and strangle him? But even on the aeroplane Jamie had begun to realise that he couldn't sustain outrage in this setting. Instead he embraced this portly chap and thanked him effusively for the plane ticket. Chunk said, "Hey, it's a pleasure man. So cool to see you after so long," and, as Jamie dumped his bags and removed his overcoat, they made small talk about jet lag and yellow cabs.

Later that night in a pool of light in an ocean of apartment, after a beer and pizza from Joe's round the corner, Chunk led Jamie over to the end of the room where two huge speakers linked via a mass of snaking wires to a desk stacked with recording equipment. After much fiddling with levels and inputs, Chunk pressed a finger to the keyboard of the laptop which sat at the heart of the tangle. Out of the speakers flowed a recording of Chunk's latest electronic improvisation, recorded to accompany a show of blotting-paper doodles by famous writers at The Drawing Centre, played at a volume that tickled every nerve of Jamie's body. "Wow," he mouthed, meaning, that's strange.

"Glad you like it. I'm relieved. You're a man of taste. Plenty of my friends find my compositions strange. 'Complete bullshit' is the expression they tend to use." He guffawed at his joke. "But there's something I else I wanted to play you. It's kind of why I asked you over." Click. A little scrap of song, recorded on a cassette player, vocals acapella, followed by laughter and thumping and eventually the kerchunk of the cassette recorder being turned off. It was the three of them: Jamie, Chunk and Freya. Silence. Next an electronic pulse. A single note swelling gradually into a fulsome chord, out of which the same tune emerged, but recreated with electronic strings, bass, congas, kit, swirling guitars... and then the vocals, their original burblings sampled, looped and enhanced. This plaintive ditty utterly reimagined.

"Wow. That's our song."

"Kinda. I added a lot of layers."

"Still my song."

"Exactly. I wanted to ask for your permission to use it. I think such a lot about those times. And when Mart sent me the MP3 of The Longstockings album, I remembered that night and a cassette I knew I had in storage somewhere." He too had been digging in the archive. "I wanted to play it to you and Freya in person. I was going to ask you both to come over, but I hear you've parted company?"

"Mmm."

"You don't like it?"

"Sounds amazing."

"I thought I might put it out on the album I'm working on if that's cool with you. I doubt it's a track that's gonna top the pop charts, but hey. If by any chance it makes any money I'm happy to split the proceeds."

"Yes, whatever." Chunk busied himself with the hifi, head down, fiddling with knobs and leads. Jamie prepared to accuse.

"But I hear you're writing new material yourself, man. I'd love to hear some." So, of course Jamie went to his bags and pulled out his laptop, connected it to Chunk's set up and clicked 'play'. They listened to a string of Jamie's songs, and Chunk said 'Cool' after each one, which Jamie decided to take to mean Chunk thought they were awesome.

Conversation fizzled then, and Jamie asked where he was going to be sleeping. Chunk led him to an area of the huge open plan room where sheets had been hung between shelving units to create a private space around a futon. There was a bedside table and light, a clean towel folded on the duvet – all very hospitable. He brushed his teeth in the bathroom as jetlag kicked in and his brain turned to porridge. As soon as his head hit the pillow Jamie was asleep, waking just as suddenly a few hours later to lie in the dark, head spinning.

The next morning they went out to the smart shops of SoHo, the thrift stores of Williamsburg. Jamie tried on hats, coats, glasses, tried the leather look, the denim, the besuited… they dressed him up and down. Jamie exaggerated the extent of his current musical exploits, chatted vaguely about the band and its gigs; Chunk told stories of hanging out with the stars, a stream of anecdotes Jamie tried to memorise for later re-telling, although they tended to lack punchlines.

"…So anyway, then Bob had to get back to the studio and after he left – Van stands there and says to Bruce, 'Bob: what a guy!'"

"Bruce. That Bruce? Anyway, not quite the same league but I was talking to Martin. Remember Martin? About the men's group."

"How is Martin?"

"Got a young son, called Stanley."

"Cute. He told me that in the email, with the music attached."

"Of course. So you know all this. That he's married again. Of course you do."

"He wrote me, yeah. Hey, I'm sorry about all this celebrity bullshit. Who gives a damn about these assholes?" Chunk's accent was wearing off gradually. Born in the Black Country, he'd moved down South to go to Uni, then later moved to the U.S.A. Jamie could begin to hear inklings of Chunk's Brummie and Cockney mingling with the Brooklyn twang, his voice like an aural passport, stamped at each destination, or like a fine wine at a tasting, swilled round the mouth to identify all the different notes and flavours that make up its character.

"I'm fascinated. Of course I am. But Martin said to say hi."

"Well as for me, coming back to England reminded me how much I miss home. Always think of myself living back in Rainbow Street."

"Rayner. Gardens," said Jamie, and realised he sounded mean and pedantic.

"Gardens. Sure."

They walked part of the High Line, a snake of reclaimed green slithering along old rusty tracks. In the afternoon they pottered round Soho and Greenwich Village. Sightseeing with a resident of a strange city was the best thing; there was no fear either of straying into dangerous territory nor of missing the best bits. Later Chunk led him down side streets, through small doorways into packed bars – one huge cavern of drinkers where he would have felt horribly self-conscious if alone. He followed confidently in his friend's wake, soaking up the atmosphere. A beer was handed to him, hospitable strangers appeared out of the gloom to pump his hand.

A cocktail or two later, mouth dry, head swimming, Jamie thought now or never. He had been waiting for the optimum point between feeling loosened up and too wasted for words. He spoke out of the blue, over the hubbub of the bar, and felt the words leave his mouth like whales coming up from the depths of his belly, in urgent need of air.

"Chunk, I know you know."

"What? Know I know what, man?"

"I know why you left the UK so suddenly."

"OK."

"OK?"

"What do you know?"

"You and Freya."

"OK." He looked down, stood in silence, then: "Was a long time ago."

That was true enough. They left the bar and walked home silently and in haste. Jamie was remembering that long time ago clearer than yesterday. He saw young Chunk giving young punky Freya a big goodbye squeeze as he set off to New York, scruffling her spikey pink hair and looking into her eyes for a beat too long, Freya curiously compliant in his bearlike grasp. They were in the doorway

252

of The Rainbow Garden, under a bare light bulb, next to the wall painted with blackboard paint and chalked with phone numbers and messages re. house meetings and demos. Jamie was next in line to hug his mate farewell, but for a second froze inside at the sight of these two in such close embrace, the flicker of something else in their eyes before they stood apart. Like yesterday.

Back at the apartment the two men couldn't speak or look at each other. Jamie went to the bathroom, locked the door, sat on the toilet for a long time. By the time he emerged, Chunk was playing a recording of an Indian raga. In the section of the room set aside for his collection of percussion instruments, he sat cross-legged at a pair of Indian tabla, tuning them carefully with a small silver hammer, then played along to the sitar, pushing his wrist against the deep drum to make it sing, tapping the edge of the small drum, correcting the pitch, producing rapid patterns which added up to gentle, flowing, complex rhythm. He didn't speak. Jamie settled on a floor cushion opposite and closed his eyes. The music ended. Long buzzing silence broken by a sudden gloop of siren on Bleecker Street. The clunk of some boiler system switching off or on in the bowels of the building. Perhaps it would be best to forget it all and crawl off to bed. No.

"You left the country so quickly."

"End of an era. I had to get out." He stood up and walked back to the kitchen area, opened the fridge and pulled out two bottles of beer, scooped up a bowl of olives. Jamie followed, took a beer from Chunk and they sat either side of the dining table.

"You slept with her, yes?" For the record, the suspect has his elbows on the table and rubs his face with his hands as he plays for time. Mouth still full of olives when he replies.

"Did she say something? After all this time?"

"I was clearing out some old files and found a letter. You slept with her."

253

"We didn't sleep. No."

"Ha." Chunk leans back on his stool and spreads his arms out like a comedian on a chat show.

"We all believed in polyamory then, brother."

"Don't brother me. You never told me."

"Hey it was a long time ago. And neither did she apparently. I could give you all the usual shit about getting stoned and it just happening. Take that as read. More importantly I skedaddled over here. She stuck with you."

"Stuck. Till now."

"Didn't stick, I mean stayed, enjoyed, had a child: the beautiful Philippa."

"Oh yeah?" Jamie stood up with difficulty, pushing himself out of the embrace of the cushion, needing some perspective.

"What?"

"My daughter. Is your daughter." There. He'd spoken it. Chunk seemed genuinely shocked by that. Seemed so.

"Hey – no way! Pippa? No no no no no no..." Shaking his head from side to side.

"You two had sex. Baby nine months later."

"No no no no. No way." More shaking.

"I worked it out." Stepping further back into the shadow of this enormous room, leaving Chunk in the spotlight.

"You worked it out wrong, Shylock."

"You mean Sherlock."

"Yeah? Like the TV show. Of course. Whatever." Chunk stood, walked back to the tabla, knelt and played another burst of beats, the drums making complex conversation, cajoling and arguing. He stopped and closed his eyes, turned his head to one side, pressed his ear to his hand like he was falling asleep or listening to the sounds of the sea in a shell. Old grey beard remembering. Jamie picked up his beer and settled on the sofa opposite.

"Maybe it was easy for you," said Chunk. "A one-off sexy threesome thing with your girlfriend and best friend. But it freaked me out. I had feelings for you, for Freya. I felt guilty about wanting my friend's girlfriend, about wanting Freya's boyfriend." He was still kneeling. He shuffled over to a bright pink floor cushion which he flopped onto.

"Felt like you two had chewed me up and spat me out. I told Freya I wanted her. She wrote me kind words about love and complications, but – you know... O God, Jamie, it was the classic open relationship, messed-up thing." He was splayed out like a paunchy starfish, legs and arms wide, a sigh rising from deep down inside. And Jamie settled back into the sofa, suddenly exhausted, chilled with shock from being here hearing this.

Charles Chunk Webster told Jamie Jackson how he'd run away from it all and come over to New York, hung around Christopher Street, tried sex with a few guys as well as girls. "I was targeted by a little cult for a while, a group who hung out in the village chatting to strangers they liked the look of, then took them back to what we called our clubhouse for... well, it was group sex basically. A clutch of us had slightly chilly couplings with each other and special guests in different formations. Breaking down the barriers of love. Except one of the tribe had herpes. AIDs was happening around us. Free love became more about the strength of condoms than feelings between people. The emotional mangle of it all. Couldn't handle it. You two were OK, back home, in your cosy goddam alternative bubble."

"Mind if I get another beer?"

"Refrigerator. Help yourself." It was going to be a long night.

from THE LITTLE BOOK OF NEARLY

In a crowded place make sounds

quietly.
Make more and more,

not so much that anyone notices
quite.

GONE

Clattering into the flat with bags of shopping, forager
Carraday bring home the week's necessaries, ready meals
and milk and the mints she like
and double sized bottle of white gloop she hoping might stop
the heartburn which rip at her throat in the night.
Gregory babbling away to the back of her head about the
queues and the weather. He dump bags in the kitchen,
click on the kettle, carry a mug to Mumma
yackyacking of the Chemist man sending his best.
And he look down at her
and she gone.
Her body still there sure, jaw clenching tight on bare gums,
skin papery, eyes closed thankfully, head back like when
she dozing. But she cold already, he putting his hand on her
brow like to check temperature, which she has none.
He stand there a longtime numb.

That it then. They be taking her, lift this flimsy body up and
cart it away.
Boomer whispering She need to be free. And so like he
planning for so so long he fetch his scissors,
cut the wisps of her thin brittle white hair, wrap it in that
sea blue scarf, spray it with the scents in her dressing table,
dusty rose smells he knowing all his lifelong, then kiss it
that bundle, then take out his lighter and click click click
till the wick flaring and the bundle setting on fire. Flames
leaping up and he drop the Mumma shape on the floor
where it quick burn wild.

Carraday watch the lick of flame amazing. But spreading
smoking now. Carpet charring and gunky. He grabbing his
greatcoat and walk out quick, try not to clunk on the stairs,
breathing and sobbing. Walk to the corner.
Walk into the wood. Walk and walk, picture the homestead
engulf in flames.
Down at the reservoir he stop. Wanting to stay still on one
leg for days but can only do minutes. Crouch he down
instead in the shelter of a big tree, down among the dogshit
and beer cans. Huddling in his coat he enter the trancelike.
Closing his eyes and awaiting the vision of his blue bird
Mumma fly free. No more dust on her eyes nor fizz in her
ears. Bird Mumma certain and returning to like she was
when she lovely and caring for him,
when she young and the future an undiscoveredplanet
she so eager to be reaching
and illuminating, making flame good.

NOO

It wasn't until he was on the train from Heathrow that it
crossed Jamie's mind that Chunk might not have been
telling the absolute truth. He turned off the Airplane Mode
on his mobile, turned on Data Roaming. Then rang Pippa.

"Hi Pip love, it's your Dad. I'm back home, safe and
well."

"Hi Dad, have you been away?"

"I told you – I was going to 'Noo Yawk'."

"Oh sorry – we're... Yes, put them down over there.
Bit hectic. Next to the igloo. Great... Sorry?"

"What?"

"Workshopping the new show. Polly Penguin on
Pluto. Working title. A hilarious adventure for children of
all ages."

"Sounds cosmic. You got funding? Bookings?

257

"Not funding. Hang on. Careful of those curtains! We're trying to be more commercial this time."

"Going well?"

"Think so. Revising the script a lot. It's all about global warming actually, but in a fun way. I feel part human, part penguin right now, Dad."

"I'm looking forward to the gala premier."

"And The Big Apple? Amazing?"

"You could say that."

"OK. Well. See you soon, Dad, eh? Love you."

"Love you."

"Oh – I spoke to Mum."

"OK."

"She's – in a bit of state."

"OK."

GONE

Next morning Carraday wake shocking cramped deep wet in the early glare. Shiver he longtime.
Arrive he backexpect to find the charred remainings of his home his mumma.But nothingnothingnothingnothing.
Except Mrs Nextdoor, mouth a red O of gossipy shock.
"Greg. I am so, so sorry. They couldn't locate you. Do sit sit. Your mum – she passed."
Seeing smoke neighbourlady found key under pot on the sill and go in. Mumma wrapped in shawl and stiff and charred Somekind of mishap with matchesbut the chair fabric was firewhatsitretardant.
Ambulance, cops and all sorts coming and going.

.

The big black telephone with its drilling ring and voices of concern with stories of how each friend being on the verge of dropping in or calling up for ages. So many different reasons stopping this from really happening.
Carraday struggling to be doing his best normalstyle:

sombre smiles and oyespleasethankyou.

O but he feel it welling up strong in him. All kinds of hokum. And the ghost. He nearly kill her, him, discussing it with MrsSeward, how he gonna help his Mumma out of stuckness into the nearlywhere. And this seeming so hatehatehateful. She gone.

He having to hide his workings, windows open for days to clear the stench of burn shovelling all the Nearly bits from the kitchen into her room and scrubbing the worktops up good and nice so that Mrs Nextdoor

saying it all so spick and span and beam at him, pat his arm approving like he a bloody six year old. "You did her proud, Gregory," she saying looking up at him with beady eyes.

And now what? Organising a funeral? The front room filling up with old friends and mostly their children, balding or plumping up themselves, events happening around him the cousins organise and not even asking him to say or do things, and others taking it for granted her hopeless son not getting it together.

Next: The Sorting. Black bin liners of clothes, old books and her leftymags. He taking them in boxes to the patch of overgrown garden and set fire to them as well.

Ashes to ashes.

He want to grind everything in the house down to dust and then sprinkle it, handful by handful, in the places she loving. But too much. The necessaries done, the neighbour sent packing, Carraday sit in his Mumma's chair

still as still. Then jump up. Take keys off the hook in the hall and round the side of the yard to unlock and pull up and over with a harsh metallic roar the door of the garage which he and Mumma be using for keeping her junk, floor to ceiling filling with boxes of it: mildewed stuff.

He fight his way into the boxes

of dross, of forgettables, stuffstuffandmorestuff of a dead one. And at the back, under a tarpaulin, to his amazement though he knowing it there really, the old VW campervan

259

his Mumma and Pappa use to drive down to Yugoslavia in
way way back. He yanking open the door, climbing in.
Tax disc from 1985. A key in the ignition.

From THE LITTLE BOOK OF NEARLY

Write an obituary
for who you nearly were.
Include quotes about you
from people you nearly knew.

SITTING DUCK

"I nearly went right off the rails when I were a teenager,"
said the buttoned-up, grey haired hippyish woman who had
strayed nervously into the Nearly Store that morning and
was sitting opposite Freya in the midst of her discount
Nearly Makeover session, holding in her hand like a hymn
book the five-point action plan they would be filling out
together over the next sixty minutes.

"And would you like to really go wild now?" asked
Freya as she tapped notes into her tablet.

"Ooh, I'm not sure about that. But perhaps once in
a while, you know, let my hair down a little."

"We can come back to that. And in your career, any
jobs you nearly took or whatever?"

"I was offered a job as a hostess once by a bloke I
met in of all places the fish shop. He took the mackerel
fillets I had my eye on and I told him so. He offered me a
drink in recompense, then made his offer. I was tempted for
a minute – he wore a very nice brown woollen suit as I
remember – but then I thought, no."

Freya looked at the clock. The Nearly Store had
been closed up since she'd been working with Tyler. This
morning she'd put the sign back in the window, thrown

away a mouldy sandwich discovered on the desk and a strange assemblage in one of the drawers, made of a hair curler, a battery and string dribbled with wax, one of Carraday's talismans. She put out the jar of Nearly badges and the leaflets. Soon afterwards this lady came in and, after a cursory glance around, started talking about her Nearlies and bought an on-the-spot starter session. Perhaps Freya didn't need Tyler after all, perhaps this was a good omen. But soon after the session started Freya's mobile pinged and up popped another message from her old boss/supporter/ and her husband's half-brother:

> Contact me. Today.

No please. No Tx sign off. Ominous. Threatening. As she tried to listen to this unlikely Nearly Hostess, it dawned on Freya that it wouldn't be long before Tyler thought to visit her office, or send someone to visit it, and she didn't want to be IN when this happened. Her new client chewed on her fingernails, picked at her Indian print dress and began to describe the career she'd followed instead of hostessing. Freya recognised that she was trapped now, a sitting duck for Tyler Jackson or any thug he might send to fetch back his money.

"Would you like to try working in hospitality then? There are plenty of options we could research." Ping.

> Or Else.

**

"I nearly... did a PhD in Lobster Hatching in the Isle of Mann. But I really fancied my Prof's research associate so I didn't go."

"I nearly... lost my mind but then discovered my backbone and became a yoga teacher (some might say I did lose my mind by becoming a yoga teacher, eg my mother who said, 'O my God Jezus, No' when I told her)."

"I nearly... became right-handed. At infant school my teacher (Mrs Robinson) tried to rid me of the 'mark of the

Devil' by tying my left hand behind my back. It would have worked but my left-handed mother found out..."

"I nearly... was born an Aquarian but for the fact that my mother sat on a knitting needle on Christmas Day... or that's the story that she always told!"

"I nearly...got married to a rich young man. His parents were very keen, my parents were very keen – but when we met he was too shy to talk to me. Later he gave away all his money and became a teacher."

**

SONGLINES & HUMLINES

He park up outside. Getting the hang of it eventually after stalling a few times and near miss with an angry lycra man on a bicycle telling him go boil his head. Pleasing to find he still remembering how this driving lark, but backing into parking space not so easy so the car behind getting bumped a bit in the process. Carraday find FreyaSeward in the Nearly Store listening to a lady who go scuttling off. MrsSeward seeming relieved.

"Mrs Seward, I've come..."

"To take me away from all this?" She laughing nervous.

"Well Mrs Seward, in a manner of speaking. Yes."

Showing her the van it belonging to Mumma. So Carraday's now. And it working. His cousin help sort out the paperwork. Carraday nearly forgotten that he passed his driving test years back, Brenda pushing him, ready for the big move that never. All insurance, MOT sorted.

Her nervous customer go hurry out real sharpish. FreyaSeward lock the door, come round the corner to view the van. Which they all going on summer holidays in like Cliff Richards in that bus, when him a kid. O to make magical mystery on the humlines of Britain and sometimes even onto the ferry and beyond, to the land of snails and onions and jenesaypah. O but how he wanting Mumma

to go swerving off sometime, thinking, let's vanish – going
awol. Like him in his panic through that night in the woods,
pacing and pacing, curling up in the embrace of a tree, coat
wrapped round, free but freezing.
Now they can doing it easy. Sliding open the door of the van
he inviting her to step up and show her the little built-in
cooker, the sink, the pull out bed, everything so dinky, like a
wendy house. She loving that. And a pop up top so one can
sleep up high, like he do with his cousins back back then.
"We could take Nearlyology out on the road," she say.
"Do some marketing." "Marketing?"
He picture them buying fresh veg and fish from stalls
in country towns.
"To promote the project. You can gather in more
Nearly stories."
"Yes!" say Carraday and he picture another kind of market.
Over the road a man in a suit been looking in at the window
of the Nearly Store, cupping his hands his eyes to peer.
"Can we go right now?" she asking
and that has Carraday gobsmack.
"Right now?"
"Up and leave."
"Well... certainly" And he open the door
and she climb herself in.

And they driving, him at the wheel, her beside,
rooting through her bag for a mirror and brush
she putting through her hair, then checking how she look,
checking too her phone each time it ping. Quick stop offs to
throw a few things in his suitcase, her backpack,
pile in beddingwashablesedibles.
Carraday having no clue where they going
but not wanting to talk in case she changing her mind.
Heading out of town see a sign for an M road and Boomer
saying M be good. Farewell. Bit scary when they get to it,
nudging through all the jams then onto a slip road where
having to drop down gear, speed up quick and

slot between lorries. Some hooting involved but MrsSeward
hardly clock it. She textexting in her phone which make
ping and whoosh as she sending her words out out out and
then get some in again. Another sign now: The West.
Wild one with wicked witches perhaps. And them in this
bulletbus heading off there as evening falls. Yes.
The mobile ringing with that old-fashioned ring
like Mumma's bakelite telephone having.
She smiling apology as she take the call and sliding to the
window side of the long front seat to concentrate, cupping
her ear so she hearing whoever.
Lots of earnest talk to follow, inaudible mostly but like it
matters. Carraday concentrating on the road and a sky full
of clouds astounding and all this green as the city gone,
cows and crops and freedom. Then he turn back to
FreyaSeward who sobbing sobbing.

SATNAVLADY

Carraday pulled over into a Motorway Services where he
turned off the engine and sat looking at her as if he wanted
to hold her but feared she might emit an electric shock if he
dared. Freya looked at him hard. Does he comprehend the
weight of her guilt, sat in her gut like a rock, bandaging her
body, pressing into her shoulders, poisoning the air around
her? She explained that it was Jamie who'd phoned and
they'd talked about the situation and it was all very
complicated. She'd told Jamie about her and Carraday
taking off in a VW to gather Nearlies and Jamie said maybe
he could come too and sing songs to attract attention in the
places they stopped in the van, and Freya had said, yes,
that might be cool. Carraday didn't look so sure.

"No room I'm afraid, MrsSeward."

"The pop-up top? Maybe you could sleep up there in
the penthouse suite and he and I could share the
downstairs? If it doesn't work we can always find a B&B."

"B and B?"

"Bed and Breakfast. Where were you thinking of going? Sorry Mister Carraday, but I was telling Jamie about our plans and he was so excited, and the idea of having music seemed... well, a good idea."

They met Jamie in a station car park. It was dark by this time and Carraday had been having a struggle finding a route through the one-way system despite the voice of Freya's Google Maps app delivering stiff instructions a bit too late to follow them, so they knew exactly how lost they had become. Freya had searched on her phone for campsites in the area and booked online a place by the marina where they could park the van for the night.

"Turn left then you have reached your destination," spoke the Sat Nav lady, and Carraday indicated left and swung the van into the forecourt. There stood Jamie under an orange streetlight, holding a backpack, and a soft black bag which was the shape of his ukulele. Freya smiled apologetically at Carraday.

"Sorry and thanks." She leant over and quickly kissed her Shaman's cheek, opened the van door and slid out to help her husband install himself and his luggage in the back of the camper van then squeeze and wheeze into a seat belt. Carraday stared ahead.

"Hello Mister C. Thanks for meeting me. You're sure this is OK?"

"What?"

"Me coming with."

"Hmm."

"Really. Very kind. And what an amazing vehicle. Has Freya told you that she reckons she was conceived in a van like this. In Sweden?"

"Hmm," muttered Carraday, stony-faced.

"It sounded like Freya could do with some support."

"She is supported."

"By you – yes of course. But."

From THE LITTLE BOOK OF NEARLY

Place a handful of nearlydust
on a square of fabric,
fold this up to form a bag and tie it with ribbon.
Wear this around your neck
And when the moment arises
bite on the bag.

CHEESED

Once upon a time in the dozing the sky grew darker and
darker with the energy of unacted desires and near misses
and urgent wishes and hard grief generating their own sort
of electricity which hissed and sizzled in Carraday's ears
and the Doctor called Tinnitus this music of the
Nearlysphere, the snowstorm of Nearlydust.
Shaman Carraday have an idea and this one a cracker:
that he set off to go travelling from town to town with
musician JamieTheHusbandifhemust,
and Freya Redcoat Seward the amazing and they stop in the
market squares and such other places they come across
and set up the plastic table and chair and put up their sign:
Nearlyology: Please Tell Us Your Nearlies
Carraday bring the Nearly Grinder –
and also have with him the purse of his Mumma's
he find in her bag at her passing. Good at living on
not much him. Jamie and FreyaSeward go stick their cards
in the money machine and punch in numbers till the tongue
of cash sticks out and they yank it and fold notes quick into
their pockets. Carraday watching Jamie's eyes widen as he
read the paper receipt which he crumple and stuff away.
Bit of shopping next for provisions, tins of toms,
onions, rice, coffee, fruit. Basic but good supplies. Then go
find a campsite and prepare for the Nearlying.

FLOAT YOUR BOAT

They passed through a village that seemed bustling with tourists and residents, parked the van by the village green and set up their stall. Jamie sang songs which helped gather a few people round, Freya dished out her flyers and did her spiel. Carraday sat at the fold-up table with the laptop and transferred the stories Freya brought to him onto their blog. Then he put the cards into the coffee grinder which they'd charged up overnight, and whizzed. Of course a guy from the pub opposite came over pretty sharpish to get bolshy demanding to know what was going on and if they had permission. Oh yes, it's all official said Freya with great conviction, a letter from the Council somewhere in her paperwork but not quite sure where. The publican snorted and backed off.

Not many people stuck around long. But a few who passed by seemed instinctively to know that this Nearlyology was for them. A young woman told Freya angrily that she never did anything nearly. She had no regrets. Then looked into the distance for a while, scribbled down the story of how she was nearly convinced to leave the country for a boyfriend who was two-timing her and intended to dump her as soon as she arrived. Freya talked to her for a long time, offered her Kleenex and a cup of coffee from her thermos before bringing her and her card to Carraday for whizzing and scattering.

Jamie encouraged them to colour in their cards, draw a picture to go with it maybe. It was all a bit bloody play scheme-like for Freya who instead helped them to write action plans. So you nearly moved to Germany? Would you like to move now? How about a week's holiday? Or maybe take lessons in the language first – or eat more schnitzel and watch Wim Wenders movies. Whatever floats your boat. Carraday overheard that, experimented with folding the sheets of paper into origami boats – another of his forgotten skills – which he placed on the surface of the village pond and pushed away into the water where they soon got upended. Actually they looked more like the contents of a litter bin than the Nordic funeral rites he seemed to have envisaged, so he tried to fish them out with a dead branch, and when that failed, he pushed them down into the depths to rot. Freya watched him and tried to think of the paper boats as her panic, brought on by each new *ping* on her mobile as another message arrived from Tyler Jackson's associates. She breathed in and exhaled slowly. Caraway's stick caught the paper and prodded it down. Freya tried to bury her worry. But it was hard. Especially later when the cash machine at the motorway service station ate one of her cards.

SOAK UP

At the campsite it was a bright fresh dew-heavy morning. Freya hurried to the toilet block in bare feet over chilly, sodden grass and hard gravel. She expelled the liquids accrued from last night's tasty vegetarian curry prepared by Carraday, an expert at cookery on a budget to feed his mum. She washed in cold water then walked on tiptoes back towards the van, stopping where she could see across the fields to soak up the extreme colours of the day, the dark green of trees against plain blue sky, the greys and browns of rock and wood, the filigree precision of each twig and leaf. A crow cawed somewhere, a waking teen moaned and groaned from inside a tent, somewhere a van door rolled shut. Around the toilet block she smelt a whiff of tobacco smoke, sensed a possibility of one of Tyler's men watching. Her feet felt like blocks of ice now, but she didn't want to move, hunkered down on her haunches and wrapped her coat around her, feeling the sun on her face and breathing in fresh air tinged with disinfectant. What an unexpectedly fine morning this was for the time of year when expectations are low; a treat to be out in this. She looked back at the camper van, its roof raised at an angle, pictured Jamie and Carraday snoring together, one on each level.

This was crazy. This later life *ménage à trois* involving not sex but plenty of groaning as the older man creaked his way into the upper bunk and her husband grumped and fidgeted under the duvet they shared down below, back to back to avoid physical contact. All the experiments along the way in communal living and open relationships had at least left them with the flexibility, in spirit if not body, to arrange things between them however they chose.

She climbed a stile, walked down the path towards the road, firm, moist mud reassuring against her frozen feet, tried to shrug off the fear of Tyler's henchmen shadowing. Then to her surprise saw in the next field Carraday, up and about after all, doing his exercises: stick man waving his arms and hips, making shapes in the air, making his words. He heard her approaching and opened his eyes.

"Sorry to disturb you, Mister Carraday. I thought you were still asleep in the van." For a moment he seemed cross, then gave her his smile.

When they arrived back at their pitch, Jamie was sitting outside at the table with a bowl of muesli, cup of tea and a notebook on his knee. He looked contented enough, but a shadow of annoyance crossed his face as the duo approached.

"Where did you two get to?"

"Walking," said Carraday stiffly.

"I came across Mister Carraday communing with the infinite." Her mobile pinged and she clicked on the screen to read the morning's threats.

"I was thinking about communing myself this afternoon actually. Freya, would you be up for another walk – on the cliffs?" said Jamie.

**

"I nearly... turned into middle aged lane towards elderly cul
de sac, but then I realised I could turn the other way."

"I nearly... became a rockstar! I toured America as the only
white man in a black blues band... but I had to come back to
the UK."

"I nearly... had the perfect love. We both felt it. We both
wanted to wait for the perfect moment before we said it. But
you changed your heart before that perfect moment came.
You changed your mind, but I can't change mine. I am
grateful for what we have now, an unusual but beautiful
friendship, one that I could not possibly live without. I will
always love you, and forever wonder 'what if?'. But I know it
is never going to be me, and I have to let go of that part of
you, however wrong that feels. I hope she realised she does
not deserve you, and I hope she never hurts you again as she
has before. Most of all I hope you find happiness. But for
now, I will let you go."

"I nearly walked into the street with my shirt tucked in my
knickers, but a kind man stopped me (as I walked across a
crowded café) and told me about my deshabille faux pas!"

"I nearly... thought I loved x, but it was lust instead. Huge
relief."

**

DISHEVELLED

They set off over the fields towards the cliff tops, the two of
them. On a narrow path where he could talk at her without
having to watch her reactions, Jamie called out to Freya.

"By the way." He couldn't believe he'd said that. By
what way? By the way of nothing, but out of an infinity of
blue. "I should've said: I've been – not telling you something.
A problem I've had with my..."

"With your what?"

"Parts. You know. Libido. Well, genital region."

"Jamie, what are you talking about?" Freya stopped in her tracks.

"Something called Hinchcliffe's. A condition. It's harder to get it up."

"Get what up where? Oh I see." And she walked on.

"It. Up. This condition makes it hurt, shrink, bend. Not good. Sorry, I should have – I just… didn't tell you."

"Back when we were..?"

"Together. Yes."

"What exactly? Explain." And he did. Sort of.

"You should've told me," she said over her shoulder, sounding cross.

"You could've been easier to tell," he said crossly to her back, but she didn't turn round to argue. He burbled on about having been issued a pump and how with this he hoped to gradually unbend and expand himself. This plastic device would be an invaluable aid for old age. He would pump and pump till his cock ballooned so much that he could fold it into the shape of a dog and other animals. He imitated the horribly squeaky sound of a balloon folder and noted that Freya's shoulders were shaking. He was capable of making her laugh at his woes, and this was a boon.

She stopped, turned towards him, still laughing. He walked straight into her arms and they held each other tight for a long time. Wind off the sea tore the words from his mouth and blew them away over the clifftops, but she heard them first before they were gone. And in the fug of the pub where they stopped to get warm, she squeezed his arm and said she understood and, eyes fixed on the open fire, told him a bit about her financial woes. When she talked about money his pulse quickened and he grew dizzy, like he had to grip onto the table top to stop himself rising into the air. Panic tinged with something like arousal. She'd always had this way of describing her plans as if she was preparing to throw the everyday over her shoulder like a judo adversary,

271

leaving their life on the floor winded and bruised. Well, it was on the floor now and quaking. Both clocked how angry they could get with the other but decided to shelve it. Things were what they were. They both agreed there must be a way through all this. They left the pub, moving out of the reassuring dark into blinding light, and just then Freya's mobile rang. She glanced at the screen and hurriedly switched it off before Jamie noticed. She took his hand and arranged his arm around her shoulders like a warm scarf. They walked together into the dark; he pressed her closer to him and let his fingers gently stroke the swell of her breast and that felt very nice.

Arriving back at the van they found no trace of Carraday. Without any comment they unfolded the bed, pulled the curtains across the side windows, climbed in, wriggled out of their clothes, held each other and began immediately and hungrily to make love. It took some effort to find the best positions for this and that; fingers and the whispering of familiar fantasies were employed, penetration achieved, and soon Freya came in an onrush of lust and affection. He was all set to cum too when she yelped in pain from a cramp in her foot. Making love was good but pausing in the middle was even better, when they lay together naked knowing just how the other liked to be held. Freya pulling a funny face when Jamie farted. Then took his arm and wrapped it round her belly. A memory popped into Freya's head of one old boyfriend she'd never, ever told Jamie about, who had wrapped his arm around her just like that, o so many decades ago, in a campsite in Paris, on a summer's night just too fleetingly special to mention. And this sudden recollection of a secret love served as a seal on things, a confirmation of her independent self, a key to opening up her heart to Jamie once again. Maybe.

"I'm so so sorry," he said, looking down at the top of her head. "I should've talked to you before." He kissed her shoulder, squeezed her bum, wrapped his leg around her leg, pressed himself up close, ready to resume.

"I understand, Jamie love." She nestled into his belly, smiled apologetically up at him. "There are other things I should have told you too."

From THE LITTLE BOOK OF NEARLY

Say what you nearly think
Hear what they nearly mean.

?!!

"HOW MUCH?!" shouted Jamie.

"I didn't know what else to do," shouted Freya.

"From my brother? From. My. Own. Sodding. Brother?!"

"He can afford it."

"He's a bastard."

"I didn't know what else to do."

"Oh yeah, like you didn't think to... bloody well ask me?"

"I'm sorry. I couldn't. I'm sorry."

"Or tell me after. You took... HOW MUCH?!!"

"Took? Took? It is my money too."

"It was. All gone now. Yes, took. Without telling me. Used up all our savings. Pippa's money. Her – our – future."

"At least I tried to do something, tried to make a go of the business. You always leave me to sort out the hard stuff.

273

You lost your job and gave up, expected me to keep us afloat."

"And that justifies robbing your family? And stealing – stealing from Tyler, that utter…"

"Look, I'm sorry but…"

"HOW MUCH!?!" shouted Jamie.

BITING

Peaceful here
with only the Nearlies of fish rocks and birds in the air,
sea sounds like the inner Nearlyhiss. And the stories
of the stones which moving up or down beach,
carried by breakers over centuries or buried for aeons or
scooped by a passing child with bucket and spade and flung.
This is where he should be always maybe,
throwing pebbles making fires doing scribbles to keep
matters in balance. At the washing place talking to a fella
running a campsite of his own down the coast say
he needing a handyman.
Carraday thinking own hutch to live in odd jobs to do
and fresh air.
Seeing Mr&Mrs canoodling dawdly back from the clifftop,
vanishing into the van, locking the doors, cutting out the
light to do fuckstuff.

Carraday creep up quiet and sit cross-legged nearby on the
grass. Getting chilly, hearing the murmurs and laughs and
the chassis creakcreakcreaking making him shudder and
cover his ears.

SILENCE

Then eruption of howcouldyou & whydidn'tyou Oh whyowhyowhy what racket what rant what recrimininations emanating Carraday stand up on one leg deep listening to the swearing and shouting and weeping and wailing. Things he wish he never hearing midst the muttermuttermuttermuttermuttermuttermuttermutter muttermutter *O get off the moral highground, I did what I did. Am who I am* muttermuttermuttermuttermuttermuttermuttermuttermut termuttermuttermuttermuttermuttermutermutter muttermuttermuttermuttermuttermuttermuttermuttermut termutter*With that goddam nearly nutter* muttermuttermutter muttermuttermuttermuttermuttermuttermutter *Being crooked? What does that mean in contemporary capitalism? Don't talk such horseshit! Don't you tell me how to bloody talk!* muttermuttermutter muttermuttermuttermuttermuttermuttermutter muttermuttermuttermuttermutter muttermuttermuttermuttermutter

Carraday in the drizzle dark thinks about knocking on the door and climbing in they bloody forgotten him the shits instead crouched shivering at the front of the van under which the remains of last night's campfire, logs, newspaper and twigs in the fire bucket keeping bone dry, a big box of firelighters.

And it comes to him sudden urgent: the need for ablazing. The time. Return them to the Nearlyverse. Carraday arrange a heap of kindling under the van engine Snap chunks of white firelighter in, then more chunks, then the rest. Reaches into his coat pocket for tobacco and papers for making a roll-up and his lighter Muttermuttermuttermuttermutter. Muttermuttermuttermuttermuttermutter muttermuttermuttermuttermuttermuttermuttermutter

gone quiet inside some more kind of rocking and moaning
now some kind of getting together

still flaming forgotten him tear up the paper spark up the
lighter wave it under the paper which blooms sudden into
big fire drop it onto the kindling a hurting needed a ridding
an ending mummamummamummamummamum deep
listening to the cosmic hiss the cosmic whimper jamie's
comic cumgroan
muttermuttermuttermuttermuttermuttermuttermutter

after the weeping and the gnashing of teeth

the making up the moving on

the discarding him.

SPINNING

Tyler'll get me arrested. I'll be rotting in jail. Serves you
right. He'll send some hitman to get me. No he won't. He'll
write it off against tax, forget all about it. No he won't. He's
an arsehole but he's not a gangster. He's a crook. You
reckon? We have to pay it back. We have to offer to. Don't
you dare go blaming me. Not blaming you for stealing his
money? Who else? I mean, go making up to that smug git of
a brother of yours. I'm so sorry sooooo so sorry. We could sell
the house, if we had to. Move… to round here? No maybe
Cornwall no Wales no Sheffield no Barcelona no Alaska no
Mars. The simple life – just the view of the sea and a walk
to a corner shop. A new house with a different view. Another
city, another country, new horizons. The economy picking
up I'm sure I could do it next time with proper investment.
Where's Carraday? Gone wandering off like usual. Must
make sure Pip's alright. She is, we did good there. You and I
never talked though about how we felt when she came out
and would get so cross like when I said by mistake she was

LGBLT. LesbianGayBaconLettuceTomato? She laughed about it after. Yeh but you and me didn't talk did we. Well if you hadn't avoided it. Me avoided it don't make me laugh. You can talk. No, you can talk. No, you. No, you you you...

And they started arguing again, babbled and shouted till they were hoarse and had to calm down and eyes red with tears and weariness, they lay in the van looking up at the drab grey felt ceiling, each of them projecting onto it so many scenes of broken dreams and future nightmares, memories and possibilities, faded friends and missed flings and lost misadventures, paths not followed yet or ever. Jamie reached out again overwhelmed with a hot jealous sexiness and Freya pulled him into her. Afterwards they gabbled about Pip as a baby as toddler wide open wide a crowd of versions of her and each other as she was might and never, pictured themselves arriving together at so many places, better and worse, but together, fragments of new lives, together yes, by the sea in new cities cramped flats cold farmhouses in prison in penthouse in campers in gutters. And now everything in their past present and future was humming and spinning. Wind down the window wondering where Carraday's got to. And on the cold, fresh night breeze, the stench of paraffin and smoke, flecks of spark, an orange glow. Something's burning.

**

"I nearly... died once. And really nearly another time.

"I nearly didn't exist... In our family was the story 'we were supposed to have travelled on the Titanic'."

"I nearly... didn't find my husband. I'd seen him on a train, somewhere between Ludlow and Leominster. I felt as if I knew him. He was on crutches. I was trying to write a speech

for my best friend's wedding the next day. We spoke briefly and didn't exchange names. Three weeks after the wedding, a friend was on the loo, idly flicking through the small ads. She spotted one that referred to a man on crutches, a woman writing a wedding speech, a train journey through Herefordshire. That was how our lives came together again."

"I nearly... got murdered by a mass murderer – twice. I lived in the street where the Yorkshire Ripper got arrested. And I lived in the street where one of the victims of Frederick West disappeared. I remember being approached by a man at night when I was walking home in the dark. I always wondered if it was Fred."

"I nearly... made a great discovery. Or I spent a year of my life believing I was near to a great discovery in physics; since I never succeeded I can't say I nearly did it, just that I felt it was something near. I was in my late 20s, a post doc in Cambridge and I felt there was a secret somewhere among all the facts and calculations that made up my work at the time, a secret, an idea that could illuminate the whole subject. I remember the feeling, the uncanny sense of excitement, of anticipation. Although it makes no sense, I felt like somewhere in the abstract world enclosed by my mind a chain was slipping through a hole, like a chain being dragged off a deck by an anchor; that sense of movement. The idea itself though never came clear, my thoughts my calculations followed round and round in tighter and tighter circles but in the end enclosed nothing. For a long time afterwards my work felt like an afterword, a footnote to a text never printed."

"I nearly became a story on the evening news. Young mother and baby hijacked on the M40 by a man wearing only a pair of jeans."

**

A BIGGER SKY

"Pass me the margarine."

OK. Jamie is beginning to get it now. Concentrate hard. He stares at the yellow plastic tub, feels the hydraulics on his chest stirred to movement. Nothing.

"Pass it to me, Jamie. You know you can."

Sunshine falls on a round loaf of sourdough bread, salad leaves and tomatoes in a blue ceramic bowl, a wooden platter of cooked meats and local cheeses, a tub of spread made from olive oil. All good things.

And yes, as he focuses, the mechanism hums and jolts, levers turn. He tenses his forehead, does something with his mind, like on waking when we try to recollect a fading dream, and that effort translates to this metal and plastic limb attached to his chest, moving, pincers opening, closing carefully around the sides of the margarine tub, fork-lifting it up. He looks down and the contraption freezes. He tries to focus once again on the movement itself and, yes, the thing whirrs into life again, extending out then down to unlock and place the marge beside his wife's slice of artisanal sourdough loaf.

"There!"

"Wow – excellent."

And the prosthetic springs back, clunks down beside his other hands on the table top where real fingers wrap themselves around bionic. Jamie looks up and smiles.

"Magic," says Freya, buttering her bread and, with her own arm, carving a slice of a perfect ripe Camembert that Pip's brought along.

279

"So Mum, you're absolutely sure these gizmos are going to sell?" asks Pip. "

"The next big thing. A surefire money spinner." At that moment Jamie's NearlyArm jolts and sends the salt cellar flying. "Once the techies have ironed out the glitches."

THAT MENTAL THING AGAIN

The house is divided into three small flats these days, one each for Freya and Jamie, giving them absolute independence from each other, this having been carefully negotiated over weeks and weeks of talks after the explosion, the hospitalization, all the operations, the months and months of painful recovery, the gradual repair. Freya loves her top floor flat, decorated precisely how she likes it, but they tend to spend most evenings and nights together. The ground floor flat was sold off, to pay off the debts, a proportion going towards Pippa's puppet theatre, a dilapidated shop being transformed into a miniature venue for children's shows and workshops, a proportion invested by Freya in the smart body parts start-up, LimBoCo.

Freya, who sits now slightly stiffly next to Pippa sat on the garden bench opposite wearing dark glasses, tells her daughter that Jamie's been getting his NearlyArm programmed to play amazing lead guitar. He's still composing songs, humming tunes and words into an app on his phone which he can email as sound files over to New York and which Chunk returns as far better music than he could ever have produced alone, over which he records another, final vocal, sends these back to Chunk who overlays harmonies, keyboard and so on and so forth, over the weeks the layers becoming richer and richer, like a slice of agate stone with its rings of variegated colours polished till the surface glows. Still, nobody much wants to download them, but who cares. He's world-famous in 10 Rayner Gardens.

Pippa smiles politely at mention of the songs, but he doesn't think she's actually listened to any, not so far. All a bit embarrassing perhaps, a singing Dad. She's telling her parents about her company's next production.

"It's about a woman who runs a travelling puppet show. She's accused by the King of putting on seditious plays. The police arrest her, lock her up, but when the case comes to court the judge says he can't imprison the actors because they're inanimate lumps of wood. The puppets are relieved, but also furious. The judge turns to sentence the puppeteer. In the dock she pulls up her skirts and shows the jury that she has a wooden leg. Then the judge says he can't imprison her either, because she's one quarter puppet." She asks her mum and dad if they'd be interested in writing the music for the show, and they enthusiastically say they'd absolutely love to; they've been playing together again recently and would so enjoy a joint project. But then Pippa changes the subject.

Jamie stands and leans over the table and does that mental thing again to grasp the wine bottle with his third arm and tilt it carefully so it pours more wine into the glasses of his wife and daughter, and they thank him and carry on chatting, about that bastard Martin who Jamie hasn't spoken to since he discovered his supposed best friend has left Connie and is having an affair with Paola whom he met at a party round at Rosalind's, about Carraday who vanished on the night of the explosion and was never seen again, who was done for arson and hung himself in his cell, who lives and works on a campsite doing odd jobs, hair shorn, beard clipped to a shadow, muttering no more gibberish outpouring, talking almost properly, the ringing in his head all gone.

Who would have thought that Tyler would keel over with a stroke like that leaving his fortune to his brother and his wife? Would order that hit man to demand the money back with menaces? That Dan would reappear at Freya's door with a bottle of bubbly, a bunch of flowers and a business plan? That the lilies he brought would turn out to be the kind which Freya sniffed in a corner shop in nineteen eighty something and sparked such a violent allergic reaction? Who would have thought Pippa and Sophie would split and Pippa would meet and fall in love with Paola, Pippa expecting a child now with sperm donated by a friend of theirs, a character you've never even heard of? That Chunk's album would sell like hot cakes, win awards, lead to the band reforming and, of course, re-splitting? That Martin's website would grow and grow spawning a new consciousness, a medical breakthrough, a line of male toiletries and fragrances? That Martin would divulge that he slept with Freya that night long ago after they'd massaged each other around the gas fire at The Rainbow Garden? That Carraday's absence would haunt them so, now everything was so strangely ordinary again? Freya often walks in the crematorium where his ashes were scattered after he was found dead in a shop doorway during the cold snap last January. There's a hostel round the corner from Rayner Gardens where he stays sometimes. Still manages to look like the Shaman, so say friends who see Carraday sitting like a skinny Buddha outside Waitrose with a paper cup of change and his old suitcase open beside him. Walking past Freya's revamped and expanded Nearly Store, a space where readers can pick up advice on what to read online or on paper, buy coffee of course, light snacks and humorous postcards and a curated selection of Kindle covers, and – thanks to Connie's new techy contacts – pay to have stories downloaded directly into their memories through a headset they attach in the store, like an old-fashioned hairdryer, this enterprise destined to make pots of money for sure when the Nearlylimbs go into production.

No, really. Martin and Connie much more together now have split up or almost have or haven't, Freya so happy sad after Bremainers won lost the referendum, Trump lost won the White House, one tiny speck of virus did didn't pass from animal to passerby. O but surely not. And the Nearlysex website is mega now, hundreds of thousands of visits from all over the planet, hundreds of squillions of feelings expressed. Well, dozens. From hereabouts. To which Jamie posted too of what did or didn't or might just have all those years back back back.

MOUND OF SOIL

More wine? Jamie grasps the bottle once more and shares out the rest of the bottle. It's getting dark. Pippa has picked up Freya's invitation to the launch of Rosalind and Carraday's next exhibition and uses the card as a fan, wafting it in front of her face in the still, balmy evening. The show features an installation in which Rosalind, painted with mud and straw, lies on a mound of soil in which Carraday has planted nearly spells they'd made together and invite visitors to plant their own. They moved to Australia and settled in the West End area of Brisbane where he found work in a bookshop until, sadly but perhaps inevitably, it folded.

ABOUT THE AUTHOR

Chris is a writer of fiction, songs, digital literature, plays, blogs, articles and poetry. In 2018 he was awarded a PhD in Creative (Digital) Writing by Bath Spa University, and has an MA from De Montfort University in Creative Writing & New Media. His 2008 digital novella *In Search of Lost Tim* was described by the Independent on Sunday as "a jeu d'esprit and, just possibly, the future of fiction."

In 1984 Chris won the George Orwell Prize for his play *We Two Boys*. He wrote *The Sheffield Street Show* for Stephen Daldry's Metro Theatre Company and a comedy book, *The Thoughts of Betty Spital* was published by Yorkshire Arts Circus and Penguin Books. Later with Cindy Oswin he wrote a pilot script for *The Twerlies,* a sitcom based on Betty Spital's radical pensioners. The BBC optioned this and commissioned a second episode. By the time the script was completed, a new Head of BBC 1 was in place and the show was never made – but nearly.

Chris worked as Community Arts Officer in Sheffield Libraries and Head of Imagination Services for Birmingham Libraries before becoming Director of The Poetry Society and then BookTrust. In 2008 he founded if:book UK, a charitable company exploring the future of the book and digital possibilities for literature.

In 2012 Chris was a participant in Tino Sehgal's installation *These Associations* at Tate Turbine Hall and became a founder member of *Academy Inegales* in 2016, working with a diverse ensemble of musicians co-ordinated by composer Peter Wiegold. Recently he became a Nearlysmith, having participated in the annual *Schmiede* maker festival in Hallein, Austria.

Chris is Chair of *Modern Poetry in Translation* magazine, on the steering group of the annual if:book New Media Writing Prizes with Bournemouth University. He podcasts, writes and performs his songs with Chris & The Ifso.
Read and hear more at www.nearlyology.net.